IN THE HILLS

ABOVE THE

GRISTMILL

By

KALVIN ELLIS

In the Hills Above the Gristmill by Kalvin Ellis
Published by Infinite Key Media PO BOX 351501
Westminster, CO. 80035
KALVINELLIS.COM
© 2020 Kalvin Ellis All rights reserved. No portion of
this book may be reproduced in any form without
permission from the publisher, except as permitted by U.S.
copyright law.
For permissions contact Kalel@kalvinellis.com
Cover by: Mexeleina / Serhat Ozalp
Hardback ISBN: 978-1-7342526-2-0
Paperback ISBN: 978-1-7342526-1-3
Ebook ISBN: 978-1-7342526-0-6

My First Dedication

For
Brittany, Jordan, Maddison, and Misty
You told me I could, and then you stood beside me
while I tried.

1

It takes eight pounds of pressure to rip off a human ear. Considerably more force is needed for an arm or a leg. Surprisingly little effort, however, is needed to pull the guts out of someone and hang them from a tree. The shadowy figure that lumbered after Peggy Mae through the trees in the Great Smoky Mountains just above the town of Grey Water Ridge was a monster capable all of those atrocities and more. Peggy, or Peg to the few friends she had back home, was an aspiring musician on her way to Nashville to become the next big thing. Her impressive vocal range could not save her from the fury of the figure behind her. Her screams, more primal than melodic, were dampened by the dense wilderness surrounding her.

When she could run no more she fell to her knees on the soggy mess of dead pine needles and moss and began to beg. Only the thing which pursued her had no empathy. It had no morals, no mercy to give. It was a fiend who prayed on the weak and killed for pleasure. The figure towered over her and she looked up at the silhouette framed by the light of the setting sun. A large hand reached out, wrapping long fingers around her neck and shoving her to the ground. She clawed at the thing's hand and wrist, but it was too strong. A spark of pain burned as her fingernail caught something hard buried beneath the tangles of fur and tore free. It was the pain in her finger that she focused on as the world began to fade to black around her.

2

Driftwood battered the shore deep below where Paisley Mott stood on the cliff overlooking the ocean. She couldn't remember going up to the bluffs, but she found herself standing there looking down on a particular spot. A spot she had seen many times in the past few years. The revulsion hit her in the gut like a hook shot from a boxer and she stumbled backward. She had promised herself, and her father, that she would not go up there again. It was too painful, and there were no answers to be gained there. Her mother had been there in her final minutes. Before she went over the edge she was hurt and afraid. Paisley often wondered if she knew that she was going to die. The coroner said that she had been stabbed before going over the cliff, but that the cause of death had been the impact on the sharp rocks below. Her body had crashed repeatedly into the rocky shoreline at the base of the cliff before getting hung up on the rocks. That was the only thing stopping her from being dragged out to sea and disappearing like so many other bodies.

Paisley dropped to her knees at the edge of the cliff and screamed into the abyss.

"Why?! Why did you take her? She wasn't like the

others," she yelled. Her mother had been a good woman, a kind woman. The other people that disappeared that year, and were thought to be victims of the same killer, were less savory individuals.

"She wouldn't want you up here." A voice somehow broke the wind that whipped around Paisley.

She turned to see her father standing there. She looked around. His car wasn't sitting in the pull-off a few hundred feet away. She noticed her car wasn't there either. Her hyper focus was kicking in. Her father was wearing a shirt that she hadn't seen in years, but that he wore in a photo of the two of them he had taken when they had gone camping at Crater Lake. He had thrown the shirt away a few months ago when he got motor oil on it while working on her car.

"What am I supposed to do?" she asked.

"I wouldn't say no to a hand job," a distant voice replied.

3

"I wouldn't say no to a hand job," the man seated next to Paisley said to the flight attendant standing in the aisle. The attendant chuckled uncomfortably. She looked at Paisley, who was struggling to remember where she was as she woke from yet another dream about her mother. Paisley had been a lifelong sufferer of anxiety attacks, and though she had found her ways to stave them off, when she was caught off guard it was much more difficult.

"Miss, can I get you anything else before we prepare for descent?" Paisley was frozen, her thoughts caught between her brain and her mouth as if they had to trudge through mud to get there. The anxiety crept from deep in the pit of her stomach where it lived and began to fill the corners of her mind with darkness.

Paisley looked around. The airplane was nearly full. The fellow next to her was a lump of a man. To her he looked like a potato that had been soaked in water, dropped in a bag of hair, and shaken vigorously. He smelled of alcohol and hot dogs. She looked around the plane. She could also see a man, a few rows up on the aisle, who wore an Elvis Presley shirt and was turned around glaring at a child, presumably his own, who had his feet up on the seat. A woman across the aisle had a tablet computer and she appeared to be watching one of Paisley's favorite movies, *10 Things I Hate About You*. Other than the tuber next to her, everything seemed normal.

Paisley looked up at the flight attendant. She was a pretty woman with a practiced smile she wore on an empathetic face.

"I'm sorry, what?" Paisley managed. She hoped this would buy her enough time to figure out what to say.

"Would you like anything else from the beverage cart? Another gin perhaps?" the flight attendant asked, ignoring the fact that the scumbag who had made the inappropriate comment was currently staring at her chest.

"Oh, no, thank you. One is my limit," she said. Though she had considered another just to take the edge off of her nerves about the days to come, but after passing out after just one, she thought it best to abstain.

"I'll say," the drunk asshole next to her said. "You were passed the fuck out. You were moaning and everything."

"I'm sorry," Paisley said turning her eyes down and away from the gaze of the drunk and the flight attendant.

"Don't be," he continued. "It was fucking hot. I thought about slipping my hand over there and seeing if it was having the same effect on you as it was on me," the man said as he adjusted his crotch, "but you know, nine eleven and all."

"Are you two traveling together?" the flight attendant interrupted.

"No, we are not," Paisley said. She had pushed herself against the window side of the seat to get as far away from the creep as possible without being obvious. The flight attendant looked down at the man. The friendly smile that had been on her face had been replaced with the look of a stern teacher about to pass out discipline.

"Sir," she said sharply, "I must ask you to refrain from speaking like that to this young lady or you will be detained upon landing for creating a disturbance while in flight. Do you understand?"

The drunk looked at the flight attendant, then back at Paisley. He made the face of an infant who just got caught jamming a cookie into the Blu-Ray player.

"What did I say?" he asked. "I won't say it again."

"How about we just agree that you won't say anything for the rest of the flight, okay?" the flight attendant said, placing a hand on his slumped shoulder.

"Okay," the man said quietly, defeated.

"Fantastic," the flight attendant said. Then, with ease, the smile slipped back onto her face. "So, miss, is there anything I can get you from the beverage cart before we begin our descent?"

"No, but thank you," Paisley said. She mouthed another, very obvious, thank you. The flight attendant nodded and threw in a quick wink before moving up the aisle to finish her round.

Paisley sat undisturbed looking out the window as the endless sea of green unrolled below them. Her nerves were starting to get to her. This was her first real story since deciding to quit her job at the bookstore, after her mom died, to vlog full time. Her YouTube channel, Paranormal or Not with Paisley Mott, had a fair number of subscribers thanks to the number of unexplainable things that happen in her home town of Jigsaw Bay, Oregon. It was, after all, the home of the most haunted lighthouse in the world—at least, according to her vlog it was. Her subscriber base jumped when she hopped the fence outside the old lighthouse and crawled through a broken window to get inside. Someone online had stumbled onto her live stream and tweeted out the link with the caption "Hot chick breaking and entering to hunt ghosts LIVE!" By the time she got in and managed to check the stream, she had more than five thousand active viewers. Since then the video had scored more than a million hits. Paisley was shocked that so many people had watched it. She was twenty-two and had been posting new daily videos for two years, and the highest number of views was just over a thousand. That was on a video in which she went exploring in a cave off the south jetty just down the shore from her house. She liked to think that the video did so well because she was searching for evidence in a string of murders, but, if the comments section was to be believed, it found an audience because she looked good in her bikini. Paisley didn't want to think that was the only reason, but she also wasn't willing to discount that it helped.

This was the first story for her channel that required her to get on an airplane. A backwoods preacher named Hollis Grimm had emailed her about coming out to the Great Smoky Mountains to investigate a series of strange and brutal deaths. He claimed to be an expert in the case and said he would be happy to share everything he knew about it as long as she was willing to post it to call attention to what he said was a "crisis of biblical proportions." At first she didn't understand why he would be contacting her-she hosted a paranormal vlog, not a crime vlog. She had searched the internet after receiving his first email and found a news article that explained why he would have chosen her. The headline of the story read "Local Preacher Links Sasquatch to Multiple Bodies Found in Hills above the Gristmill." The story was in the *Pitt County Observer*, and was written by a man named Boyd Gunnerson. It intrigued her. She was either dealing with a bona fide serial killing bigfoot, or a bat-shit crazy, redneck, preacher. Either way it would make for some good content.

After opening the link, she had been taken aback by the photo attached to the story. It wasn't a sasquatch or a mangled body, but instead it was a picture of Hollis Grimm, the preacher, himself. He was a tall, thin man with wavy black hair down to his shoulders. He wore a plain black suit and an even plainer white button-up shirt underneath. He wasn't rugged in the traditional ways but there was a sharpness to him. He had a little facial scruff, but not yet a five o'clock shadow, that she found handsome. There was a strength in his posture; he stood bolt upright with a confidence that came through even in the photograph. He stood with his arms folded in front of him, his head cocked back slightly, and his piercing blue eyes looking down over his high cheekbones. She knew this man was a preacher and now she understood why. She had only seen a picture of him and she was ready to be baptized in his holy water.

But it wasn't Hollis's looks that brought Paisley all the way from Oregon to investigate the death of seven women; it was what the article claimed he had seen before one of the bodies was found. His statement to police claimed that he had seen a figure nearly nine feet tall, muscular and covered head to toe in fur of brown and dark red, moving through the trees. Hollis believed that the murders were not murders at all but sacrifices made to God by a creature he determined was a sasquatch. How could Paisley not go and do this story?

The remainder of the flight went smoothly and the creep next to her didn't say anything more. She managed to get off the plane, get her bags, and make it to the train station in time to catch the only train that went to the tiny town of Grey Water Ridge for another week. Hollis had said that if she missed it he would just drive the four hours out to get her, but she really didn't want to put him through that much trouble. Plus, she wasn't sure if she was ready to spend four hours alone with him. She had determined that he was intelligent by their email correspondence. She had seen how attractive he was in the photo. And she had a strong feeling that he was highly charismatic given his status as a preacher at just twenty-eight years old. She worried that she would stumble over herself like she did when she was a teenage girl asking Bill Chizmar, the usher at the single screen movie theater back in Jigsaw, if he wanted to watch the John Carpenter Double Feature with her as he tore her ticket. He had looked around like she was joking and then pointed out that he was working. Propositioning a preacher was probably along the same lines. She assumed that when you worked for the big guy, you were always on duty.

4

Courtney Teere, or KingCourt to the few friends he had online, had just powered up his computer when he got the tweet notification. He knew that it had to be one of three accounts that had posted. He followed nearly two thousand accounts on Twitter, but most of them he just trolled looking for fights. Only three, however, had he set to send notifications to his phone. One was a pro-wrestling podcast that he listened to, because they always seemed to have the scoop before anyone else. The second was a website that had daily codes that could be used to access porn for free from his favorite websites. The last was his latest obsession, some fine piece of ass who craved the eyes of her betters. She was some chick who claimed to be a rich bitch who lived in the mountains somewhere. She never showed too much in her pictures, but it was just enough to get him going and he knew that once her subscribers got sick of watching her take boring pictures she would have to start showing some real skin. He liked to think about what he would do with her in her fancy living room, or ridiculous fucking library. He bet she was the type to pretend not to want it but that would really enjoy whatever you did. Fucking women, always with the games.

By day he was Courtney Teere, Emergency Roadside Assistant for RH Trucking. He drove around the Nashville Metro area in his shitty little black Ford Focus hatchback putting air in the tires of dumb women who thought that just because the low tire indicator came on on the dashboard of their overpriced Lexus that they needed to pull over immediately and call a man for help. Or helping careless women who never changed the oil in the car even when the indicators on the dashboard of their overpriced Mercedes came on to tell them they were low. He hated his job-he hated his life-during the day. But by night he was KingCourt. He was a max-level undead rogue with end game gear, the sickest mount, and was the second-in-command of his guild. People worshiped at his leather-clad skeletal feet. He had once single-handedly wiped out an entire party of Light Bringers who had tried to infiltrate the Tombs of Desolation and cast Holy Divinity at the Altar of Ula'Tar. Had the enemy succeeded, his guild, TRNL, which stood for Thick Rod No Lube, would have lost a quarter of their guild points and would have had to run all the final patch raids again. But he shut those bitches down.

Courtney was not a large man by any stretch of the imagination, but he was strong, as most who spend eight hours of their day working on cars are. Always pushing or pulling something, turning some wrench, lifting some part. It was a tough job and you built a lot of muscle doing it. He may not have been a bad looking man if he took care of himself. He only showered when he had to for court or something, which, between his driving record and the two sexual assault charges, was often enough. Greasy hair that was speckled with motor oil hung down in his face and around his neck. It had been more than a year since he last

17

shaved it off, and it likely hadn't been washed since. He wore small, round, metal framed glasses. The kind Harry Potter wore, which annoyed him every time someone pointed out the connection.

The tweet notification was from the hot piece of ass. She had posted another pic of herself. This time she was sitting backward on a chair and she had her back to the camera. Her ass hung over the edge of the seat just a little. He felt something stir inside of him and he adjusted his crotch. He had been following her just long enough to gather a little information on her, and soon he would know where she was. He might even pay her a visit sometime and see if she tasted as good as she looked.

Courtney smiled at the thought and flipped the clasp on his belt.

5

As Paisley came out of what passed for a train depot in Grey Water Ridge she recognized Hollis at once, even before she saw the sign with her name on it. She had been under the impression that people only did that in the movies. Her first thought was that Hollis was even better looking in person than he was in the photo. He had a charisma that radiated off of him like heat off a feverish child. When he saw her he smiled, and there it was, the reason people followed Hollis Grimm. Between those electric blue eyes and that Cheshire grin it would be impossible not to. She wasn't prepared for the triple threat that came next.

"Well hello there, Miss Mott. It is a great pleasure to finally make your acquaintance," Hollis said in the smoothest southern drawl she'd ever heard. His voice melted like warm butter on hot cornbread. Her knees quivered and she had to take a moment to steady herself. He reached out with his palm up, and even though no one had ever extended this greeting to her before, she knew what it was. She placed her hand gently in his, and he kissed the back of it. His hand seemed soft but strong, and she could not help but to make the mental correlation between those long fingers and another part of his anatomy. She blushed.

They stood for a moment in silence before she realized it was her turn to speak.

"Oh, yes, thank you. It is nice to meet you too, Mister Grimm," she said hoping he didn't notice the color in her cheeks.

"Please, call me Hollis," he said with that drawl she wanted to hear more of. "Is it okay if I call you Paisley, or do you prefer Miss Mott?"

"Oh jeez, no, please, call me Paisley, or Dylan, that's my middle name. My friends used to use it because I didn't like my name," she said. Though no one had called her that since middle school. "Or Dill, but only my dad calls me that."

His grin widened. She felt a flutter in the pit of her stomach.

"Dill? Like the pickle?" he asked playfully, adding a wink that nearly knocked her off her feet.

"Yeah, I guess so," she replied.

"Only sweeter, I would wager?" he said and stuck out his hand again. "May I carry your bag, Pickle?" he asked.

She handed him the bag without a word. She was not the type to feel smitten, but she just couldn't help it, Hollis Grimm was a lady killer.

6

Paisley raised the camera to eye level; she flipped out the LCD screen so she could frame herself up properly; she tapped the small microphone pointing at her from atop the camera to check the levels on the screen, and when she determined everything was in order, she hit record. Paisley and Hollis had just walked away from the train depot and she thought there was no better time to start recording than now. She had done a bit of B-roll on the train, but she'd been sitting next to an older woman who Paisley figured would not want a camera interfering with her crossword puzzles. Paisley instead took the opportunity to work on her latest knitting project, a cute little monster that she planned to use as her mascot. He looked a little like Bigfoot, so it seemed fitting.

"Hey, paranormal party people! Welcome to Paranormal or Not with your girl Paisley Mott!" Paisley noticed that Hollis tensed a bit when her persona came forward. Paisley was quiet most of the time. Not because she had nothing to say, she just didn't normally feel like saying it. She instead would just silently judge everyone else. But when the camera turned on it was like she was someone else. She was strong, confident, sexy, and powerful. She felt an energy when she knew she was on screen.

"Do I have a treat for you folks! As promised I have made the trek across the country, all the way from the Pacific Northwest to the Appalachian Trail buried deep in the Smoky Mountains of Kentucky. I'm here in a little town called Grey Water Ridge to investigate something dark, sinister," Paisley pulled the camera in for an extreme close up, whispering, "and possibly, paranormal." "I'm off to dig in and see what we can find. Stay tuned." Paisley flipped the screen closed and powered off the camera.

Hollis was leaning against the fender of a beautiful black 1968 Plymouth Fury. It was a long car with two doors and a rag top. It was shiny and clean and Paisley thought it was the perfect car for him. She wouldn't have been able to identify the make and model, but she thought it looked close enough to the 1967 Chevy Impala that the Winchester Brothers drove in one of her favorite shows, *Supernatural*.

"Wow," she said.

"Thank you," Hollis said stepping back and looking at the car. "I restored her from the ground up."

"She's beautiful," she said, meaning it honestly.

"I try not to revel in sinful pride, but it is hard not to feel it a little after putting all the work into this car," Hollis looked back at Paisley with a sly look. "But don't tell God, okay?" he added. He bit his lower lip sheepishly and Paisley felt that warm feeling in her stomach again.

"Your secrets are safe with me," she said as she walked over to the passenger side door that Hollis had opened. Hollis held the door and took her luggage, but she held onto her camera as she slipped into the front seat. The black leather was warm in the afternoon sun. The car was immaculate and smelled like it had been detailed. She was starting to think that maybe Hollis was in fact trying to impress her. That warm feeling crawled up into her stomach like a kitten in a hammock and she smiled.

The original plan was for Paisley to stay at a motel in Grey Water Ridge, but Hollis had insisted that she stay "somewhere more suitable" and arranged for her to stay with someone in town. She had been hesitant about staying at a motel because Hollis had told her that the internet service in that part of the state was spotty at best. Cell phone service was relatively new in Grey Water, and the data service was still trying to catch up. If she did stay at a motel she didn't know if she would be able to upload her videos daily, but she figured the worst-case scenario was that she would have to edit everything when she got back to Jigsaw Bay and upload it in parts over the next few weeks. That wouldn't be the worst idea, though, because she had a feeling that after this she might need an actual vacation. From the looks of Grey Water Ridge, it was going to be a long few days.

As the Plymouth carried them through the thick woods and into the Great Smoky Mountains, Paisley felt a shift in culture. A sepia tone coated the landscape, save the trees, which were a brilliant green, like someone had come and washed the dirt that covered everything else off of them. The old buildings, the vehicles parked on the lawns of the few remote homes they passed, and the red dirt that ran alongside the road, all appeared to have a rust coating.

The town of Grey Water Ridge was old, but cute. Main Street was flanked on either side by two-story brick buildings. It reminded her of a backwoods copy of Stars Hollow from the show *Gilmore Girls*. It surprised Paisley how functional the town looked. She had tried to find information about it online, but it seemed that no one really ever visited Grey Water, and the people, not having internet, probably didn't feel the need to post anything about the town. That thought made her smile. If she did a good enough job on this story, maybe she could put Grey Water Ridge on the digital map.

As the car slipped between the buildings an eerie sensation came over Paisley. She looked around, and saw that everyone in the windows of the shops was staring at them. Their big, cautious eyes peered from behind dirty windows stained with soot from years gone by. There was a general store, a pharmacy, a barbecue joint, a fish joint, a soda shop with a big light-up ice cream cone attached to the awning, a barber shop, a bar, a butcher, and a handful of other stores that were not very distinguishable. Paisley thought that, if it weren't for the Twilight Zone feel of the occupants looking out, it would be fun to wander down the street and look into the shop windows.

The place was a true mountain town. Tall mountains stood on every side, and the town nestled into the crook of a bend, as if the mountain had grown up around it.

When they passed the buildings on main street the structures were fairly sparse. Here and there, a large property with a trailer home sat back in the trees. A ramshackle house leaning slightly off center looked like the large pile of firewood next to it might be load-bearing. A man sat on a makeshift porch that appeared to be an old pallet with a piece of plywood thrown across it. He wore torn jean shorts, a pair of boots that were more hole than leather, and a lone-toothed grimace that hid under a ratty gray beard. As they passed, the man watched with a single, yellow-crusted eye. Where the other eye had presumably once been there was just a small hole peeking out from under a heavy eyelid bulging with purple veins. Paisley couldn't help but stare back. The man looked like something from some old prospector's tale. When they got far enough down the road that she had to turn her head back to watch him, the man spit in their direction. A massive glob of dark mucus spewed out with impressive distance and left a kite string tail that fell on the man's bare torso and came to rest in his wiry, white chest hair.

"Ugh," Paisley said. It was an unconscious statement.

"What is it, darlin?" Hollis asked.

"That man, I just," Paisley stopped. She was worried if she started her stay here with an insult, the rest of the trip might not go well. Though now she wished she'd turned her camera on and gotten a shot of the old man. It would make for some good scene setting.

"You just what?" Hollis asked after she failed to finish her sentence.

"I was just upset with myself for not having my camera out to get a shot of main street for the vlog," she half lied.

"Oh, well, I bet Hyacinth will be more than happy to take you back into town later, after the shops are closed, to get some shots," he said.

Hyacinth was the woman that Hollis had arranged for her to stay with. She was apparently the heir to some sort of mining fortune or something. Hollis had mentioned she had enough money to have a lot of power in the town, but that, in his words, "her dinner bucket was full of rocks and no stew, if you know what I mean?" Paisley hadn't known exactly what he meant, but she could assume he meant to say that this woman was rich but not very smart.

Paisley wasn't sure what to expect from the house that Hollis insisted she stay in. She thought maybe he knew someone who had a nice cabin in the woods, or maybe an apartment above one of the shops. Perhaps even a larger house on the edge of town with an extra bedroom. At no point in the planning of this trip did she expect to see, let alone stay in, what she found when they arrived at their destination.

A long drive led through a massive iron gate. A large marble raven sat on either side of it, which gave way to a large stone wall that seemed to stretch into the trees as far as Paisley could see in both directions. The gate was open and Hollis slid the car through and onto the property with practiced ease.

When the house came into view it took Paisley's breath away. As they rounded a bend in the drive the trees gave way to a clearing, and there in front of them stood the most amazing Victorian Gothic mansion Paisley had ever seen. Steep peaks held the sharp angles of the slate roofs. Ornate decorations circled the windows of the massive brick building.

It sprawled out in every direction, but Paisley's focus was drawn to the four-story-tall tower that stretched into the gray sky. It had a balcony on each floor surrounded by a wrought iron fence. She could not help but think about the house from *The Addams Family*. She wondered if this was what it would have looked like if it wasn't inhabited by a family of monsters.

"Whoa," Paisley said. She couldn't think to say anything else.

"Pretty fancy, right?" Hollis said.

"What is this?"

"This is Hyacinth's house. This is where you will be staying while you are with us."

"Seriously?"

"Yep. That there is Raven Bloom."

"Raven Bloom?" Paisley turned away from the house for

the first time to look at him.

"The family's last name is Bloom. And Craven Bloom, Hyacinth's great grandfather, who built the house, was not the most loved person in the town." Hollis pulled the car into the massive turn around in front of the house. "When he took over all the mining operations up here from his father, Wilbur, who was beloved by the town, the people here gave him a chance. Then, once he tried to expand the town and make it some sort of big city place, they turned on him. He built that house to shield himself, and his family, from reality. A few generations of Bloom have been raised here, each one more sinister than the previous."

"And Hyacinth?" Paisley asked. Hollis paused for a moment. Paisley was good at reading people. Hollis was taking very careful consideration about how he described this woman. Was it because she had money and power and he didn't want to get on her bad side? Was it because he was trying not to influence Paisley's opinion of her? And then it happened, and she thought she knew. His eyes looked down at his nose, his lips pursed out, and then he raised them as if smelling his upper lip. He was deciding whether or not Paisley could handle something. She had seen this look before. It was a look she had seen a few men give her in the past when determining if she, as a woman, could handle the same information that a man could.

"She," he started, "she is a special woman."

"Oh come on, spill it. Remember, you asked me to come down here, and I trusted you enough to do so," she said. "Now you need to trust me enough to do what I do, and I can't do that if I'm busy trying to decode the things you tell me. So you need to shoot me straight and I'll make sure you come out clean on the other side of this thing."

He looked at her for a long moment. She could see the

wheels in his head turning. She still thought he was cute as hell, but she was annoyed that he was playing the same stupid games that the guys in Jigsaw Bay played.

"All right, fine!" Hollis said. "You are a tough one, aren't you?"

"Damn straight," she said, before remembering that the man in the driver seat next to her was a preacher. "Oh, shit, sorry," she said. "Crap, I said shit. That probably makes it worse. Sorry." Hollis laughed.

"Oh, don't worry about that. God always knows what you're thinking anyhow. How those thoughts fall out of your face makes no never mind to him, so why should it to me? And it isn't like the good book doesn't have passages that would make a made man blush," he said, that wonderful smile creeping back across his face.

"I'll try harder," Paisley paused. "Swear to God." She burst out laughing. Hollis laughed too. "So what's the scoop on this lady?" she said, jerking her thumb at the massive house.

"Hyacinth is a good woman. Her intentions are pure, but she doesn't have the head or the heart to affect the change she is capable of making," Hollis said. "That's off the record," he added.

"Of course," Paisley lifted the camera to show that it was off. "Does she know I'm a vlogger? Will she be cool if I'm running around with a camera in her face the whole time?"

"She has been briefed, though I don't know that she understands exactly what a vlog is. I told her you were like a documentary filmmaker," he said.

Paisley looked back at the house. Her face scrunched up. The house was intimidating, and she had a feeling that if the woman that lived in that house was half as intimidating then she was going to have a very hard time staying there.

She was lost in thought staring at the house and didn't hear Hollis get out of the car, so when he appeared in front of her window she jumped. He opened the large door and leaned down to look at her.

"Are you okay?" he asked. She didn't know if she was or not, but she nodded and got out of the car. The house felt even bigger when you were standing in front of it. She lifted the camera, pointed it at herself, and hit record.

"So, guys, guess what? I am here in Grey Water Ridge and I'm standing in front of something amazing. You guys are not going to believe this but the house I'm staying in is like something directly out of Silent Hill or something. It's insane. It's a house so big that it has its own name. Behold: Raven Born!" she said as she spun the camera around. She panned and tilted slowly, with the expert touch of a practiced hand, showing off the impressive house.

"Raven Bloom," Hollis said in that charming, Southern voice. Paisley spun the camera back toward her face. She bit her bottom lip, and raised one eyebrow. She looked deep into the barrel of the camera for a moment before speaking.

"Right, Raven Bloom, I apologize." She didn't turn her face from the camera, but looked toward Hollis, and then back into the lens. "All right, people, you've gotten a sneak peek at this beautiful house, but now it's time to meet the man who brought me down here with his tales of a monster that lurks in the woods above this tiny, peaceful town, murdering women and leaving them strewn about the forest." She paused for a moment for dramatic tension, part of the theatrics of it all. "Paranormal or Not fans, please welcome to the vlog, the one, the only, Reverend Hollis Grimm." She said this but didn't turn the camera toward him. Instead she left it pointed at her face. She bit

29

her lip and raised her eyebrow again as she looked at him without turning her head. She looked back into the camera. "Ladies, brace yourselves." She raised her eyebrows at the camera and then spun it to see Hollis. His dark dress boots were crossed as he stood leaning against the back fender of the Plymouth. He had his arms crossed low on his chest and the long fingers of his right hand wrapped around his left bicep. He was dangerously good looking. He smiled at the camera and waved using just the fingers that were on his bicep.

"Howdy, y'all," he said. Paisley could feel women all over the world melting somewhere down the stream of time when they heard that voice.

"Hollis has just filled me in on a little bit of the history of this place and I will in turn do the same for you folks when I get some more detail. But for now, I think it's time to meet the Lady of the House," Paisley said, aiming the camera at the front door and then back at herself.

She began walking with the camera in her face and Hollis followed her. Paisley was careful to frame it so she was in the foreground on the left and Hollis could be seen over her right shoulder. She looked into the camera, and then cast her eyes over in Hollis's direction. Then gave the old double eyebrow raise that says "Hey, check this guy out." As they ascended the stairs, Paisley watched her feet so as not to trip and fall with her camera in her hand, and so she did not see the door open, but she heard it. It creaked like something out of a horror movie. When she looked up and saw the woman standing there she was caught almost as off guard as she was when she saw the house for the first time.

"You have got to be shitting me," Paisley said. Hollis let out a laugh. The woman in front of her stood nearly six feet tall. Her wavy red hair fell like a waterfall around her alabaster neck and shoulders. Her eyes caught the bright afternoon sun and reflected like shallow ponds with beds of pure emerald. The woman's body was lean and held the curves everywhere a woman wanted them. Paisley's mouth hung open. Sometimes when she saw women that were the stereotypical beauty types it caused a twinge of jealousy, but this time she found that she was just attracted to her the way any mortal might be attracted to Aphrodite. The gorgeous woman smiled at Paisley and as she opened her mouth to speak Hollis introduced them.

"Paisley Mott, meet Hyacinth Bloom." Paisley continued to stare for a moment after Hollis's introduction. The woman stepped forward and stuck out her hand to shake. Paisley slowly pushed the lens of the camera away from her own face and pointed it toward Hyacinth.

"Very nice to meet you," Hyacinth said. "I am so excited to have you staying with me." Paisley took her hand and shook it. It was the perfect amount of soft skin and firm grip. Not intimidating, but it felt like the hand of a woman who has used her hands for something worthwhile.

"The pleasure is mine," Paisley said. "Thank you so much for inviting me to stay. This is an amazing house."

"Thank you," Hyacinth said. Then she looked directly into the camera like a seasoned pro and said, "And this must be your audience?" She smiled and waved at the camera. "And thank you all for coming too!"

Vlogging is hard work. Most people think it is just as easy as walking around pointing your camera willy-nilly, but Paisley knew how difficult it was. You carried this heavy thing around everywhere, talking to yourself, and feeling the weight of judgmental people all over. So to have this beautiful, rich woman embrace what she was doing made Paisley feel wonderful. She smiled in the very genuine way that rivaled Hyacinth's beauty.

"Oh my," Hyacinth said, "you have such a beautiful smile." This made Paisley blush and get that warm feeling in her stomach for the third or fourth time that day.

"Me?" Paisley said. "You two look like you were cut from the cover of some sort of expensive Harlequin romance novel." She rotated the camera from Hyacinth to Hollis and back. "Is everyone in this town gorgeous?"

Hyacinth and Hollis both laughed.

"She's funny, too," Hollis said to Hyacinth. "You two are going to have some fun out here."

"And get ourselves into some trouble, I wager," Hyacinth responded with a small wink at Paisley.

"I like trouble," Paisley said. It was the only thing she could think to say. Her mind had stopped working altogether. She spun the camera around and gave the lens a deep look that said "Can you believe this shit?"

"So, can I offer you a tour of the house?" Hyacinth asked.

"Heck yes!" Paisley responded, careful this time not to say *hell* in front of Hollis.

"If you ladies don't mind, I am going to get over to town. I've got some things to attend to before the sun goes down," Hollis said as he walked down the porch steps and opened the trunk of his car.

"Oh, you aren't going to join us to see the house?" Paisley asked, pointing the camera at him.

"No, I've already seen it, but thank you." Hollis pulled Paisley's bags from the trunk and headed back up the porch.

"Well thank you for arranging all of this, Holly," Hyacinth said.

"Holly?" Paisley asked, surprised that such a man would

allow himself to be called by such a name.

"Sadly, yes. Thanks, Hiney," Hollis said, sticking out his tongue.

"Oh, there is history here," Paisley said, panning back and forth between the two beautiful people.

"It's not as interesting as you would think," Hollis said. He set the bags down and extended his hand to Paisley. "Miss Mott, it has been a pleasure getting to chat with you. I look forward to doing it again very soon."

"Please, call me Paisley," she said.

"Paisley, a pleasure," he said and shook her hand. "Hiney, see you around."

"Not if I see you first," Hyacinth said with a smirk.

With that, Hollis strode back to his car as both women watched him go. They didn't say anything as he got into the car, started it up, and drove down the long drive. Finally Hyacinth broke the tension.

"So, Paisley, shall we?" She had picked up Paisley's bags.

"This is a weird place, isn't it?" Paisley asked, not sure if the question was rhetorical or not.

"You have no idea." Hyacinth led Paisley through the front door of the mansion.

ナ

The interior of the house was equally as impressive as the exterior, if not more so. There were high ceilings, arches, huge sweeping staircases, and that was just the foyer. In the middle of the marble floor stood a twelve-foot-tall raven, carved out of a single piece of black marble. When Paisley saw it she gasped. It was an intimidating looking thing to walk in and see.

"Oh, sorry about that. He scares people sometimes," Hyacinth said.

"I'll say," Paisley replied, staring at the creature. It reminded her of a bird that had given her nightmares as a child. It was in one of her favorite books, *IT* by Stephen King. In the story a giant bird attacks one of the kids out by the site of an old fire at an iron works. She wondered if King had seen this terrifying piece of art and used it as inspiration. Paisley pointed her camera up at the behemoth that was towering over her.

"Paisley?"

"Huh? Yeah, sorry. I was distracted by this thing."

"Can I ask you a gigantic favor?" With how beautiful Hyacinth was, Paisley was worried that she would say yes to anything without hesitation.

"Of course," Paisley said. She had a feeling she knew what it would be. Hyacinth was about to ask her not to film in her house.

"When you post your videos, would you mind tagging me in them?" Hyacinth looked almost timid asking this, which didn't seem normal for her. Paisley was shocked.

"Tag you?" Paisley stared. She assumed that no one in this town knew what tagging someone meant, let alone was in a position to request it be done. "Of course."

"Oh goodness, thank you!" Hyacinth said. "Unless I come out looking like a fool, then you can just blur my face out of every shot." Paisley turned off her camera and looked at Hyacinth.

"Okay, I was under the impression that you guys didn't have internet up here. How do you even know what tagging means?"

Hyacinth laughed. "Oh, Paisley, you don't think I would live up here, so far away from civilization, without internet, do you?" She paused. "Let me show you something." She put the bags down on the marble floor and led Paisley down a hallway. At the end of the hall was what must be the most beautiful library in the world.

"Holy shit," Paisley said, then caught herself. "Oh, sorry."

"Don't be. It doesn't bother me a bit," Hyacinth said. "What do you think?"

"You know what it reminds me off?" Paisley said. She had hoped that Hyacinth had seen *Beauty and the Beast*, or she was going to look like a fool for referencing a children's film.

"The library from *Beauty and the Beast*?" Hyacinth asked.

"Yes! Exactly! Has anyone else ever said that?" Paisley asked as she turned her camera back on and started scanning the room.

"Well, actually, it was based on the library in the Admont Abbey, in Austria. It is the oldest, most beautiful monastic library in the world. When I was a little girl I loved *Beauty and the Beast* so much, and I loved to read, so my father had our old library torn out, and he built this one for me. It's my favorite room in the entire house." Hyacinth smiled as she looked around the room.

"That's incredible! What a dad. He must be an amazing man."

"He was," Hyacinth said. The smile was still on her face, but pain now sat where nostalgia had been.

"Oh no, I'm so sorry."

"It's okay. He was very old when I was born, so it wasn't a huge shock, but it still isn't easy."

"I don't have to film in here, if you'd rather I didn't?" Paisley asked. Hyacinth seemed to rebound.

"Oh, of course you can. I'm sorry, he just passed a few months ago, so I'm still processing it. Feel free to film anywhere in the house you'd like. The house is full of mystery and I bet it would make for a great vlog. It would easily rival the episode you did about the old mansion south of Eugene in Oregon," Hyacinth said. Again Paisley was caught off guard.

"You've seen my vlog?"

"Of course. I'm subscribed and have seen every episode. I even listened to the podcast you were on a few months ago," Hyacinth gave an embarrassed smile.

"Are you kidding me?" Paisley said.

"Nope, serious as a..." Hyacinth started. Her eyes moved around the room and a sad look overtook her face. "A heart attack," she finished.

"Oh God, Hyacinth, I'm so sorry. Is that what happened

to your father?" Paisley asked. Now she felt awkward about the filming, but didn't want to turn the camera off and have it become even more awkward.

"Yes. He died of a heart attack, in this room. In that chair." She pointed at a wingback chair right behind Paisley. Paisley turned and looked at the chair and then took a step back from it.

"I'm so sorry," Paisley said. There was a moment of painful silence, and then Hyacinth laughed.

"I'm totally fucking with you," she said. "My dad isn't dead. He lives in France with his new wife. The thing about him building me the library was totally true, but he isn't dead. Very much alive, and very much a pain in my ass," she laughed. Paisley did too. A raucous and loud laugh.

"You are such a bitch," Paisley said, still laughing and trying to point the camera at Hyacinth. Hyacinth just winked and made finger guns at the camera. "Oh, we are going to have some fun."

"I agree. Now, the reason I wanted you to come in here," Hyacinth said, and walked over to a wall. She stopped at one of the curved shelves covered in books. She reached up and pulled on a book. There was a click and the entire shelf slowly slid out and revealed a secret passage that lead into a large room. Hyacinth lifted her hand to usher Paisley in.

"This isn't where you murder me and hide my body, is it?" Paisley said, walking into the room with the camera outstretched in front of her.

"Nope, I do that in the guest room, where you'll be staying."

The room inside was a state-of-the-art office. There was expensive computer equipment, lights, tripods, a brand new hectocopter drone, and the newest Sony camera complete with the best lenses money could buy. The whole setup made Paisley drool.

"Oh I get it, this is where you film the porn," Paisley joked, then realized that it could have been completely plausible and set down a fancy camera lens she had picked up.

"Ha, nope. This is where I run my marketing business," she said. She hit a button on her computer and a massive monitor that hung on the wall lit up and displayed a webpage. There were amazing images of the woods, a river, other beautiful places off the beaten path. Most of the pictures showed a variety of stunning women, which Paisley noticed, included Hyacinth herself in about half of them.

"What is this?" Paisley asked, surprised yet again.

"Well, it started with this." She handed Paisley her smartphone. It was opened to an Instagram page.

"Holy shit! You have five hundred thousand followers?" The phone showed images similar to the monitors, as well as a lot of pictures of Hyacinth around Raven Bloom, including some inside the library. In the pictures she was in various stages of dress and undress. Nothing that Paisley would call porn, but some were fairly suggestive without being offensive.

"Yep, that's me," she said.

"How did Hollis not mention you were an internet celebrity?" Paisley asked.

"Because Hollis doesn't know. No one around here knows. They don't know what Instagram *is*, let alone how to use it," Hyacinth laughed.

"Well hot damn." Paisley turned the camera back toward her face. "Folks, this day just keeps getting weirder and weirder." She turned the camera to Hyacinth. "I think it is you who needs to tag me. You have way more followers than I do."

"We can tag each other," Hyacinth said with a suggestive wink at the camera.

"Well, I think I just gained a hundred thousand subscribers with that wink alone," Paisley said with a laugh.

The rest of the tour wasn't nearly as exciting. The house was unreal, but they just toured the main floor and then Hyacinth showed her to the guest room on the second floor, which was easily twice the size of her own apartment. Paisley wanted to shower before dinner, and Hyacinth wanted to cook for the two of them. She claimed the posts of her cooking always got a "crap ton" of likes.

The shower was amazing. It was a claw foot tub that stood in the middle of the expansive bathroom, surrounded with a curtain. She had seen things like this in movies, but didn't think they actually existed. The faucet and shower head seemed to be made of pure gold. The extravagance was overwhelming. But Paisley wasn't complaining. What had she done that led her to this point? She didn't know, but again, she wasn't complaining.

♱

When Paisley woke to the sound of a light knock on the door she had forgotten where she was. She thought the bed was so comfortable that it could be a dream. Then reality hit her and she reluctantly sat up. The light coming in through the window made it easy to assume that it wasn't too late in the morning, but Paisley couldn't be sure.

"Come in," she said. Hyacinth did. One would assume that she had just woke up, but she didn't look like most people when they get out of bed. Her hair was up and tousled but she looked like she was ready to walk out onto a fashion show runway. She wore designer capri-length sweatpants and a cropped sweatshirt that hung off one shoulder. Paisley could see why people loved looking at this woman.

Paisley pulled the hair that had stuck to the drool on the side of her face away and she figured she looked like she'd been dragged through a hedge. Before she could say anything Hyacinth ran across the room and dove onto the bed.

"Good morning," Hyacinth said as she slid to a halt next to her.

"Good morning," Paisley replied. "Do you always look

like this first thing?"

"Nope, sometimes I look good," Hyacinth said. Paisley knew it was a joke, but she also liked Hyacinth so much that she was okay with the humblebrag. "You have to get up, you had a call."

"A call?" Paisley reached for her phone on the bedside table. She had four missed calls from a number she didn't recognize. "I must have slept through it, I'm sorry, did the ringing wake you?"

"Oh lord no. My room is all the way on the other side of the house. It took me ten minutes just to get here. No, when Hollis couldn't get a hold of you he called the house phone and it woke me up. Any time the house phone rings I know it's someone from town. Since most of them don't have cell phones they seem to always think I don't and they call the house."

"It was Hollis?" Paisley said trying to fix her hair as if he were waiting in the hall.

"Yeah, he said he needs you to be ready in a few minutes. There was another murder," Hyacinth said. Paisley noted the casual way in which she said it, like she wasn't surprised.

"Seriously, another murder?" Paisley said. She wasn't so used to the idea that it didn't still shock her.

"Yep, out near the river, in the hills above the gristmill," Hyacinth said. "Not far from the last one."

"Was it the same thing?" Paisley asked. Then realized she hadn't actually had the chance to talk to Hyacinth about the reason she was here, other than them talking about being internet stars and such. "I mean, do you think they are related?"

"You mean, do I think it was Bigfoot?" Hyacinth asked.

"Ha, well yeah, I guess. What are your thoughts on that

whole situation?"

"I think some sick fuck is murdering people in the hills and the people around here are too up their own asses to accept that it is not some mythical creature coming down out of the hills to punish them," Hyacinth said.

"Wow, well that was blunt," Paisley said. She liked this lady. Hollis had said that Hyacinth wasn't smart, but Paisley felt that he was mistaken. She assumed Hollis just didn't understand her. Or maybe Hyacinth liked allowing people to have that perception of her. Like perhaps she felt it gave her a power over them because they would underestimate her.

"Oh gosh, I'm sorry. I know you're here to hunt Bigfoot. I didn't mean to shit in your cereal," Hyacinth said, placing a hand on Paisley's knee.

"Oh, dude, you're totally cool. I don't really believe it's a bigfoot either," Paisley said, though she did secretly hope she would be the first person to prove the existence of such a creature. To do it on her vlog would mean fame and enough subscribers that she would be set for life. "I just thought it would make for good content. I figured the people that believed in it would be hilarious."

"They are, trust me. Just don't let Hollis, or any of the people that attend that ass-backward church of his, know that you don't believe, without a doubt, that there is some monster in the woods. They may be more dangerous than whoever is actually doing the killing."

"What do you mean?"

"The people around here don't do well with change. That's why this place still looks exactly like it did in the fifties. Same stores, same families, same everything. They refuse to accept that times change."

"How does a community even exist like that?" Paisley

asked.

"That's just it. They have a will like I've never seen to keep things the same. So they all believe this crap, and it could be very dangerous to openly question them. If you intend to poke fun at them, don't do it live. Once you're safely away from this shit hole town you can narrate or do whatever you want to show these people for the joke that they are, but for now, for your own safety, play along." Hyacinth had lost her jovial tone. Paisley had a feeling that Hyacinth had had to deal with some of these crazy people before.

"I'll be careful, thanks for the heads up," Paisley said. "So what am I supposed to do today? Why does Hollis want me to be ready?"

"He wants you to go out there with him and film it," Hyacinth said climbing backward off the bed.

"Film what?"

"The crime scene."

"What? Why?"

"Fantastic question. Hollis is an odd one." Hyacinth said as she walked toward the door.

"I don't know that my viewers want to see a dead body," Paisley said.

"I don't know, people are messed up. But what do I know? All I ever show people is avocado on whole wheat toast and this fall's newest line of designer leggings." Hyacinth stuck her tongue out at Paisley before pulling the door to the guest room closed behind her. Paisley could hear her walking down the hallway. She was whistling. Yep, Paisley liked Hyacinth Bloom a whole lot.

Ten minutes later, Paisley was dressed, her hair and teeth were brushed, and she was ready to go. She just had no idea what she was in for.

1

"Have you ever seen a dead body before?" Hollis sat behind the wheel in such a casual way that it reminded Paisley of her father. Not because they were similar, but for the opposite reason. Hollis leaned back when he drove. He sat with a few fingers from his left hand resting on the inside of the bottom of the steering wheel, his right arm draped across the bench style seat. He had his knee pulled up between the steering wheel and the door. He looked more like he was a supermodel posing on a couch and not a preacher driving a car. Her father had driven their family cars with his hands at ten-and-two, back rigid, head on a swivel. The juxtaposition was amusing.

"I'm sorry, what?" Paisley knew he had asked a question, but she was so lost in her thoughts that she could not remember what that question had been.

"Have you ever seen a dead body?" Hollis repeated.

"Oh, I've seen one in a casket, does that count?" she asked.

"I guess, but I meant have you seen one before it's treated?" Hollis asked.

"Oh, no, I haven't," she said.

"Are you ready for this?"

"I don't know. Will it be messy?"

Hollis paused for a moment. He seemed to be considering his answer. Paisley assumed it would be messy, but she had hopes that maybe this one was different.

"I think it will be a bit of a scene," Hollis said.

"What happened to her?" she asked, not knowing if she really wanted to know.

"Well," Hollis started before Paisley stopped him.

"Wait," she said, then pulled out her camera and pointed it at him. "Okay, now go ahead." Paisley thought she saw Hollis roll his eyes a little, but she couldn't be sure.

"The victim was found a few hundred yards off of Route 441, near Bachman Gulch. It's a secluded wooded area near Alum Creek. It isn't visible from the road," Hollis had a way of falling out of his normal charming demeanor and into a more business-like tone when the camera was pointed at him. He had even sat up and put both hands on the wheel.

"And who found her?" Paisley asked, off-camera.

"A man said that he had stopped to relieve himself on the side of the road when his dog ran off. When he went looking for the animal he found the body," Hollis said.

"That seems odd."

"It is, for a few reasons."

"What reasons?"

"Well, for one, the bodies are normally far enough into the woods, and in spots that locals don't normally go, so they're not typically found for at least a few days after they were killed. This young woman appears to have been killed within the last twenty-four hours. Two," Hollis stopped and looked at the camera. "This isn't live is it?"

"Nope, just shooting some stuff to be able to cut in to

make a good narrative."

"Good, because this is an active investigation and I don't think that Sheriff Northfield wants me talking about all of this before he makes the official announcement."

"No worries, it won't be out until after everything is said and done and my investigation is complete." Hollis seemed to smirk at that part, but Paisley tried not to take it personally.

"So another reason that it's suspicious is that the guy wasn't back there to use the bathroom, as he said he was. He's a known moonshiner, and it's the Sheriff's thinking that the man was looking for franchising opportunities. Which, given his criminal history, could make him a suspect in the murder."

"History? It's a pretty big leap from bootlegging to murder."

"It's just very curious that he found her so quickly, so that throws up some red flags. And he already has a questionable track record."

"Sure, I get that, but just because someone likes shitty booze doesn't mean that they're going to kill someone in the woods."

Hollis smiled. "Oh, I know, and I don't think he did it either. The M.O. fits the creature, and I believe that it alone is responsible."

"Right, the bigfoot," she said.

"The sasquatch," Hollis corrected.

"Right, sasquatch." Paisley said. "So, do they know who she is?"

"Well, if this is in fact the same thing then we probably won't know for some time still. Of the seven women found two have been positively identified, four we have no idea about, and the last we know was a young woman who was hitchhiking across the state, according to a trucker who was the last to see her alive."

"And the trucker, is he a suspect?"

"No, he had a solid alibi for the time of death. He had dropped her at a truck stop about six miles from where she was found up in the hills a week or two later."

"So someone else must have taken her after that."

"Some *thing* must have taken her," Hollis corrected.

The two sat silently for a moment. Paisley put the camera down and just watched as the trees went past her window.

Hollis pulled his large black sedan as close to the crime scene tape as he could, but thankfully Paisley's view was blocked. He got out of the car, Paisley did not. She sat with her camera turned off and sitting in her lap. The shock of being that close to a dead body, even though she couldn't see it, terrified her.

"Are you coming?" Hollis asked.

"Um, no, I think I'll just run commentary from here, if that's okay?" Paisley said.

"But you won't be able to get a shot of the body from here."

"That's okay. Sometimes not seeing is more frightening. Like Jaws. Or herpes." It was Paisley's way to make jokes when she was uncomfortable. She couldn't help it. Hollis stood up and looked over the scene. She thought that from where he was standing he would be able to see the body. He leaned back down and looked at her.

"Okay. Well, do you want me to go get some footage for you?" he asked.

"Uh, no, thank you. That's okay." She didn't know how to tell him that she didn't even want to see the body when she was editing. Then the idea hit her. She knew how to sidestep the conversation altogether. "I can't actually show anything like that on my show because it's a violation of the terms of use. No bloody stuff, no dead bodies, and no nudity."

Hollis stood again to look at the scene. "Well, then, you are three for three on things you can't show here. You hang here and I'll go take care of this. I'll be right back." Hollis closed the door and ducked under the crime scene tape.

10

"Was it him again?" Hollis asked. He already knew who had killed the girl.

Grover Northfield, the county sheriff, looked back over his shoulder from his place by the body. "I'm sorry, you say something, reverend?"

"Yes, sheriff, I was asking if it was 'him' again," Hollis said, making air quotes around the word.

"Who? Jesus Christ?" the sheriff said with a giggle. Hollis didn't seem to find this amusing.

"No, him, the one who killed the other girls. The sasquatch." Hollis said the name quietly, giving it as much respect, if not more, than he would when he said his closing prayer in front of the congregation this coming weekend. They would no doubt be discussing the young lady and the discovery of her body. Hollis was sure that someone would soon report that she was a prostitute or some other lost soul. "You know he likes to leave them up here."

The sheriff turned to face off squarely with Hollis. The look on his face made Hollis angry. It was clear that his suggestion was not being taken seriously.

"Now Hollis, I've asked you to stop spreading rumors

that these murders were done by some forest monster. It gets people excited and makes conducting an investigation much more difficult."

"Grover, I grew up in these woods, I know every inch of 'em, and I've personally seen the beast four times not more than a ten mile radius from where we stand. And this case fits the pattern."

The sheriff stepped closer. Grover Northfield was a well-built man, but he wasn't as tall as Hollis, so he had to look up at him. Hollis liked this.

"I don't believe we have shared the details of this case with anyone yet, so I don't think you are qualified to make that determination," the sheriff said in his best "shut him down" voice.

"I'm just trying to help," Hollis said. "And I would like to remind you that it was your office that called me."

"To perform last rites to this young girl, not to try and convince me that the boogie man is killing women on my mountain."

"And I would like to do just that, if you don't mind," Hollis said, pushing past the sheriff. He waited until he was past the lawman before allowing a grin of satisfaction to creep across his face. He hoped that Paisley could see this exchange from the car. The sheriff turned and looked at her.

"Did you bring your girlfriend to a murder scene?" the sheriff shouted after Hollis, but Hollis just kept walking toward the mess.

This crime scene met all the other criteria for it to fit the profile of whatever killed the other girls. The head showed a large blunt object had smashed into it repeatedly until the orbital socket disintegrated from the force and the face of the pretty young blond had collapsed in on itself. This time the guts were hung in a nearby tree, a creative choice, Hollis thought. They looked like a deep purple beehive hanging from the branch.

Hollis approached the remains. He couldn't think of them as a body anymore-there wasn't really enough of her left for that. He looked back over his shoulder to see if the sheriff was within earshot. He wasn't. They never liked to hear the last rites. It was a sacred thing and they never seemed to want to be part of it. But the people in the hills had strong faith in the Lord and would never think to move a body, or what remained of one, without someone of the cloth performing the last rites. Hollis knelt and leaned in close to the woman's face. What Hollis knew, that the law enforcement in the area did not, was that last rites are given to the living and not the dead. Hollis had convinced them otherwise when the first woman was found dead. After having such a big hand in Grover being elected sheriff, the newly appointed county official had trusted him and never questioned the process. The people up here believed anything Hollis told them, as they believed he was the closest to God of all the members of their congregation. Instead of last rites Hollis would give a prayer from the Catholic ritual book *Pastoral Care of the Sick.*

"Loving and merciful God, we entrust our sister to your mercy. You loved her greatly in this life; now that she is freed from all its cares, give her happiness and peace forever. Do not judge her in heaven as we have judged her on Earth. Allow her punishment here to be enough. Welcome her now into paradise, where there will be no more sorrow, no more weeping or pain, but only peace and joy with Jesus, your son and our savior. Amen." He always felt he should kiss the forehead of the deceased at this point, but he was smart enough to know that it was an active crime scene and he always took special care to never leave anything at crime scenes. Though he knew the worthless law enforcement up here wouldn't know a murderer if he knelt in front of them and confessed. So instead of kissing them he would bow and kiss the palm of his right hand, and then release it into the air.

As Hollis bent forward to perform this ritual he noticed something sticking out of the dirt a foot or so from the mangled body. It was metallic, and the light from the morning sun glinted off the polished metal surface and poked his eye like a needle. It was as if God himself wanted him to see it. He reached down and brushed the dirt away. And there, looking up at him, was the white face of a man's watch. Hollis glanced back over his shoulder to see if the sheriff was watching. They wouldn't know what to do with a piece of evidence even if they found it. Hollis kissed his left palm and as he reached up to release the kiss he scooped up the shiny piece of metal with his right hand. He dropped it into the inside pocket of his jacket before standing up. He used brushing the dirt from his knees as an excuse to wipe the dirt from his hand before the sheriff noticed it. He walked back toward the car and he could see that Paisley was narrating, but this time she had her phone up. Hollis wondered if that meant she was streaming live.

"Thank you, sheriff," Hollis said. "I have performed her last rites and believe that she will now be resting at the right hand of our Lord and savior."

"Well, thank you. It is much appreciated," the sheriff said. Hollis walked back toward his car, ducking under the caution tape and shooting a smile up at Paisley. He felt he got the best of Grover again. They had been friends once, but now Hollis didn't trust him. He thought Grover was involved with people he shouldn't be and that his priorities might be questionable.

11

Paisley watched as Hollis walked up the hill and started talking to an officer. The officer was a little bit of a pleasant surprise. She had worried that this area would be so old school that they would be a bunch of racists or something. Maybe she had watched too much television and that painted hill folk in a negative light. So she was happy to see that not only was an African American man living here, but that he was an authority figure.

The officer didn't look happy to see Hollis. Paisley set the camera in her lap and pulled out her cell phone. Hollis had said there wasn't really cell service in Grey Water Ridge, but she had fine service, even up here. She checked her hair in the rear-facing camera and then hit the live stream button on the phone. She filmed Hollis and the officer as they puffed their chests at one another.

"Well, people, here we are. Shit got real. There was another murder, and I am here at the scene of the crime. And no, I'm not kidding. The man you see here is Hollis Grimm. He brought me out here to film the scene, but we're not about to do that, that's crazy, right? Like why would anyone want to see that?" she said. Then she thought for a moment. People may actually want to see that. As sick as that sounds. She turned the camera toward herself again.

"You guys don't want to see this stuff, do you?" she asked. It normally didn't take long when she went live for viewers to start popping in. There were already a few and the comments had begun.

WhyItHurts - *"He's cute."*
dillholeherpes - *"show us the bloody"*
Mit316 - *"Hey girl!"*
WhyItHurts - *"I wouldn't mind seeing the crime scene as well."*

"Hi Mit, hi everyone. Well I can't show you much, but let me see what I can do." Paisley leaned across the front seat. She could see Hollis walking up toward where she thought the body might be. She scooted behind the wheel. She could see Hollis kneel down, but from where the trees were she could only see his back. She aimed the camera at him and zoomed in as far as the phone would allow. He seemed to be talking to someone. She could tell that the body was just out of view.

"Okay, I'm going to see what I can get," she said. She stretched the phone to the corner of the dashboard behind the steering wheel. She couldn't see the screen, so she wasn't sure what it was catching, but she hoped it was something good. She saw Hollis look back over his shoulder then lean forward and say something. It looked as if he had caught something, whispered to it, and then let it go. Hollis stood and turned back toward the car. Paisley quickly slid back to her side of the car. "Okay, so I don't know what I got, but I hope it isn't gross. I don't want anyone to see that." She held the phone up so she could read the comments while still filming the scene.

Dillholeherpes - *"I didnt see nothing"*
WhyItHurts - *"Did he pick something up!?"*
Mhtx4040 - *"Wait, who is this tall sexy man, again?"*

Hollis was ambling down the hill.

"He's coming back. He is freaking gorgeous, I'll give you that, but the fact that he was just next to a dead body, and one that I hear is not in good shape, really affects his sexiness meter." She looked back at Hollis. He smiled at her. She smiled back, then looked into the camera. "But yeah, I totally would."

Hollis opened the door and slid in behind the wheel of the Plymouth.

"Poor girl," he said.

"Was it bad?" Paisley turned in her seat to point the camera at Hollis. "You don't mind if I'm live streaming right now, do you?"

Hollis looked over at her. The corner of his mouth rose in what seemed to be an unconscious reaction.

"No, I don't mind." He sat up straight and then turned toward the camera in his seat. He had to put his knee up on the bench seat, and Paisley was very aware that his knee was now less than an inch from her own. She tried hard not to look down at it. She tried hard, but failed. She glanced down ever so quickly. She had hoped that her face was concealed by the phone, but right after she did it Hollis adjusted in his seat and his knee slid that final inch. She could almost feel his power in that touch.

"Internet, this is Hollis Grimm. Hollis Grimm, the internet," she said.

"Hello internet," Hollis said, flashing that award-winning smile. The comments rolled in.

Mit316 - *"Looks like a scuz."*
Tiff1993 - *"oh yes I would too."*
WhyItHurts - *"But seriously, did he just tamper with a crime scene?"*
Dillholeherpes - *"was she naked? Can we see it?"*
Txtxatat - *"Well hello, Hollis!"*

"So, um, was it bad?" she asked again, trying to reclaim her professionalism.

"The Lord makes no mistakes," Hollis began. His voice was strong, but comforting. Like the preachers you would see in a movie. "He sees us for who we are, and understands our deepest, darkest moments, and he forgives us those moments. Whether they be evil in thought or in deed. But like the butcher, or the gas man, once you've run your tab eventually payment comes due." He looked down. His face went from being that of a stoic figure, deserving of honor and devotion, to that of a wounded man, sad and contemplative. Paisley subtly zoomed in on his face and tapped the screen on the phone to focus on his eyes. They flicked back and forth as if he was searching for an answer to all of it. Then he closed his eyes for a moment. Paisley realized she was holding her breath. She was capturing a moment. She didn't know if she was more excited about being the person that this amazing man was sharing this moment with, or the fact that this was making for an amazing live stream. As she stared at the phone display to keep focus, she noticed a single tear squeeze out from between his eyelids and stream down his cheek. It came to rest on the corner of his full lower lip and pooled there like a rain drop on a leaf after a late afternoon storm. Paisley felt a lump creep up her throat. She felt her own tears coming on. She sniffled them back. The sound caused Hollis to open his eyes. He looked up into the camera, and then over it into Paisley's eyes. He saw the tears there. Without a word, he reached around the outstretched phone and over Paisley's arms to wipe the tears from under her eye with one large, soft thumb. First the right eye, and then the left. His hand rested for a moment on her cheek before pulling it back and rubbing the tears between his fingers until they were gone.

"Thank you," he said. Then he turned back to the steering wheel and started the car. Paisley looked at the phone and before she could end the stream she saw the last two comments.

WhyItHurts - *"You've got to be shitting me."*
WhyItHurts - *"But yeah, totally would too."*

12

Main Street was busier than Paisley would have thought this early in the day. Hollis had driven them straight in to town after delivering the "last rites." He knew that there would be questions, he knew people would be scared, and he knew people would need him. He was right on all three counts. As the car pulled into a parking space in front of the butcher shop, they swarmed. People were asking questions. Some were crying. Some seemed nearly hysterical.

"Reverend, was it the beast?" called out one older man with a faded red shirt, equally faded blue overalls, and what appeared to be a John Deere hat from the turn of the century.

"Reverend, what do we do now?" a woman of about fifty asked, through the hands covering her face and trying to hold in her tears.

"Are we in danger, Reverend?" another voice from the crowd shouted.

"Was it another one of the whores?" said another man. Paisley hit the stream button on the phone and started to catch it all.

Hollis put a foot out of the car and people moved back to

give him room. He rose from the car like black smoke from an oil fire. Once he was out and his door shut, he lifted his arms as if to offer a hug to all those who would take it. Paisley thought she could use one. She did her best to film him holding his makeshift service here in the street from inside the car. People surrounded him, ducking under his long arms to be next to him. Some hugged him, some just leaned close, others placed their hands on him and bowed their heads.

The shops on Main Street emptied as the occupants flooded the street to surround their lamb of God. It was getting hard for Paisley to see him, so she slipped out of the passenger side of the car and up onto the steps leading to the town library. From there she could see the crowd growing around him. They pulsed inward toward him. It reminded her of the crowds she had seen on television trying to get into Walmart on Black Friday. With the camera pointed at the epicenter of the crowd, where Hollis stood easily a head above everyone, Paisley waited to see what would happen. She could not believe the sight, or the sound. The people were so loud. So many questions all at once. People weeping, some shouting for prayer, but then Hollis did something that quieted them all almost instantly. He raised his right hand in a fist, and then opened it with his palm to the sky as if he were letting go of an imaginary butterfly. The crowd went silent. Paisley could hear their shoes shuffling, people sniffing tears, one woman coughed. Hollis held his hand there and then looked up at it, and then to the sky past it. When he spoke his voice was soft, like that of a father telling his child that there was in fact a boogie man under the bed, but that he would never let it get him.

"Lord, we have heard your message. Yes, we have heard

it loud and clear. And though we may not understand your methods, we must honor them without question. We are your humble servants, and we wish nothing more than to serve you with righteous fervor. We don't know yet if it was your agent who came to collect the young woman in the woods this morning. Maybe it isn't for us to know." He kept his hand raised but he looked down at the crowd surrounding him. "Who are we to question you, O Lord? Who are we to try and guess what lessons you have for us?" He lowered his hand and pointed a long finger out over the crowd. "Not one among us feels that proof of your power is required, oh Lord. We will find your message in our every breath, and we will be glad that you have given us that breath." Hollis lowered his head and his hand. The crowd followed his lead as if they were trained to do so. "Dear heavenly Father, who art in heaven, hallowed be thy name. I, Reverend Hollis Grimm, of your town of Grey Water Ridge, do humbly ask for your forgiveness for those among us who would question you. For those among us who presume to know what is your will and that which is not for us to know, but that which is for us to trust. So forgive them Lord, I beg of you, in your name alone, Amen."

The crowd responded with an ashamed call. "Amen," they said.

"Now go, and on Sunday morning we will convene at the church and perhaps he will grace us with answers. Bless you all," Hollis said, and the group scattered as quickly as they had come.

"Well, fuck me," Paisley said, luckily only loud enough that a few prude women who were walking back up the street could hear her and shoot her an awful look. Paisley stopped the live stream.

Hollis looked into the car and saw she was no longer there. He looked around and spotted her perch on the stairs. And as if none of that just happened, he said, "So, lunch?"

The cafe was right in front of where the crowd had gathered for their weird demonstration. Paisley still wasn't sure what to make of it. She was in awe of Hollis. The way he commanded people. The way they trusted him. She had a friend who always talked about how hot single fathers were. The way they always cared for their little ones. She wondered if the way she felt about Hollis was a similar feeling, like this was a guy you could trust to take care of you.

Walking into the cafe, all eyes were on them. The place was full save for one small table in the front by the window that looked out over Main Street. It seemed odd that it would be available even though there were people waiting to be seated.

Hollis walked right past the folks that were waiting and up to the table, and Paisley reluctantly followed. He pulled out a chair for her, she sat, and he took off his jacket. It was the first time Paisley had seen him without it. He was very tall, and the dark jacket made him look thin, but without it she could see the definition in his muscles. The white cotton button-up was tight across his chest and even tighter around his biceps. He had the powerful build of an athlete. Her breath caught in her chest and she coughed. Hollis had not sat yet and he reached over and put a hand on her shoulder.

"Are you okay?" he asked.

That hand. It was so big, and so strong. She didn't want him to move it. Well, she did, just not away from her.

"I'm okay, thank you," she said. Hollis sat across from her at the table. The light from the large window illuminated him perfectly. It looked like he was setting up for a portrait session. She instinctively pulled out her camera. She flipped open the screen and started shooting some footage. She began with Hollis as he moved his silverware and napkin to the edge of the table out of the way of his arms. Then she slowly panned across the diner. She was watching the view finder closely to make sure everything was in focus when she noticed that all of the patrons in the diner were staring at her, and not in a friendly way.

"They may not take to kindly to being filmed," Hollis said quietly. "The people up here are very private. They like that the outside world is just that, outside."

Paisley turned to look at him. He had unbuttoned the cuffs on his shirt and was rolling up his sleeves. His incredibly toned forearms were covered completely in tattoos. She could not help but stare. He noticed.

"Surprised?" he asked.

"What?" she said, snapping out of her daze and putting down her camera.

"Do the tattoos surprise you?"

"Um, well, honestly, yes," she said. "But I suppose you probably weren't always a reverend."

"Actually, I've been studying theology nearly my whole life. So I feel like I was born into this life. But the tattoos came after my confirmation," he said rolling his arms so she could see the ink.

Some of the tattoos looked new, like one that appeared to be a large footprint, whereas others looked faded, like a large one of a cross covered in vines, though the vines had a number of leaves on them in various stages of fading.

There were also verses that appeared to be in Latin, weird relic symbols, and a beautifully done rendering of the entrance to a mine shaft. The tattoos covered all of the visible space on his arm coming down to about four inches above where his cuff would stop. She couldn't help herself, and reached out and touched his ink-covered left arm. She ran her fingers down his arm to his bare wrist. The transition from ink to skin was not subtle as the skin there was much more pale. She understood that the tattoos stopped where they did so that a shirt could properly cover them. She stopped on a small tattoo of a lighthouse. She recognized it.

"Is this..."

"It is," he said. "That's actually how I heard about you for the first time. I had spent a few months in Oregon a while back. I had gone to that lighthouse and thought it was absolutely beautiful. So before coming home I went to a little tattoo shop in Jigsaw and got that done."

"Which one?" Her fingers traced the lighthouse from base to tip.

"I don't remember the name, but--"

There was a crash as a glass hit the floor. Paisley jumped, Hollis did not. She pulled her hands away from Hollis's arm and turned to see a waitress standing with an overturned tray and a single glass of water in her hand. It looked as if she had taken one glass off the tray to put on their table and tipped the tray in the process. The waitress said nothing to Paisley, she just leaned across her to put the glass of water in front of Hollis.

"Here you go, Hollis. Sorry about the mess," she said, never acknowledging Paisley. She turned and walked away, stepping over the broken glass and spilled water.

"What the--" Paisley started and caught herself before

saying something profane, "heck?" she finished. "What was that all about?"

"What?" Hollis asked as he slid the glass of water that was set in front of him across the table to Paisley.

"She completely ignored me. I don't think she liked that I was touching your arm."

"Oh, I don't think that's it. Like I said, people in this town don't like people from outside. I'm sure Renee just doesn't know how to deal with all the newcomers yet."

"Well, Renee needs to learn some customer service," Paisley said. Then she thought for a second about going on about how rude the lady had been, but then caught on to what Hollis had just said. "What do you mean all the newcomers? Has there been a lot more than just me?"

Hollis appeared to consider his answer.

"There has been an uptick in tourism lately," Hollis said. "It's good for the town financially, but they aren't ready for that yet. We're working on it."

After a moment a teen boy came out to clean up the mess. Paisley turned to him.

"Thank you so much," she said to the boy whose dirty blond hair looked like it could stand a good scrub. He looked up at her and it took everything in her not to recoil or react. The boy looked like a normal, albeit dirty, teenager except for the large jagged scar that ran down from his scalp on the right side, across his right eye, which was now the milky white of bacon grease left on the stove, and down to the corner of his mouth. He said nothing. He just looked with his one good eye from Paisley and then to Hollis, and then back down to his chore. He swept up the broken glass and wiped the water with a wadded towel, and then he was gone as quickly as he came.

"Thank you," Paisley called after him. He never turned

back. Paisley watched him go and once he was through the batwing doors that lead into the back she turned to Hollis. "What is with people here?"

"Don't mind him either. Renee is just trying to figure out how to deal with people. That boy, Garrett, is trouble, and he knows it. So he tends not to say much around me." There was a moment of quiet tension. "Maybe he's afraid I'll tell God," Hollis said with a wink. That broke the tension and Paisley laughed.

Renee brought Hollis another water and a few menus. The rest of the meal was pleasant, other than the sinking suspicion that someone had spit in her caesar salad. They spoke about Paisley and her work, but Hollis didn't want to talk about the murders. He said that it wasn't great conversation for a public setting.

13

Paisley hadn't grown up in a tough area by any stretch of the imagination, but she was raised with a strong respect for things that were, to her, out of the ordinary. The note on the front door rang some alarms deep in her. She froze.

"What is it?" Hollis called from behind the steering wheel of the car that was now parked at the base of the steps leading up to Raven Bloom. "Everything okay?"

Paisley stepped forward to read the note. She wasn't sure if it calmed her nerves or if she should be more worried. She heard Hollis's car door open and close, then, within seconds, he was next to her.

"Is that a note?" he asked.

"Is this normal?" She pointed at a note with very fancy handwriting on it.

"Had some errands to run, be back soon. The door is open," Hollis read out loud. He left off Hyacinth's signature, but Paisley supposed that was normal. When her anxiety kicked in she often stressed over details like that.

"Do people up here just leave their doors open and notes for people to just stroll in?" she asked. Hollis pulled down the note. He grabbed the large, ornate handle and opened the door. He paused and listened.

"Hello?" he yelled into the house. "Hyacinth?"

Paisley noticed that Hollis took a step into the house before calling out. Most people would keep their feet outside the door and lean in to yell. Just another pointless detail that her overactive mind picked up. She wondered if Hollis may have a closer relationship with Hyacinth than the two let on. Hollis took another step into the house and disappeared behind the massive door. Paisley held her breath and waited.

"Yep," Hollis said as he popped back around the door. Paisley was startled but managed not to jump. "All is clear."

"Are you sure?" Paisley asked. Hollis had only been out of view for a few seconds, so he clearly didn't check the entire mansion.

"I'm certain," Hollis said. "People leave their doors open up here all the time. There's little to no crime up here in Grey Water Ridge."

"Other than the women who are brutally murdered and strewn about the forest on the regular," Paisley said with a nervous chuckle. Hollis did not seem to find this as amusing as she did.

"People are dead, Paisley," he said with a serious look. He stepped out of the doorway and onto the porch, raising his arm so that Paisley could step into the house; she did. Her shoulders slumped as the guilt from what she said washed over her. "And if the guy in the kitchen has anything to do with it you may be next. Kbye!" Hollis said, running for the stairs, laughing as he went.

In that moment Paisley went from sad, to scared, to mad, to laughing.

"You're such a jerk!"

Hollis stopped at the bottom of the stairs and turned around.

"Hyacinth always leaves her door open. I don't always agree with it, since most people in town dislike her, but she doesn't care. You shouldn't worry though--every person around these parts is afraid of Hyacinth and her family. No one would dare meddle around here."

Paisley looked back into the house. For as big as the place was it looked inviting and warm, even though it was dark in certain corners.

"Do you want me to come in with you and check the place out?" Hollis said. He looked down at where a watch should be and then realized he wasn't wearing one. He pulled his phone from his pocket and checked the time. "I know there are going to be a lot of people asking a lot of questions about the girl in the woods, so I should probably get back to town, but..." He trailed off.

"No, I think I'll be okay, but thank you." Paisley pulled her own phone out of her pocket and held it up. "I've got some friends that can come in with me." She smiled.

"I don't know what that means." Hollis said.

"I'll do a live stream," she said.

"Oh, okay, I get it," he replied. "Just be careful."

"Why?" she asked as she stepped farther into the house and slowly started closing the door. "It's not like anyone would ever try anything at the fabled Raven Blooooom," she trailed off as she closed the door. The last thing she saw before it was shut was Hollis with a confused look on his face. She laughed and turned on her phone. A few clicks later she was ready. She took a deep breath and tapped the "stream" button on her screen.

14

Courtney walked through the door of his shitty little studio apartment to the familiar scent of stale cigarette smoke, even more stale dirty socks, and moldy cheese from the nachos he fell asleep eating a week or two before.

It took a minute for his eyes to adjust to the dim light that managed to sneak past the moving blankets he had stolen from work and hung over the small windows high on the wall that looked directly out onto the sidewalk of the apartment complex.

He didn't need to be able to see to find his computer, though. He could navigate to it with his eyes closed if he needed to. It drew him like a magnet. He spent almost all of his time there when he wasn't working. He sat and his hands fell directly in place over the W, A, and D keys. The standard position for movement of a character in a role playing game on the computer. It was like he was melding into his second life when he sat down there. Though his priorities were such that it was more likely his first life, and everything else was second.

As soon as the computer came to life he clicked the icon on the desktop that represented his game.

"What the actual fuck!" he yelled. A message had

popped up in place of the character loading screen. It notified all players of a maintenance closure to patch a bug.

Courtney was furious. The game had scheduled maintenance on Tuesday in the early morning so it never interfered with his gaming since he was always at work at that time anyway. This was bullshit, and he intended to let them know about it.

Another tab opened and his Twitter page popped up. He composed a quick message to the developers.

"Dear sirs. If you fucking cunts knew how to fucking program you wouldn't be shutting servers down at peak times causing everyone to consider switching to your competitors as the place we spend money every month. Kindly get my game back up and then go fuck yourself with a chainsaw." He followed this message with four middle finger emoji. He hit send and smiled.

He glanced quickly at his feed to see if anyone in his guild had tweeted to say that they knew when the game would be live again. A new notification came in.

The notification was from Hyacinth Bloom, who he had been tracking for a bit. It was a retweet from someone he had never heard of, who was doing a live stream of Raven Bloom, which Courtney now knew was that fine piece of ass's house. He had clicked on the link and saw that it was some other cute chick walking around Hyacinth Bloom's house. He had seen enough porn to know that if one hot chick was walking around another hot chick's house, chances were she would find that hot chick in the shower and shit would get very real, very fast.

The woman that came up on his computer screen was hotter than he expected. She had decent little tits, and her face was probably a good six or seven. He couldn't see her body, so he couldn't tell if she was fat or not; she was no

Hyacinth, but he thought he would fuck her anyway. According to the info on the video page the chick's name was Paisley Mott, and she did ghost hunting or some shit. It was weird seeing the house without being curated for a specific picture. Hyacinth never did videos, just photos, so he had always wondered if she just went to a local library after hours and took the pictures she posted of the massive book room. Or if maybe it was an apartment complex with really nice amenities and the whole thing was a scam. To see the house, and its incredible size, made him want to meet Hyacinth even more. He looked around his shitty little studio apartment and then back at the seemingly endless halls and rooms of the mansion unfolding before him on screen.In life, you had to make your own luck, and if he were going to get Hyacinth Bloom then he was going to have to take her.

15

"Hey everyone, thanks for being here!" Paisley said, and then looked at the small eyeball icon that indicated how many people were currently watching live. The number was moving right around a hundred. That was slightly above average for one of her live streams. After she posted the videos they normally got a lot more, but it was still nerve-wracking knowing that there were that many people watching her right now. There was no editing. Just people watching her every move.

"So, guys, you aren't going to believe this, but I am in fact staying at this incredible Victorian Gothic mansion with the most amazing woman, and she has given me permission to film in here." Paisley looked around as if she was taking everything in. She figured it would add some drama to the shot. "So I figured I would give you guys a sweet tour."

Notifications from Twitter normally increased after she tweeted, as people would retweet her, but this time as the flood of notifications came in she noticed a major spike in her viewers. She was up to a thousand and then fifteen hundred. Within a minute she had more than five thousand people watching her.

"Wow, welcome everyone. I'm not sure where you all came from, but hello!" Paisley stepped deeper into the grand foyer. As comments flew in at the bottom of the screen she tapped and held one, locking it in place so it couldn't vanish with the others.

Photodog8226 - "*Hyacinth Bloom just tweeted that you were giving an exclusive tour of her house, so you are probably going to get mobbed by Bloomers.*"

Sure enough, the number of viewers climbed quickly. Paisley had to concentrate on not looking at the number and focus on the tour. After all, that's what everyone was here to see.

Paisley flipped the camera to reveal the amazing black marble raven standing sentry in the foyer. She panned slowly, showing the double staircases sweeping up from either side of the statue.

"And this, my friends, is Raven Bloom," Paisley said as she did her best to pan up the menacing statue.

Tix8785 - "*Holy shit!*"
Augustblush - "*Daaaaamn son! That's sick!*"

The comments flew by so quickly that it was hard for Paisley to make them all out.

"Now, kids, hold on to your britches because I am about to show you something truly amazing." Paisley turned and walked across the foyer to the hall leading to the library.

As the library came into view of the camera the comments increased.

"*OMG*"

"Hole. E. Shit."

"It's Belle's Library!"

"Oh yeah, Hyacinth shows that a lot, but never a full view like this?"

"Does she have any first editions?"

"Can I live there?"

"Booking flight to where ever that is."

Paisley tried not to let it distract her. She angled the camera downward, away from the architectural wonder that was the shelves, toward a gorgeous, ornate rug that lying in the middle of the room.

"That rug really ties the room together, does it not?" she said, then paused for fake laughter before swinging the view back to the shelves and their bountiful, beautiful content.

She moved around the room, showing off the incredible curved design that went around both levels of the room. One comment caught her eye.

"Does she have the ladder?"

"Someone just asked if she had the ladder," Paisley said as she stepped up onto the bottom rung of the ladder and then shoved off. Books whirled by like comets in the night sky with Paisley in the center of the frame for all the viewers to see. She laughed as the well-oiled ladder cruised around one corner and then another. It slowed to a stop and she jumped off. She filmed the ladder as she pushed it back in the other direction, watching it move sans rider.

"So, what else do you guys want to see?" Paisley asked the camera. She read as many of the comments as she could as they flooded in, but she caught and read the following comments and their users.

WWKKD - *"The Kitchen!"*
BoatGuys286 - *"Totally kitchen"*
NY152 - *"Just stay in the library. I love books."*
KingCourt - *"Ur tits"*

Paisley stopped and released the comments so they could disappear with the rest.

"Oh, okay, well that isn't going to happen KingCourt, sorry." She tried to laugh it off, but she was shaken. She had people make inappropriate comments before on her videos. She would normally just delete the comments from the thread, but this was the first time it had happened live. She persisted.

"All right, friends, let's go find the kitchen!" she said. She figured the kitchen would be a big draw. When she had looked at Hyacinth's Instagram account she had noticed a large number of the photos were taken in there, and rightfully so; it was a beautiful room made of stone and dark wood. It looked to Paisley like something out of a resort in a movie.

Paisley spent another half an hour touring around the kitchen, the den, and a few different living rooms. She had noticed that there was a distinct lack of recent family photos. Not that they hadn't been there, but that maybe they had been but they had been removed. There were gaps in the hallways, on mantles, and on shelves where the symmetry of the design had been thrown off by a missing frame. It may not have been as noticeable if Hyacinth's house was not so perfectly curated. She never mentioned it to the viewers, and she didn't know if they had noticed themselves--she had decided not to look at the screen so she could avoid another sexist troll.

As Paisley left one of the living rooms she heard a door open at the front of the house. She looked down into the camera on the phone.

"Someone is here," she said. She had started out pretending to be frightened, but as the idea set in that she left the door unlocked and that it could be anyone, the fear became real and her heart rate spiked.

"Hello?" Paisley called out. There was no response. She heard a few muffled footsteps. "Hello?" she called out again. "Hyacinth?" There was no response.

Someone was in the house with her, and they were not responding. It was getting hard to hide her fear. Her first thought was that she was about to be murdered in front of a ton of people. How many, she wasn't sure of, but for some illogical reason it seemed important for her to check. She flipped the screen so she could see it. There were more than fifteen thousand people watching. But it wasn't the number that caught her eye. It was the comments. The comments all said the same thing over and over again. Two words. Scrolling up the screen and filling the text box.

WhyItHurts - *"Behind you!!"*
Djradmaddi - *"bhind u"*
LilDirk2002 - *"behind you"*
Hybloom - *"BEHIND YOU"*

Paisley froze. She heard a floorboard creak behind her.

The phone dropped. Paisley dove forward, tucking her shoulder and rolling. She kicked the phone as she did and it spun, so that the audience saw the impressive maneuver. She came out of the roll and popped up onto her feet, with her hands raised in a defensive position.

"Jesus fucking Christ!" Paisley said.

"Oh shit, Paisley, I'm so sorry. I was just messing with you," Hyacinth said.

"You scared the shit out of me!" Then, realization set in. "Hybloom, right." One of the comments was from Hyacinth, though part of her may have known that, and thought maybe Hyacinth had been watching and trying to warn her.

"Yeah, I tuned in when I got back. When I saw you were way back here I thought I would sneak up on you. Sorry, hon."

Paisley turned the camera to address the viewers.

"What do you think, should I forgive her?" she asked. All of the comments coming in were versions of yes with the occasional "No way!" thrown in for good measure. But then KingCourt caught her eye again.

KingCourt - *"Make her strip and give her a fucking spanking."*

"Ugh, why does someone always have to ruin it?" Paisley asked, showing Hyacinth the comment.

"Oh, dude, Court, grow the fuck up, you pig," Hyacinth said. "Don't make her block you too."

"You know this guy?" Paisley asked. Hyacinth pulled the camera up and looked directly into it.

"Yeah, he's a fucking trash person with a tiny dick, no friends, and zero respect for women," she said. Paisley laughed and turned the camera back to herself.

"Well, friends, that's going to be it for now. I've got some crazy stuff to show you once I can get in and edit everything, and I have a feeling there will be a lot more crazy stuff to come. I'll do my best to keep in touch while

I'm up here in the hills, but you take care of yourselves. Until next time. Mott out." Paisley clicked the button to stop the live stream.

16

As the bitch with the decent tits closed the stream he could hear the two of them laughing. It echoed in his head. A cold feeling ran through his chest as if he had just taken a big gulp of ice water. He knew where they were. He'd been following Hyacinth Bloom long enough to have done his homework. The idea of visiting her had presented itself a few times, but if he went now he could get the two-for-one special. The gears began to turn.

17

Paisley had been out looking around for about an hour, and it was a good thing the Canary Yellow Hummer had a working navigation system out there in the middle of nowhere. If it hadn't she would have been in deep trouble, as she had absolutely no idea where she was. She had the window down and was listening to the sound of the gravel under the SUV's large tires. She could hear birds chirping, wind through the trees, and some source of water off to her left. For the first time since getting to Grey Water Ridge she felt at home. The forest out there wasn't the same as the forest she was used to in Oregon, but it was close enough. Paisley was very happy that Hyacinth had offered the use of the Hummer so she could get out and get some air therapy. Hyacinth had offered Paisley her choice of vehicle from her stable of luxury cars and trucks, but the Hummer stood out so much that she just had to pick it. It also helped that it had four-wheel drive but wasn't the behemoth of a truck that Hyacinth herself loved to drive. She was told to just grab whichever keys she wanted from a box in the garage. Another shocking moment of security that made her wonder who these people were.

As she drove she wondered if the source of the sound of

water would show up on the navigation system's map. She placed her thumb and forefinger on the screen and pinched. The terrain on the screen got smaller as the point of view launched upward as if the camera was attached to a rocket approaching escape velocity. She could now see every road, mountain, and body of water within a three-mile radius. It appeared that there was a stream that ran parallel to the same road she was on. She saw that up ahead the river was going to take a left turn and terminate at a lake about a mile off from the road. So when she saw a small clearing right after the river turned she pulled the Hummer in and parked. It looked like someone had used this spot to park before. Probably someone that had plans to go to the same lake she was going to.

Paisley looked at the smart watch she wore. It was still midmorning and she had planned on stopping in to talk with Hollis at some point, so she couldn't spend all day out here, but she had some time to kill. Looking in the direction of the lake she could see that a small path had been worn over time. She figured that someone had trekked to the lake enough times that it probably wasn't too hard of a hike. She pulled out a waterproof neon green backpack that had seen more than its fair share of hikes in the hills along the Oregon Coast. It was stuffed with hiking gear. Being well prepared probably wouldn't keep the anxiety she often felt at bay, but it might buy her more time to get in front of it when it started. She threw the backpack on and then grabbed her portable camera case. She started a live stream as she set out to find this hidden lake, and began talking.

"I'm up here in the hills, and it is gorgeous. I don't know that this means anything for my investigation, but I think it gives me a sense of the terrain I will be dealing with out here. Now, you may be asking yourself, dear viewer, why, if I am out here investigating the murders of now seven women, by a suspected monster in the very woods I currently find myself in, am I out here wandering about? Well, let's review the information thus far." Paisley stopped and held up one finger in front of the camera. "One, all of the murders took place overnight, in the dark, and it's not even noon yet." She held up a second finger. "Two, the victims that have been identified were all allegedly women of questionable moral character. Now I'm not saying that I am a saint, by any stretch of the imagination, but if the rumors are true then the beast only wants to kill those who sin openly. And sadly, I have no plans to sin in these woods today," she said, flashing a smile. She held up a third finger. "And three, I grew up in the woods. I'm not afraid of anything they have to offer. I have found that a proper respect for your environment is the best way to ensure that you will make it home safe." She thought to herself for a moment and then finished with, "Plus, I've got you guys with me, so I think I'll be just fine." She ended the stream and sent it to her account to be posted in her feed, then she slid the phone into her pocket and focused on the hike. She wasn't familiar with the terrain, and she wasn't going to do something stupid just for the sake of a good shot. She would make time to set up the camera and do the whole production of it all when she came to a nice spot that she could scout out. For now, she would be all about making it to the lake safely.

The trees stretched up to the sky like thousands of hands hungry for light. They were so tall that once Paisley stepped onto the path the temperature dropped as well as the available light. It was a feeling she was used to, but in this instance she felt the weight of the dark blanket of shadow that fell over her.

The woods were quiet, save for the birds, the sound of distant water, and the breeze through the leaves. Back home in Oregon Paisley would see more of a mix of deciduous and coniferous trees; here they were mostly just deciduous, so there were not as many pine needles on the ground, which she missed. She liked the way they felt under her feet when she walked. The sounds were just different enough that the farther she got from the safety of the Hummer the more uneasy she felt. Her confidence level began to drop, and she knew herself well enough to know that once it started it often didn't stop until she was an overly anxious mess and that she could freeze up and be in real trouble. Each step felt like she was getting closer to that. That all-too-familiar point where she would just want to sit down and give up. After all, she had never done anything this major by herself. What made her think that she could do this alone? What gave her the idea that she was a good enough vlogger, or a good enough investigator for that matter, that she should be out here trying to cover this story? Her feet shuffled like a reluctant preschooler heading for the nap corner as she moved along the path. She pulled her arms close in to her body. Her head, normally on a smooth swivel, keeping an eye out for potential danger in the woods, was now jerking back and forth at every little sound. Visions of all the days in elementary school when she would have anxiety attacks and hide under the slide hoping the world would forget she existed danced in her head.

Paisley felt like the world was now closing in on her. Her breath started to catch in her chest as she walked. She knew she was getting to the point of no return on this anxiety attack. She knew that if it hit she would end up sitting on the nearest rock she found until it passed, and then she would hike back to the Hummer, likely after dark. Distracted by the fear of being out there alone with whatever beast roamed those hills, she didn't see the drop-off in the path and took a hard step down. Her knee shook and her weight shifted, causing her ankle to roll. She managed to save herself from a serious injury, but there was pain nonetheless. That felt like it might be the last straw. Her eyes began to sting as she tried to fight back tears of stress and frustration.

"Make the choice," a voice said. It made Paisley jump. Then she realized the voice was her own, that she had said it. She said it again, "Make the choice." She felt a jolt of adrenaline radiate through her body. She raised her head, her jaw clenched. She had been in this situation before, and she had trained herself to deal with it. It didn't always work, sometimes it was too much. "Do what you know how to do. Be Paisley Mott. Own it." The words came like an iron sword out of a stone. She lifted her head and let the feeling wash over her. When she lowered her head a moment later she was a different person. She was no longer little Paisley Mott, who would hide under the slide. She was the Paisley Mott who created her own destiny. This was part of the ritual of being okay. There was one last thing that always pulled her back from the brink. Part of the ritual that had ultimately saved her life. She pulled out her phone and hit the stream button. Looking right into the lens she felt powerful.

"Hey guys! So this place in incredible! It's unreal. I highly suggest making the trek out here if you ever get the chance." She was approaching normal. She had a secret that she kept when she talked to the camera. The secret was that she wasn't talking to the audience. She was talking to her twelve-year-old self. That poor little girl who thought that she would never be like the other girls. The poor little girl who thought that it might be easier to just give up. That poor little girl that just needed someone to show her that twelve was not the pinnacle of life, but instead just a stepping stone on which you could boost yourself. She hoped that some little girl, or boy, was watching her and thought that they could do anything too.

10

The lake was everything that Paisley had hoped it would be, and more. As she came through the final thicket of trees it unrolled in front of her like a tapestry. The water was so clear and calm that Paisley could see the bottom for nearly twenty or thirty feet out. She stood on the grassy shore looking out over the magnificent view. Mountains surrounded the lake on all four sides, and it appeared that trying to get here any other way than the way she had come would be very difficult. She turned on the camera and started shooting some B-roll before aiming the camera at herself.

"This is it, folks. This is what heaven looks like. It's beautiful. Now I'm not going to say it's more beautiful than what we've got in Oregon, but I can say that it's pretty darn spectacular." Paisley looked back over her shoulder at the lake, then back at the camera. "Stand by for some tasty drone shots!"

Paisley set her camera on a rock so that it was still recording her while she took her drone out and got it airborne.

The lake looked even more stunning from the air. She watched the live shots on her phone which was clipped to the drone's controller. As the drone climbed high into the air she slowly pushed it out over the water and got a variety of shots she felt were absolutely incredible. As it soared across the lake something caught Paisley's eye on the screen. Something moved on a bank to the left side of the lake. She turned to look but the trees were too thick between her and the movement, so she turned the drone and flew in that direction. She assumed it was probably a deer, which would make for a good shot, but what if it was actually a sasquatch? A shot of it would make history.

The drone tipped forward and darted for the shoreline. It was the fastest she had ever flown it, and she was both exhilarated and terrified of crashing into the trees if she couldn't slow down quickly enough. As she approached she could see something in the trees. It was a shadow in the darkness--she could see as it moved that it was large and stood upright. It was no deer. She couldn't tell how large it was, or if it was a person, a bear on its hind legs, or Bigfoot, but whatever it was saw the drone and went running back into the dense woods where she could not safely fly it. She begun to pull up to slow down, and then thought about the possibility of being the first person to catch the legendary creature clearly on video. She smiled and the drone barreled toward the thick trees once again. She could no longer see the shadow figure, but she had seen the dark path that it went down and thought she might be able to follow it if she was careful.

Worst-case scenario was that she'd crash the drone. If that happened she would risk losing it, and the 4k video on the memory card, but she would still have the preview video saved to the phone. If it did crash and was unable to take off again, she would find a way to hike over to that side of the lake and recover it.

The woods were so thick here that even with the wide-angle lens she could only see directly in front of her when she flew down the path. There could be something right next to the drone and she might not know it.

The light on the camera shifted--something had moved behind the drone. She tried to spin the drone around but before she could something smashed down on it hard and it crashed to the ground. Paisley screamed. She watched the screen as the camera slammed into the ground and bounced once, ending up in a pile of leaves. She tried getting it to lift off, and she could see leaves blowing away from the camera, but then there was another jolt and the wind stopped. The camera continued to run. Paisley gripped the controller, frozen with fear. She screamed again as the camera angle tilted and the drone was lifted. She thought quickly and tried to turn the camera on the drone's gimbal, but when she moved the controller sticks to do so she could see that the camera stayed pointing the same direction, but the drone itself spun. Whatever was holding it was holding it by the camera. She watched helplessly as it began to crash through the woods.

Paisley looked in that direction and then realized that the thing may be coming toward her. She snatched up her camera, and with it in one hand and the drone controller in the other she took off running toward the Hummer, her ankle sending a knife of pain up her leg with every step. Fear propelled her and she could think of nothing other than being torn apart and left in a tree for someone to eventually find.

After what felt like an eternity of running, the yellow glow of the Hummer was finally visible through the trees. A cramp had begun to form in Paisley's side, but ran faster at the sight of Hyacinth's car. She broke through the tree line and slid to a stop at the driver side door, ignoring the burning pain in her ankle. Paisley had left the door unlocked, which she was grateful for in the moment. She pulled the phone out of the controller and looked to see if it was still recording. It was, and whatever had it was still carrying it. It was pointed away from the figure, but now the elevation had changed. She watching as the image approached a clearing in the trees, and she realized that it wasn't following her--but what she saw puzzled her even more. It was a cliff. Then the drone appeared to be flying again, though not in the smooth straight line she was used to watching; this time it was jittery and tipped end over end. She tried to catch a glimpse of whatever had been carrying it, but instead caught a glimpse of bright yellow-- and then the drone smashed onto the hood of the Hummer. It crashed like thunder and was followed by the sound of rain as plastic parts exploded and ricocheted off the vehicle.

"Holy shit!" Paisley sat frozen for a moment before jumping out of the car. She looked up, but the cliff was too high and she couldn't even figure out which point the drone had come from. She gathered as many of the pieces as she could, then jumped back into the Hummer and sped away.

Even with the adrenaline pumping through her veins, the little observational magic trick she did when anxious was still in effect, and she couldn't help but notice the thin line of red paint buried in one of the scratches on what was left of the drone's body.

19

The small white church sat atop the hill like a glowing crown against the dark green of the trees surrounding it. It stood alone save for the old red Toyota pickup truck filled with firewood that was parked alongside it. When both the truck and the church were in full view Paisley thought that the door to the church, painted a stark red against the white of the building, was colored to match the beat-up truck. An odd thought for such a moment, but the anxiety had not yet lifted completely and her perception was still heightened.

Paisley parked next to the old pickup. The paint on the old truck had been scratched vertically as if someone had been dragging a key along its side twice a week for a few decades. It was the type of vehicle that helped a person do their work so they just never got rid of it. She jumped out of the Hummer with part of the busted drone in her hand and grabbed her camera bag, slinging it over her shoulder on the move. Sense memory groped at her, and when the sound echoed off the hills it caught her. Something familiar. A noise buried deep in her subconscious. She stopped and let the memory twist its fingers into her hair and drag her in. Then the smell caught up with the sound and the memory came like a high wave on a thirsty beach.

Her grandfather singing Sinatra songs as he swung his axe. The smell of the fresh cut wood. The sound of the head driving into the wood as it cracked and split. He would stand with his plain white tee shirt tucked into his khaki pants with his axe in his hands. He would have her put a log on end on the large stump behind the cabin he had built from the ground up by hand. After he split a few he would take a little break while Paisley would gather them up in a bundle and stack them next to the cabin. Her grandfather would often tell her stories of her grandmother, who had passed before she was born. It always made her feel so close to him. Now the sound, and the smell, of wood being cut could take her back to that place.

Paisley went around the corner of the church and saw Hollis there chopping wood. He wasn't anything like her grandpa in his clean white tee shirt. No, Hollis wasn't wearing a shirt. He was wearing dark blue jeans, tan work boots, and, from what she could see, red Hanes underpants that peeked out from the waist of his jeans. His chest and arms were cords of muscle. He looked to Paisley like a swimmer who loved to lift weights. His shoulders were broad and powerful. They rotated like a machine as he brought the axe down with expert precision. She could see his tattoos didn't end with his arms. He had a large piece on his back as well. It appeared to be cursive script. Paisley wasn't sure at first how he had not heard the Hummer pull up, but as she got closer she could see a cord bouncing off of his chest: he had headphones in. She could hear the loud music playing but she couldn't identify the song. She stopped, thinking it wise not to startle the large man holding the axe.

"Hollis? Hollis!" She waited until she could hear the song end and tried again. "Hollis?"

He heard and turned. She was surprised that he wasn't startled. He pulled the earbuds out of his ears and hit stop on the cord.

"Well hello there, Pickle. To what do I owe this incredible honor?" he said, looking past her.

"It's just me," she said. Normally she let men's thoughts run their course and then explain their actions. She had seen this so many times that she knew what would happen. He would look around her to see if Hyacinth had come with her. Then he would do some sort of "um" or "huh" to show that he had made an observation, and then he would explain why he had made the assumption that then lead to the observation. She had let him get away with things similar to this already, but that was because he was freaking adorable and even though he was a man of God and most likely off limits, she liked him. At the moment, however, she was freaked out.

"Okay, I just wondered," he started.

"You wondered if Hyacinth brought me out here, but she didn't. She loaned me a car, and the address to the church wasn't hard to find."

"Oh, all right," he said. Paisley thrust the broken drone toward him. He leaned back so he could focus on it. "What's this?"

"It's my drone. It's destroyed," she said.

"Your what?" He gingerly took the broken thing from her.

"My drone. A flying camera," she said.

"Oh! I've seen those online. They're pretty neat." He studied the wreckage with interest.

"Well, it *was* neat, until something attacked it."

"What do you mean? Like a bird or something?" He looked up to see if there were any large birds of prey visible in the sky.

"No, by something in the woods. It knocked it out of the air and ran off with it. Then it Pluto Nashed onto Hyacinth's Hummer from up on a mountain."

"Pluto what?"

"Bombed."

"I don't get it."

"Whatever," Paisley said. Her sense of humor barely worked in the civilized world--she wasn't sure why she thought such an obscure reference would play out here in the sticks. "Something threw it down on the car from up on a mountain."

"Are you serious?"

"Yes, of course. It was terrifying."

"Did you see it?"

"Yes," she said. Hollis's eyebrows went up and seemed to pull the corners of his mouth with them. "Well, no, not exactly." Hollis looked like a child who had been given an ice cream cone just to find out that it was broccoli flavored.

"Well did you or didn't you?"

"No, not really. I got the outline of a shadow. I don't know what it was. I was trying to find out when it attacked."

Hollis looked at the drone closely.

"Looks like it was hit with a stick. I bet the creature used a branch from a tree."

Paisley took a moment to consider if she wanted to point out the paint transfer on the side of the drone. She wasn't convinced that it was a branch that took the drone out, but perhaps a baseball bat or an axe handle, something that was painted red or had words printed on it. If it was

Bigfoot that hit it she doubted that it would have had the foresight to keep the camera pointed away from itself the entire time as well. It was a person who took it out. And a person who threw it on Hyacinth's car. It was a message. A message not to go around there anymore, but she didn't know if she should tell Hollis any of that. She didn't know if his friendly demeanor could handle her correcting him again, and she still hoped to get some information out of him. She held out her hand showing she wanted to see the drone. He handed it back to her.

"Oh yeah, look at that. I bet you're right," she said. She pulled her phone from her pocket, opened the video from the drone, and hit play. It wasn't the best quality video, but he could see what happened. Paisley had queued it up to right when she flew into the trees to find it. Then fast forwarded it to the point right before it had been thrown off the cliff.

"Wow," Hollis said. "Pretty clear proof that it was the beast." She worried that he was drawing too many certainties about the incident and she didn't want him asking to use the video in his service or anything else to prove something she didn't yet believe in. One of the reasons she went to see Hollis was in the hope that he would debunk the video immediately. One of the most important things when investigating the paranormal was making sure that the people who are driving the investigation don't use every coincidence to protect their theory. Hollis seemed to be doing just that.

"Hey, do you have a few minutes to sit down and talk about the murders?" It was an abrupt tone change, but Paisley hoped he would follow her on it.

Hollis looked around, and this time Paisley wasn't sure what he was looking for. It was obvious they were alone.

"Sure thing. We can go inside and have some lemonade and talk, if that's okay?" Paisley nodded. Hollis smiled and extended his hand. "After you."

"You probably don't need that," she said, pointing at the axe he still held. "At least I hope not."

He chuckled at his forgetfulness. He looked back at the stump where he had been chopping wood. It was now a good forty feet away. He winked and then spun. The axe made a slicing noise as it ripped through the air. It made a few fast revolutions before sticking deep into the side of the stump.

"Holy shit," Paisley said. She wasn't sure what impressed her more, the accuracy with which the axe was thrown, the strength it must take to exert that much force, or the confidence he must have to even attempt that sort of thing.

"Thanks," Hollis said with a smirk.

"Oh, God, sorry," she said, covering her mouth. Hollis smiled and pointed at her in an adorable manner. She thought about what she said. "Oh no, that was probably worse. Sorry!"

"It's okay, I'm just messing with you. Though you may have some penance to pay when we get inside." She flushed at what she felt was obvious flirtation. If it wasn't, then Hollis Grimm was the most oblivious man she had ever met.

The inside of the church was much like the outside. No frills. Everything from the floor and walls to the pews were slat wood. It looked, on the inside, like an old cabin. She supposed the outside would too if it hadn't been painted white and had a steeple. The wooden pews were set on either side of the narrow center aisle and Hollis walked between them toward the pulpit at the front of the church.

On the wall above the pulpit hung a large crucifix with a very pained version of Christ nailed to it. It wasn't the normal somber-looking face of the savior. No, this iteration was screaming in pain. Hollis turned and saw her looking up at the figure. He snatched a black tee shirt from the front pew and pulled it on.

"We like to remember the true sacrifice made for us. So the pain is important," he said.

"Well, it would be hard to forget his sacrifice. He looks like he's suffering a great deal," Paisley replied.

"Oh, it isn't his sacrifice we honor. I mean, we do, but it's his father's sacrifice. The sacrifice of God." Hollis walked across to a table that had a few bottles of lemonade, some packages of crackers and cookies, and a small coffee station. The coffee maker was shiny and new, and looked very out of place in the old building. She didn't see anywhere in the building where there was running water, including the very obvious lack of a bathroom. The building was not up to code, that was for sure, but she suspected that the people in this area had little use for building codes. With the lack of running water it would be safe to assume that someone brought water to fill the machine on mornings with service. Paisley tried to turn off the part of her brain that was over-analyzing everything so that she could focus on what Hollis was saying, but her anxiety was still in overdrive. Hollis picked up a bottle of lemonade and brought it over to her, then continued his lesson.

"God needed man to understand his love, so he sent his son for them to love. And man did. Man fell in love with the son of the savior. He gave us something to believe in. Something to give us hope after centuries of sin and desperation. So when he had his own son tortured, and murdered, for us, it was to punish us. Not to forgive us. And that is what we need to remember." It was quiet in the room as his words hung in the empty building like a noose from a weak beam. When Hollis popped the cap on his own lemonade Paisley jumped from the start. That made Hollis laugh, which broke the tension and made Paisley laugh in return.

"So, speaking of punishment, can we talk about the girls?" Paisley asked. Hollis took a sip of his lemonade, made a face, and nodded his head. "Do you mind if I record?" Paisley pointed at the camera bag on her back. She knew that if the camera was rolling it might calm her nerves and quiet the anxiety.

"Of course not, go right ahead. That's why we're here, right?" Paisley pulled the camera out and got it set up. She hoped to get a lot out of him that she could use for the vlog. She knew it would be either incredibly interesting or completely bat-shit crazy. Either way would be okay with her. She could sell either side of that particular coin.

With the camera on a small tripod over Paisley's shoulder, and the microphone pointed at Hollis, Paisley began.

"So, Reverend Grimm, can you give the people that may be watching a brief introduction and maybe a bit about the town before we get into everything?" Paisley said, pointing at the camera. Hollis turned up the charm. Paisley thought that he could say the craziest thing anyone had ever heard and there was a good chance that people would believe it. He looked into the camera.

"Hello, my name is Reverend Hollis Grimm of The First Evangelical Assembly of the King's Redeemer, in Grey Water Ridge, Kentucky. Before we get in to the sightings around town, perhaps a short history lesson about Grey

Water, and then how I got involved with the church. What do you say?" Hollis smiled at the camera. Paisley could feel hearts breaking somewhere down the stream of time again when people watched this video. Hollis began.

20

Grey Water Ridge hadn't always been named as such. It started out as a mining camp. It was named Harris Ridge, after the first person to settle the area and stake claim to the riches of coal buried deep beneath the beautiful mountain vistas of the area. Gerald Lee Harris had discovered the coal and was determined to pull as much out of the hills as he could. The modest camp quickly turned into a town when Harris purchased nearly every acre of the county and dropped mine shafts into the earth to start pulling the coal up in very quick order. Those who came in the early days made a lot of money, but those who showed up late to the game were often hired by the stakeholders who didn't want to split their shares as equally as may have been fair. Like many mining towns that have outgrown their ability to produce, the town became overrun with poverty. Poor labor practices caused deaths in the mines, and a few out of it. Anger in the town grew and there were talks of the laborers marching into Harris's home to grab him and drag him out to one of the shafts to drop him in.

With the townspeople in an uproar something needed to be done. So a man named Wilbur Bloom stepped forward with a suggestion. Bloom was a young man who had moved to Harris Ridge, with his pregnant wife, to try his hand at entrepreneurship. He sank every last dime he had into building a small gristmill at the head of the river coming into town. He had chosen a location where the water wouldn't yet be contaminated by the coal dust downstream. It was a modest set up, but if he kept a good pace he could turn out a few bags of flour a day. He went down to the saloon one night to try and enlist the help of a young man to help him run the mill. Instead, he happened to be in the right place at the right time to talk some sense into an angry mob set on murder, stopping in while they were figuratively sharpening their pitchforks and lighting their torches. Bloom asked what was happening and they told him they were about to take the town back.

"Take it back from whom?" asked a tall thin man dressed in clothes that were probably very nice before they were sold second hand to the man who now wore them. Bloom.

"G.L. Harris, the slimeball who's stolen all of our money," one drunk man wielding a club said.

"Well, did Harris steal your money or did he steal the town?" Bloom asked.

"He stole both."

"How?"

"He--" The man stopped and thought. "Well, he doesn't pay us enough."

"Well, that isn't exactly the same as stealing from you. Did you agree to work for the wage you've been paid?"

"What does that have to do with anything?" another man shouted. The crowd cheered their agreement with the question.

"Well, if you agreed to the low wage, then you're as guilty as the man who offered it. Was it Harris that offered it?" Bloom asked.

"Well, no, it was the managers," the first man said.

"So why string Harris up for your negotiations with a third party?"

"Well, because he's up there making money off our backs," the man countered.

"And was it your money that was initially invested to set up the camp and drop the shafts?" Bloom asked.

"No, but..."

"Did you know that Gerald Lee Harris put every last penny of his family's fortune to get this camp going?" Bloom asked.

"But now he's making that and more," the drunk argued.

"Actually, he hasn't even made it back to the starting point in his finances yet. He's still operating in the red, as they say," Bloom pointed out.

"And how do you know?" the drunk asked.

"Because I, sir, am an accountant," Bloom said with pride. He hadn't said he was Harris's accountant, and he didn't say that he was only an accountant in the fact that he did his own books, he just said he was an accountant and had an understanding of numbers. He knew Harris had likely borrowed money to start the camp and had not tapped into his family's wealth. He was also fairly certain that Harris would have skipped out on repayment of those loans had the mines not proved out.

"That don't mean he can treat us like this," the drunk said, eliciting another cheer from the crowd.

"I agree completely, and I, on your behalf, with your blessing, will talk to him about this matter tomorrow, if you will allow me that honor?" Bloom had been looking for a way to get noticed by the mining company, and saving the owner's life and quelling a potential labor strike should do just that.

The drunk looked around at the crowd.

"I think we best just have our justice tonight," the drunk said, earning yet another cheer from the crowd.

"Okay, how about this..." Bloom looked around and made a quick estimation of the number of people in the room. "How about you stay your anger for tonight, you let me talk to Harris in the morning, and if you agree to be patient and allow me to negotiate on your behalf, I will buy the next round of beer for everyone in here." The room was silent. They looked at their unofficial spokesman, the drunk.

"You'll buy everyone here a drink?" the man asked.

"I will," Bloom said. "But you have to all agree that killing Harris isn't the right way. At least that tonight it isn't."

"Well, okay then!" the drunk yelled, and the crowd once again cheered. Bloom stepped up to the bar and got the bartender's attention.

"Are you crazy?" the bartender asked.

"I don't have enough to cover this tonight," Bloom said, handing the bartender what little money he did have. "But I'm good for it, I promise. If you allow a tab to be run, I assure you that I will be back here tomorrow with the money, along with a healthy gratuity for you."

The bartender thought about this for a moment. "One drink each?" he asked.

"Yes, please?"

"Okay, but tomorrow..."

"Of course, thank you so much," Bloom said before running out the door.

Bloom went to see Harris the next morning. It took him a long time to gain access, but after word had spread about what he had done in the bar, and how he had potentially saved Harris's life, he was allowed an audience with the man. He explained the uprising and told Harris of the labor unions forming around the country and warned of what would happen if they got to that point.

By the end of that year Bloom had negotiated a fairer price for the workers, created a holding corporation to manage the miners, and removed the current stakeholders from operations and paid them out dividends on their stock instead. Then, after all of that, he ran for mayor and won, as no one would oppose him. Bloom, now a figurehead in the bustling town, closed up shop on the gristmill.

Harris ran his mining company for a few more years until an explosion in a mine killed thirty-six people and blew the side out of a mountain. Investigators claimed that a miner had placed a set of charges in the wrong spot. Bloom asserted that the workers being overworked and unsupervised had caused the placement to go unchecked and that had caused the mine collapse. That accident caused loads of soot and coal dust to pile up in the river. The town was flooded, and eight more people died and three homes were lost when a makeshift dam gave way. The slurry from the mine runoff then made it to the river, devastating it. The river turned black and the water was considered poisonous. Towns downstream wanted Harris's head on a pike for causing sickness and distress for their people. The families of the miners that were killed sued the company. Harris was at the end of his rope. That's when Bloom stepped in again to save him.

Bloom had owned stock in the Harris's company as part of his deal with the workers, and using his newfound financial influence had purchased even more of the stock. When the accident happened, and the stock prices dropped to next to nothing, Harris bought up almost every share that was held by the old managers, and then made an offer to Harris himself to buy him out. With everyone in a hundred mile radius calling for his head, Harris saw no other way out than to sell. So he did. With Bloom, the town's hero, at the helm of the company, and swearing that nothing like the accident would ever happen again, tempers cooled and business resumed.

Under Bloom's leadership the company thrived. Bloom used the wealth to expand the company, and within ten years he was one of the richest men in the South. Wilbur brought his son, Craven, into the business and would eventually leave it to him. With Harris ousted, and the town wanting to distance themselves from the horrible things he had done, but not to forget what happens when attention isn't paid to things, they voted to rename the town Grey Water Ridge in honor of the now poisonous river.

21

"What happened to the miner who blew up the mine?" Paisley asked. Hollis had spent the better part of an hour telling her, and her camera, a significant part of the town's history.

"He was arrested but never went to trial," Hollis said.

"Why not?"

"That night, facing either guilt or the idea of being lynched by the angry town residents, he killed himself in his cell."

"Coward," Paisley said.

"It was a tough time."

"Is the river still toxic?"

"No," Hollis said. "It's been clean for a very long time now. But the name is important to the residents here. Most of them have had family here for generations, and those events scarred a lot of us."

"Has your family been here that long?" she asked. Hollis paused for a moment. Paisley knew that pause. He didn't want to get into that subject but didn't want to seem like he was avoiding it either. She liked his mysterious side.

"My family has been in Grey Water since it was Harris Ridge. They weren't original charter members of the town, but they were early enough to have deep roots," he said.

"Were they here during the accident?" she asked. Hollis paused again. It was like he had to process his answer, run it through a filter and make sure it didn't contain anything he didn't want shared, and then put it out.

"Yes, my family was in town during the tragedy." But before Paisley could ask another question, he continued, his attitude changing as he did. He was that confident preacher again. "That wasn't the last time that the town was punished for its sins," he said. "The lord saw the greed that this town bathed in and he saw fit to punish us. We are not to question his methods, only to question ourselves for bringing his wrath upon us."

"You think the mining accident was punishment?" Paisley asked. This wasn't where she thought the conversation would go, but she figured it would be an interesting road nonetheless.

"I do," he said. "I also believe that the current deaths in the woods are a warning sign that if we don't start to change our ways we will once again find ourselves being judged."

"Is that what you believe the murdered girls are? Punishment?"

"Is it murder if the thing responsible for their death wasn't human?" Hollis countered.

"What do you mean?" Paisley tried to hide the skeptical look that was sure to cross her face.

"God uses all forms of tools to shape man. In this instance he has chosen a forest beast. A beast greater even than ape, or bear," Hollis said. His serious tone pulled Paisley in. It was hard not to believe him. She had dealt with a lot of liars in her day, and a lot of people who had told themselves something so many times that they actually believed it, but Hollis was either telling the truth, or he was a demented sociopath. Paisley looked into his dark eyes. She believed him. She believed that there was something in the woods.

"Have you seen it? The bigfoot?" Paisley asked. Hollis smiled. He had been asked this question a lot, she assumed.

"Sasquatch," he said.

"Pardon?"

"Sasquatch. Bigfoot is a name. Bigfoot is a moniker given to a specific sasquatch in the American Pacific Northwest, where you are from, if I'm not mistaken?" Hollis said, but didn't give her time to respond. "Our sasquatch is different from the sasquatch that you have in your neck of the woods, that you call Bigfoot. Bigfoot has darker, brown and black fur. Fur that looks more like a gorilla. Our sasquatch is..." Hollis paused. He put his hand on his chin and his eyes narrowed. He looked back up at Paisley. "Would you be my guest this Sunday at our service?"

Paisley had already assumed that she was invited and had planned on attending the service.

"Yes, of course. I would love to," she said.

"Fantastic. Bring your camera and you will learn everything you need to know about the beast that wanders in the hills," Hollis said. Paisley couldn't wait.

22

The yellow SUV backed cautiously out of the drive and onto the dirt road, then turned and kicked up clouds of dust as the girl drove away. Hollis leaned against the door frame of the church and watched her as she went. He was playing the interview back in his head. He felt like he had done well enough. He wanted her to be enthralled with the tales of the beast in the woods. He wanted her to get his story out. He turned and stepped through the door that was just an inch taller than he was, and closed it behind him. He had thinking to do.

Hollis walked to the pew closest to the door. It was the farthest from the front, which was where he gave his sermon every Sunday morning. He sat in the pew, his long legs bunching up as he squeezed in. He reached out a hand unconsciously and laid it over the pew as if he was grabbing it. His long thumb dropped down and began tracing letters that were roughly carved into the back of the old wood. He looked up as the pad of his thumb ran across the letters and he could almost see his father standing at the front of the church barking out his sermon. Hollis was ten years old again.

23

Hollis tried not to snicker as he dug the knife his father used to scale fish into the pew. His young hands were large for a boy of ten, but he had not yet hit the growth spurt that would make him the tallest man in the county. Currently his father was questioning a man in the front row about allegedly stealing a chicken from a neighbor's farm. Cecil, Hollis's brother, who was just seven years old, was watching closely so he could tap Hollis on the leg if his father looked their direction, but they seemed to be in the clear. Hollis finished scratching the capital H and then sat back and smiled as he looked at his handiwork.

"Do mine next," Cecil said quietly. Hollis looked at him, then looked up at their father, who was now strutting around the front of the church like a chicken for some reason as the parishioners scattered among the first few pews watched him. "It's a C," Cecil said with pride.

"I know, I'm not a dummy," Hollis said. He was a little sensitive about his brother telling him things. Hollis was smart, but Cecil was what everyone called "advanced." He and Cecil had learned to read the same year, but Hollis was three years older. Cecil loved books and learning new things. Hollis did too, but he wasn't as quick a study as

Cecil was. Hollis leaned forward with his eyes angled toward the man clucking at the front of the room, and began to scratch the letter C.

After the service Hollis and Cecil ducked out as soon as their father finished the prayer. The boys had chores to do, and once they were finished they would be allowed to go up on the hill behind their father's house and camp. It was just inside the woods, so they could still see the house from where they set up the tent, and their father would be able to look out the back window and see if their campfire was going.

Hollis loved to camp, and Cecil loved to go with him. Hollis would set up the tent, get the fire going, and cook a couple of hot dogs while Cecil would pull out one of the scary books that their mother had left behind when she moved out. There was a book called *Scary Stories to Tell in the Dark*, a couple of R.L. Stein books, and Hollis's favorite, a book by a man named Stephen King, called *Skeleton Crew*. On the night Hollis had carved the letter into the pew Cecil was reading the last story out of the King book. It was a story called "The Mist." In it a group of people were stuck in a grocery store after a strange mist had rolled in and brought with it a bunch of monsters. Hollis asked Cecil to stop reading until he was done setting up camp because he didn't want to miss any of the story. Cecil agreed and helped Hollis by holding the stakes while his brother hit them with a hammer. Cecil trusted Hollis completely, so he never even considered that Hollis might miss and hit him instead. After camp was set they each sat near the fire, with their blankets wrapped around them, while Hollis rotated a few hot dogs on a long metal fork, and Cecil read the story. When the hot dogs were gone Hollis would stick the tines of the large fork under the hottest log until it glowed bright orange, then he would pull it out and use it to burn marks into another log. The story, however, gripped him so much that he forgot to pull the fork out of the fire and it began to glow halfway up the shaft.

They were both captivated by the monsters just outside of the survivors' vision, and what would happen if one of them went outside. A few pages in, they found out, and it wasn't pretty. Hollis wondered if the stories in this book were too much for a seven year old, but they never seemed to bother Cecil, so he never said anything. Hollis found something else interesting in the story. There was a character named Mrs. Carmody who was accused of being a witch, but Hollis felt she was more of a preacher. She preached the dangers of disobeying God. Their father did the same thing, but not in the way that Mrs. Carmody did. Their father talked about disappointing God, but the lady in the story talked about swift and deadly wrath for those who did not believe in the almighty. Hollis was excited by this idea. He loved how the survivors in the story began to flock to her once people started to die. They needed her to save them from the vengeful God. Halfway through the story Hollis was standing up and pacing back and forth around the fire hanging on every word of the story. He was charged up. He was so focused on the story that he didn't hear the sound come from up the hill. Cecil did and stopped reading.

"Why did you stop? Keep going, it's getting good!" Hollis said. Cecil had dropped the book in his lap and was looking off into the dark that had pushed in around them unnoticed like a snake sneaking up on a rabbit in tall grass.

"What was that?" he asked. His eyes looked like pennies in the firelight.

"I didn't hear anything." Hollis said. As if on cue the noise sounded again. A low rumble followed by what sounded like stones being dragged across a metal grate. Hollis stepped back quickly to stand next to Cecil. He instinctively put his hand up in front of Cecil to protect him. A branch broke and the shadows on the far side of the fire shifted.

"What is it?" Cecil whispered.

"Shut up."

Whatever was there was getting closer. They couldn't see what it was, but they could see that it was big. The shadows shifted again and Hollis saw the slightest glimpse of firelight reflected in two small mirrors about eight feet off the ground. Then the mirrors blinked.

"Hollis?" Cecil said. Hollis held out his hand to stop Cecil. Hollis's body was so tense that his hand jerked as he raised it.

"Cecil, listen to me," Hollis whispered, trying not to move his mouth. "When I say *now* you run back to the house." Cecil looked over his shoulder back toward the house. Hollis could see the light in the kitchen was on. His dad would be down there right now. Cecil or he could scream, but his father wouldn't hear them from there. "If you get there and I'm not with you, tell Poppa to get up here right away and bring his gun, you hear me?" Cecil nodded and ground his feet into the dirt, preparing to run.

The figure was just outside of the firelight now. Hollis could see its outline against the darker woods. It was massive, and it didn't look like it was even standing up straight.

"Now!" Hollis yelled. Cecil turned and took off down the hill. The figure in the dark shifted forward as if to follow the running boy, but Hollis slammed his foot down onto the wooden handle of the long metal fork, which was still stuck under the big log in the fire.

Sparks, ash, and embers burst into the air as the log leapt from the fire and flew outward toward the shadow. Hollis watched as the aerial torch streaked through the sky toward the thing. It landed short of the figure, but it provided enough light for Hollis to see it well enough, and he would go his entire life without forgetting a single detail of what he saw that night.

The beast was easily nine feet tall, and Hollis would guess later, after understanding more about tissue and weight, that the creature weighed at least nine hundred pounds of pure muscle. It was covered head to toe in a thick dirty red hair with strips of orange weaved in sporadically. It was wide at the shoulders and chest, like a bodybuilder. It stared at Hollis, not afraid of the fire, but perhaps annoyed by it. Its eyes were black holes that reflected the slightest bit of light. Large, sharp canine teeth jutted up from a lower jaw that was pushed forward so that the long teeth could rest on the thing's upper lip. Its large head shifted as if the thing were deciding whether to attack or not. Hollis attacked first.

Hollis dipped down and scooped up the book that Cecil had dropped and in one fluid move he chucked it across the scattered fire toward the beast. As Hollis looked up to see if the book would find its mark, he was terrified to see that the thing was no longer there. He wasn't sure if it was retreating or moving around to get a better angle of attack, so Hollis did the only thing he could think to do. He ran.

Cecil was still running down the hill when Hollis caught up to him. He slowed and ran beside his brother, putting one hand on his back trying to hurry him. The boys began to yell for their father as they approached the house and barged through the back door.

Their father was sitting in the kitchen, looking angry and disappointed. A nearly empty bottle of whiskey on the table sat next to the knife he used to scale fish.

Both boys froze, forgetting about the thing in the dark. They were busted.

"Shit," Hollis said.

24

Hollis ran his thumb along the last of the four letters in the back of the pew. He was looking at the pulpit where his father preached before he died, and where Hollis would return and take up the mantle when he was seventeen. His father would preach kindness, love, and forgiveness, and he practiced it as well. Hollis had been afraid that night they saw the beast would be the first time his father would hit him, but it wasn't.

His father died later that year without ever raising a hand to either of his boys. His father was kind and loving. So when he and Cecil ran in and saw him sitting there with the knife they had used to defile the church pew they knew they had disappointed him, and they felt horrible. Hollis almost would have preferred a beating to seeing his father crying. He had told his boys that night that he was scared for them because God punished those who wronged him. It was man's job to forgive, but God's job to decide a punishment.

Later that night, when the boys were in the room they shared in the small house, they agreed that it was best not to tell their father about what they had seen. Hollis was convinced that the monster was sent from God to punish them. Cecil didn't seem as sure, but he wasn't about to split hairs. He was just glad to be safe.

The next morning the boys went back up the hill to gather up their tent and supplies, but found that all of it had been destroyed. The tent was in ribbons, their blankets had holes torn in them, and the book Hollis had thrown was gone. They left everything where they found it as sort of a tribute to God to make up for their evil ways.

They never stayed overnight on the hill again. It would be months before they would even play up there during the day, and even then they would not go near the campsite. Their father assumed that the boys associated their refusal to stay up there with guilt over that night and his disappointment over the carving of the two letters into the pew. He made the decision to not sand the letters out of the pew and left them there. He wanted them to be a constant reminder to Hollis, who always sat in that same spot on Sunday mornings.

Now Hollis looked down at the pew. The first two letters, that he had done that day when he was ten, were jagged. Next to them were two more, these ones cleaner, done by Hollis's much stronger hand when he was seventeen, long after his father had died. He touched the second set of letters. A tear formed in his eye. These letters were supposed to represent protection. The first initial of a little brother he wondered if he would ever see again. His finger then came to rest on the second, cleaner, H.

25

Hyacinth stood in the large kitchen. She wore a low-cut white tee shirt that was just one stop of opacity away from being transparent. The sun came in from the large picture window above the sink and reflected off a giant, brushed stainless steel, hood vent above an equally large gas range. She was perfectly lit as the timer on her camera chirped its countdown. Hyacinth held a pose with one hand running through her thick red hair, and the other holding a small espresso cup while she blew the carefully crafted steam into the sunbeam. The shutter clicked. She held the pose as it clicked a few more times. She was no amateur, and knew that you took multiple shots just in case something magical happened. After the shutter stopped clicking Hyacinth set the cup down and skipped over to the camera. She clicked the preview button on the expensive camera and cycled through the photos she had just taken. With a little tweaking she knew she would get her next Instagram post. She dumped the espresso into the sink as the files transferred wirelessly to her computer in the hidden office. She didn't actually like coffee, but she noticed a six percent increase in positive engagements if her photo had some sort of coffee in it. She also knew that she would get a twenty-one percent positive engagement bump on this photo because she was wearing a white tee shirt and standing in front of a light source. You could easily see her form through the shirt, but you couldn't see her skin. This was key for her. She never posted nude photos, or even anything showing more than you could see if she was wearing a bikini. She didn't need to. Though a lot of her followers would ask, if not demand, that she post nudes. Some even thought that by sending her direct messages they would be able to get her to send one privately. She never responded to these people. Instead she kept a list of those who asked, and she cross-referenced each name so if they asked more than once she would block them from interaction. It was a pain, but all part of doing what she did.

She was walking from the kitchen to the library when she heard the Hummer pull in. She peeked out the window and saw that Paisley was parking it right out front instead of taking it around to the garage. She could also see that there was a big dent and a scratch across the hood.

Hyacinth opened the door and stepped out onto the porch. Paisley was getting out and pulling her camera bag behind her. She had some busted piece of plastic in her hand, and looked upset.

"Hey, are you okay?" Hyacinth asked. Paisley raised her head, looking as if she might cry.

"Oh my God, Hyacinth I am so fucking sorry." She ran up the steps to where Hyacinth was standing, then held the drone out to her.

"Oh, girl, it's fine, don't worry about it." Hyacinth looked at the broken thing in Paisley's hand and realized it was a drone. "Did you crash your drone into my truck?"

"No, I didn't, but you aren't going to believe what

119

happened. Luckily, I have the whole thing on camera."

Hyacinth watched what footage they were able to pull from the SD card. After it was over Hyacinth wrapped her arms around Paisley and squeezed.

"I am so glad that you're okay," she said. "Don't even worry about the car. It isn't important at all. What's important is that you are safe. Plus, I've got that snazzy hectocopter in my office that I've never even opened that you are welcome to use while you're up here. It's like magic. You can just set it to follow your phone and it will fly around above you recording everything. It's amazing."

"What, you mean that amazing drone in your office? The one that's still in the box?"

"Oh, you saw it?"

"You mean the auto-adjusting hectocopter with 8K video and a multi-axis gimbal? Yeah, I think I noticed it."

"Hahaha, you're such a nerd," Hyacinth said, laughing. "Yeah, that's the one. I opened it and flew it once. Well, I tethered it to my phone and it followed me around the property like some psycho machine before I put it back. But you are free to use it if you want."

"Seriously?"

"Of course, use whatever you need. Most of it was sent to me for free anyway," Hyacinth said.

"Oh my God, thank you."

"No problem at all. Like I said, it's all just stuff. The important thing is that you're okay. And the big question of course, who the hell was that out there?"

"Or what?" Paisley said.

"What?"

"Yeah, I went by Hollis's church on the way back here, and he seems to think that it was a bigfoot."

"Wait, so Hollis saw this footage?"

"Yeah. Well, he saw it on my phone. So it was harder to see," Paisley said. Hyacinth was relieved. She didn't think that it was a sasquatch, but she wasn't ready to share what, or who, it might be with a relative stranger just yet. She liked Paisley--a lot actually; she was another internet celebrity, and the only other one Hyacinth had ever met. She felt like Paisley understood her on a level that no one else ever had. That didn't mean she was about to give up all of her secrets just yet, especially to someone who was looking into the goings on of Grey Water Ridge. Some things you had to protect. Hyacinth hit play on the computer and watched the video again. It was long, and she watched intently for some verification of what she had suspected. She glanced over a few times to see that Paisley was watching just as closely, if not more so.

After the second viewing Hyacinth got up to close the video.

"Can you play it in slow motion?" Paisley asked. Hyacinth stopped for a moment. She didn't want to. She didn't want Paisley to look any closer at this video, but she couldn't say no. That would look suspicious.

"Sure, which part?"

"As the camera sees the shadow in the trees. I want to see if we can get a really good freeze frame of it. Then maybe we can use your photo editing software to enhance it enough to at least get a better idea of what it looks like."

Hyacinth started scrubbing forward to find the part Paisley was talking about. She stopped when the drone spotted the shadow and began going frame by frame. There was a split second when the figure turned and Paisley spoke up.

"Right there, that one. Grab that frame," Paisley said.

Hyacinth wasn't a big fan of taking orders, and Paisley was just telling her exactly what she would have done anyway. Well, what she would have done if she didn't want to hide what might be there. But she knew exactly how to execute it, and not doing so would be suspicious. She narrated what she was about to do so that Paisley wouldn't be able to say it first and think she didn't know what she was doing. She always felt she had to prove herself to people; she didn't want to be that way with Paisley, but it was habit.

"Okay, I'm extracting the raw data from the frame. I'm exporting it to Lightroom, and I'll raise the shadows first, so that we don't wash everything out by just raising the exposure," Hyacinth said. Paisley nodded along with every comment. Hyacinth wasn't sure if it was in agreement or in acceptance. She wondered if Paisley had a better way of doing it.

"I am so glad you're here," Paisley said. Hyacinth stopped and looked at her.

"What?" she asked.

"I would be so lost trying to do this myself. You're amazing, thank you," Paisley said. Hyacinth smiled. She turned back to the computer and worked her magic. She used every trick in the book to pull as much information as she could out of that small section of the photo. It wasn't perfect, but when she leaned back to let Paisley get a good look, it was obvious. It wasn't a sasquatch at all. Unless this particular sasquatch wore a cowboy hat and carried a baseball bat, both which were now very apparent in the photo.

"Well, look at that!" Paisley said. "You are a rock star!"

"There we go. Just some asshole in the woods," Hyacinth said.

"He looks really tall, or is that just me?"

"I think that's just the angle," Hyacinth said. Paisley was right, he was tall, but Hyacinth wasn't ready to let on that she knew who it was. "You can't show this to anyone yet."

"What? Why not? This is internet gold! It's got a touch of crazy, a dash of conspiracy, and a whole heap of mystery. This has viral video written all over it."

"Listen, there's a lot more under the surface of these murders than just some creature wandering around out there, and I'm asking that we get some definitive answers before we start showing our cards."

"We? Our cards?" Paisley asked. Hyacinth was nervous that she had come on too strong and that Paisley would withdraw and she would lose any chance she had to try and guide this mess in to a smooth landing. Though she was pretty sure that Hollis had made damn sure that would never happen now.

"Yeah, we. I'm like the Watson to your Holmes, the Wilson to your House, the Scooby to your Shaggy. I've got your back on this one," Hyacinth said, hoping that Paisley would go for it. Paisley sat for a moment in thought.

"How about this, instead," Paisley started.

Hyacinth braced herself internally for her to say she was taking her stuff and staying somewhere else. She hoped she wouldn't, not just because she wanted to be involved in this, but because she genuinely liked Paisley, and really enjoyed having her in the house. Plus it would be easier to keep an eye on her and try to control some of the information she got if she was there. She held her breath.

"How about the Scully to my Mulder?" Paisley said. Hyacinth smiled.

"Fuck. Yes!" Hyacinth said and jumped forward onto the couch to wrap Paisley in a giant hug.

The two laughed and held the hug for a moment.
"Did you just smell me?" Hyacinth asked.
"Noooo," Paisley lied. The two laughed again.

26

The sun bit through the window and punched Paisley squarely in the face. She attempted to throw her arm over her eyes, even tried putting a blanket over her head, but with every passing minute the morning light punctured the giant window in the guest room and forced Paisley to admit that she had lost the battle and would have to get out of bed. This was her third time waking up in the mansion and she still wasn't used to the amount of light that hit the east side of the house in the mornings. Hyacinth was either used to it, or wasn't bothered by it, which Paisley found insane. Who in their right mind wants to get up that early? Paisley stumbled out of bed, still in the sweatpants and hoodie she had fallen asleep in, and lumbered down the stairs toward the kitchen and the smell of coffee and bacon. As crazy as she thought Hyacinth was for getting up this early, she couldn't be mad about the fact that for the third morning in a row she had woken to breakfast and coffee. The previous two mornings she had come down to find Hyacinth setting the scene for a very clever breakfast photo to be published for her eager fans.

The first morning Hyacinth had been sitting with her feet up on her chair, her knees pulled to her chest, her hands cupping a mug of steaming coffee. She had looked away in a three-quarter shot so her face would be mostly obscured, but her perfect hair, that was styled to look like it hadn't been styled at all, was front and center. The second morning the camera had been set up on a tripod low to the floor so that it looked up at Hyacinth, who stood at the stove with a spatula in one hand, hovering over a frying pan on the stovetop, the contents of which were unknown, but whatever it was seemed to be appetizing to her as she was making a pursed-lipped face as if whatever it was made her very happy. The highlight of this photo, however, was the very small terry cloth shirt she wore that showed off her midriff, but as she was facing the stove, only the side of her stomach could be seen. Which meant that her very shapely backside was on full display in the tight boy-shorts she wore. If Hyacinth wasn't so smart, funny, and kind, it might make Paisley feel a little upset that she was also gorgeous. Hyacinth was beautiful and used it as a strength.

As Paisley approached the kitchen she wondered what sort of picture staging she would walk into. She saw Hyacinth looking into the refrigerator and could imagine her setting the camera up in there to get a point-of-view shot from inside.

"Trying to get the perspective of the cottage cheese?" Paisley said as she entered the kitchen. Hyacinth shut the door and Paisley noticed that she wasn't as dolled up as she had been the previous two days. She still looked stunning, but it was the natural beauty and not the character she put online.

"Well, good morning," she said. "Breakfast is on and--" Paisley cut her off.

"Thank God, I'm so hungry I could eat the ass out of a

pig just to get some bacon." Hyacinth laughed and turned to look toward the table.

"Speaking of bacon..." She pointed. Paisley turned. There was a man sitting at the table. Paisley recognized him after a moment as the officer that Hollis had talked to at the crime scene. He was an attractive, rugged man. He had a square jaw, the stubble that so many men tried and failed to pull off, and deep brown eyes. His muscular frame filled out his Sheriff's uniform nicely. He stood.

"We have company," Hyacinth said. "Paisley Mott, meet Sheriff Grover Northfield."

"Nice to meet you, miss. I am so very sorry that it took me so long to get out here and make my introduction. It's been a busy few days," Grover said.

Paisley shook his hand. She had seen him briefly at the crime scene, but she couldn't see just how attractive he was there.

"It's my pleasure," Paisley said. "I'm sorry, I wasn't aware we were expecting you or I would have cleaned myself up a little before coming down."

"Nonsense. Grover doesn't mind, do you?" Hyacinth said, sliding a plate with grits, bacon, toast, and hash browns across the table to him.

"You look positively lovely, Miss Mott," Grover said, sitting down behind the plate. Hyacinth brought two more plates for her and Paisley while Paisley poured herself a cup of coffee.

"You know, Sheriff..." Paisley started.

"Grover, please," he said. Paisley stopped and considered that she had never been on first name basis with law enforcement, and she supposed she'd have to accept it as another in a long line of weird experiences that this case had brought on.

127

"Deal. And please, call me Paisley."

"Deal," Grover said.

"And you can both call me Governess Bloom," Hyacinth added. Paisley lightly punched her arm as she sat down.

"So, Grover, I was hoping to sit down with you and get an interview at some point, if you don't mind?" Paisley was half expecting him to say that since it was an active investigation he couldn't share any of the details of the case, but she also knew enough that she could ask questions and hopefully lead him into saying more than she already had.

"Of course," he said without hesitation. "My office is happy to help." Paisley was thrown off by this and just sat for a moment gathering her response. Hyacinth chimed in before she could.

"Grover is a friend," she said. "A good friend." She reached over and laid her hand on top of his on the table. Paisley looked back and forth between the two of them for a moment as that set in. It made total sense.

"Of course," Paisley said. Part of her was relieved. She had worried that Hyacinth and Hollis were an item, and she not-so-secretly wanted to take a shot at the preacher. She still hadn't forgotten the familiar way that Hyacinth addressed him as "Holly" though. She had spent a few hours with Hollis now and hadn't heard a single other person refer to him that way. Hyacinth took her hand back. Grover seemed to blush a bit.

"There are, naturally, aspects of the cases that I cannot share as it is an active investigation, but I am happy to share everything I can with you," Grover said.

"On camera?" Paisley asked. Grover considered this for a few moments.

"Okay, but one condition," Grover said.

"Which is?"

"If I say something stupid, or something that makes me look less than qualified, you can't put it online," Grover said.

"I normally don't make that deal," Paisley said.

"Grover is in a tough spot, Pais," Hyacinth said, using the nickname she had given her the night before as they sat up drinking and watching movies and talking about which fictional hero they would each be. Hyacinth chose the Gal Gadot version of Wonder Woman, while Paisley, as she had her entire life, chose Indiana Jones. Hyacinth continued, "There are people in the county that would like to see Grover lose his job. He's still an outsider in their eyes."

"An outsider? Why?"

Hyacinth looked at Grover, and then back at Paisley. Then Grover lifted his hand to show the brown skin on the back. Three looks crossed Paisley's face one right after another. First surprise, then understanding, then disappointment.

"Isn't Sheriff an elected position?" she continued.

"It is, but that doesn't mean they voted for me by choice," he said. He seemed a bit ashamed. Paisley could see it in the way he shoved the grits around on his plate.

"Why would it not have been their choice?" Paisley asked. Grover looked at Hyacinth, and she looked back at him. She nodded. Grover set his fork down and wiped his hands.

"As an outsider they thought that I would be an easy person to influence. But I'm no puppet."

"The townsfolk didn't like it when Grover stood up to a few of the older members of the town council when they asked him to close the roads into town during the peak of tourist season," Hyacinth said.

"Why would they want that?" Paisley asked.

"Because they don't want people coming in here and disturbing their way of life," Grover said. "And with hunting season, and people hiking the trail, we have a few months every year where a bunch of folks roll into town. It's good for business, but it alters people's routines. And every now and then someone decides they like it here, and they want to stay. Well, there isn't any real estate for sale here. So they offer to buy land and build. That only brings up hurt feelings and causes a lot of arguments. They prefer to just not have the outsiders roll in in the first place. So they asked that I put up signs that say only local traffic can use the roads up the hill into town. I said I couldn't do that and they have hated me ever since." Hyacinth rubbed his thigh in support under the table.

"Man, the people here are seriously messed up," Paisley said.

"You have no idea," Grover said. Hyacinth pinched him playfully under the table.

"Hey, my family has been here for generations, thank you very much. We helped build this town that you two are making fun of," she said.

"Well, yeah, your great, great, grandpa was this town's savior, from what I read," Grover said. "So I'm not talking about you folks."

"Great, great, great, grandpa. Three greats," Hyacinth corrected.

"What do you mean 'from what you read'?" Paisley asked. Hyacinth tensed a little. Paisley noticed. She also noticed that Grover noticed. They all tried to play it off.

"The *Harris Ridge Return*," Grover said, as if this would answer Paisley's questions.

"The what?" she asked.

"The *Harris Ridge Return*. It's the tiny little newspaper that ran here in town after the Civil War ended. It was basically a gossip rag for the people in this area," Grover said.

"Why haven't I heard of this before?" Paisley said. This was exciting news. This was exactly the type of thing that private eyes would always find some key piece of information in.

"Well, probably because it went out of business more than a hundred years ago," Hyacinth said.

"But they have the archives over in the library on Main Street," Grover said. "They're on that microfiche thing. Goes all the way back to 1860 or something. Tells about Hyacinth's three greats grandpa riding into town and single handedly putting an end to Gerald Harris's nonsense." Hyacinth looked at Grover. Paisley couldn't tell exactly what the look was. It was a mix of frustration and fear.

"Well, you sure do seem to know your town history," Hyacinth said. "Or is it just my family you were studying?" Paisley felt something in the pit of her stomach. This was the first time she had seen Hyacinth be anything but sweet. She didn't seem angry, it was just uncomfortable. It wasn't impossible that she was messing with Grover.

"Nope," Grover said, not noticing the tone change, "I just read up on all the big stories when I was running for Sheriff so that I could hopefully relate to everyone here. I didn't want to lose the job. I had a lot on the line." Grover squeezed Hyacinth's hand. It seemed to back her down into her normal self again. Paisley was grateful for that.

"Can I see it?" Paisley asked, cutting the tension.

All three of them jumped as a squelch crackled through

the room as if a pig had broken through the wall. It was Grover's radio. A muffled voice came on.

"Sheriff, you there?" the voice said from the black box on Grover's hip. He grabbed the microphone that was clipped to his epaulet.

"Go ahead, Sami," he said, pushing the button on the microphone and then releasing it to listen.

"Sheriff, we got us a 10-54 up by Old Hide Lake." Before the transmission was over Grover was on his feet and moving. Paisley noticed that Hyacinth looked worried too. "Looks like it got another one," the voice finished.

"I'm on my way now," Grover said as he keyed his microphone. He turned and looked at Hyacinth.

"What is it?" Hyacinth asked. If she didn't know what the code was for, and she had the worried look on her face, it wasn't the situation that bothered her, it was the location.

"Another body," Grover said. "I'm sorry, I have to go. Thank you for breakfast," he leaned over and gave her a quick kiss with a practiced ease. "I love you."

"I love you too, be careful," Hyacinth said.

"It was very nice to meet you," Grover said before turning and walking quickly toward the front of the house. Hyacinth followed closely behind, and Paisley took up the rear of the party.

Grover reached the door and grabbed a heavy coat with a fuzzy collar, the type Paisley had seen in a million cop shows; it was standard issue. Under the coat was a white cowboy hat that had a six-pointed star on the front with the county seal in the middle. When Grover put the coat and hat on he looked to be right out of *Walker, Texas Ranger*. Grover walked out the door, got into his Jeep, fired it up, and tore out down the road heading to the second dead body he had seen in three days.

27

The library was located in an old two-story building on Main Street. It shared a wall with the cafe and the barber shop. Walking through the door, Paisley was greeted with the familiar scent of old books and dust. That same smell that all bookstores and libraries that had been around for a while had. An old brass bell above the door signaled her arrival. The main floor was lined with shelves packed from floor to ceiling with books, some old, some that looked fairly new. She felt a little ashamed by her surprise. She hadn't expected that the people in this county did a lot of reading.

Paisley heard soft footsteps, but they weren't that of a person. She recognized them as those of the canine variety. By the sound of them it was a large breed. The slow cadence added comfort in knowing that the beast wasn't bounding toward her, but instead, it was likely curious to know for whom the bell had tolled. When the animal came around the corner, even with its sedated steps, Paisley found herself nervous. The dog in front of her was massive. If it were on its hind legs it would easily be seven and a half feet tall. As it was, the dog's nose was above Paisley's belly button. It had a long neck with a narrow face, but it was hard to tell exactly how large it was as the dog was covered in a mix of gray, white, and black hair. She had seen this breed on television, but couldn't remember its name, and didn't realize they were this big in person.

The animal stopped a few feet in front of Paisley. It seemed to barely fit down the narrow aisles of the library. It looked at her with passing interest and gave a single, low woof. If this dog was a person it would be a very large, very old, very grumpy man who looked at you when you walked in and just gave you a grunt for a welcome. The dog was too large to turn around and go back to where it came from, so it backed up with the ease of having done it a million times. Once in the intersection of the next set of shelves it backed in and executed a two-point turn.

Paisley could now hear new footsteps, these being a little louder, and belonging to a biped. The voice came before she could see its owner. A friendly voice, with that same friendly Southern charm that Paisley was growing to love.

"What is it, Pilot, do we have a guest?" the voice said to the now unseen dog. It was followed by another of those low woofs. The voice began its welcome before being in sight. "What can I do for you?" A small man with square-framed glasses came around the corner. He was carrying a small stack of books and reading something inside the cover of the book on top of the pile. He wasn't looking up when he came into view, and when he finally looked up at Paisley he froze for a moment. His eyes grew wide behind his glasses. He looked to Paisley to be in his mid-thirties. He was around five and a half feet tall and had a narrow build. He was wearing faded blue jeans, old basketball shoes, and an orange tee shirt that had a picture of a delivery truck on it. The lettering above the truck said

"John Doe Courier Service" and underneath, in slightly smaller letters, "What's in the box?" The man just stood and stared at Paisley until she spoke.

"Hi there," she said.

"Oh, um, hello," the man said. "Welcome to Pitt County Public Library."

"Thank you."

"What can we help you with?" The man seemed to be coming around. He set the stack of books on a small counter that functioned as the circulation desk.

"Sheriff Northfield sent me over. He said I could check out some archives of an old newspaper."

The man looked at Paisley suspiciously. "Grover sent you over?"

"He did."

"Do you live in the county? Because the archive room is normally reserved for county residents only."

"Oh, no, I don't, I'm sorry. He just told me to come look for information on an investigation."

"An investigation?" That seemed to get the man interested. He stepped closer. "Are you a Fed or something?"

"Not exactly." Paisley considered lying, but she didn't want to start going down that road. "I'm an investigative reporter of sorts."

"A reporter? For who?"

"Well, honestly, myself. I'm self-employed."

"Well, if the Sheriff said it's okay, who am I to argue?" The man had yet to make direct eye contact.

"Thank you so much." Paisley stuck out her hand. "Paisley Mott, and you are?" The man hesitated--he seemed intimidated.

"Boyd," he said, and shook her hand. After a moment he

added, "Gunnerson. Boyd Gunnerson."

"Well, it certainly is a pleasure to meet you, Boyd. I was hoping to look specifically at the microfiche, if that's possible?" Paisley thought she would love to sit and make small talk with the nervous little guy--he seemed nice enough, just a touch shy--but she had work to do. And with Grover getting a call about another homicide that morning, she suspected she would be fairly busy.

"Of course. It's upstairs in the archive room. Follow me, I'll take you up," Boyd said, and turned for the back of the building. Paisley followed. As she walked up the center aisle of the library, and past the crossroad, she glanced over to see the monstrous dog that Boyd had called Pilot.

"That's a beautiful dog you've got there," Paisley said as they walked to the back of the building and then up a small set of carpeted stairs.

"Thank you. She's pretty amazing."

"What breed is she, if you don't mind me asking?"

"She's an Irish Wolfhound. The females normally don't get that large, but the males do. She's just a freak of nature," he said with pride.

The second floor of the library was much dustier than the first. It was obvious from the prints in the dust that someone had been up there recently, but that could just have been Boyd or another librarian.

"Looks like this area doesn't get a whole lot of use," Paisley said. Boyd looked around the room. There were stacks of boxes, piles of paper, and loose books everywhere. He seemed to take this as some sort of slight. His shoulders slumped and he dropped his chin a bit.

"Yeah, I'm sorry. It's just me that works here, so I don't get a lot of extra time to work up here, so it's a bit of a mess. I had things in order for a bit, but then..." he paused.

"You know how people are. They don't put things away when they take them out."

"Was someone else up here recently, making a mess?" Paisley asked. Boyd's pause led her to think that maybe someone was messing around up there, and that Boyd knew it was better not to mention it.

"Just local kids, you know how it is," he said. Boyd walked over to a canvas drop cloth covering something on a desk. He pulled the cloth and sent motes of dust into the air. The light through the window caught the dust and created a wall of particles so thick that, combined with the sun, it was like trying to see through swamp water. Someone had been up here rooting through boxes recently, but they weren't here for the microfiche.

Boyd gave Paisley a quick tutorial on the machine, and once she was confident on how to use it, he left her to it. By the time he left, Boyd had seemed to have gotten a little more comfortable being around her. He still wasn't making eye contact, but at least he was talking and he even made a joke about "Why would anyone want to look at small fish?" She hadn't made her final judgment on Boyd Gunnerson, but she suspected that she would get along with him just fine, if he would lighten up.

Paisley turned around in the small wooden desk chair that Boyd had pulled over from a table. All of the chairs up here had cracked vinyl cushions that looked like they had seen a lot of abuse in their long years. As she scanned the room, Paisley let her eyes drift across the various stacks of things that seemed out of place. She tried to allow herself to notice patterns. After swiveling her head back and forth a few times she noticed something. There didn't seem to be a physical rhyme or reason to the pulled boxes. Which meant that, if Boyd was serious about having this place in order before, someone was in here looking for something specific. And if they were looking for something specific, and every box hadn't been pulled down, then there was some way of identifying the boxes that warranted closer inspection.

Paisley looked around to make sure that Boyd had gone down the stairs.

"Boyd?" she called out, just above a comfortable speaking volume. She waited a moment and got no response. She figured that meant she was safe to break out her camera and get some video. She unzipped her camera bag and pulled the camera and its small tripod out. She was getting to be an expert setting it up and had it recording in less than thirty seconds. The impulse to live stream was strong, but as she had no idea what she was doing or what she was looking for, she reconsidered. Instead she settled on video footage she could edit and a quick photo post to social media. She snapped a picture of the dusty room with the caption "Let the investigation begin," added a few hashtags, and posted the photo to her feed. Then she turned on the camera and began.

"So, since my last update things have taken a bit of a turn. There was another murder. My drone was attacked. Then I was attacked, with the drone, sort of. I met the sheriff. I found out that he is romantically involved with Hyacinth Bloom." She said this last bit with the emphasis of surprise she felt when it was revealed to her that morning. She thought for a moment about what she had just shared and decided that she would talk to Hyacinth before editing it, and if she didn't want her business out there, Paisley would cut it. Normally it would add drama to the story, but she liked Hyacinth and didn't want to rock her boat. She continued.

"So fast forward to right now. I am currently upstairs in the Pitt County Library, and it is seriously a creepy old place. The guy working here seems okay. He's super shy, but he's also kind of sweet. I'm up here about to scan some microfiche." She spun the camera to see the large machine, then spun it back to her face. "But I can't seem to get over something." She moved closer to the boxes and focused the camera on them. "These boxes look like they were all put away in order, and someone came tearing through here looking for something, but what? Well, I'm going to see if there's any evidence to be had." She made sure the camera was aimed at the full set of shelves and that the focus was good. She would do a time lapse or something else to show the passage of time as she searched the shelves. Maybe she would even create masks so that it looked like there were four or five of her working in different areas at the same time. That would add some production value.

The old chair showed its age with a creak as Paisley stood and walked across the room to a row of boxes with a few removed. The boxes that were out of place had been opened and the contents removed. One box that had been pulled was simply labeled "Misc. County Records." She read out the name of the box, narrating the documents she was seeing as she went. She figured she could edit out the audio, but it was better to have it just in case she found something telling. The contents of the box were scattered on the table next to it. There were a few articles of incorporation for various companies, a few tax records, and a lot of building permits, but nothing that stood out. She scanned through them to see if any names jumped out at her. She did run across the occasional Bloom, Harris, and even a hold application for a new well for the church signed by Martin Grimm, who Paisley wondered if it was

Hollis's dad. She moved along to another box labeled "Expired titles." The documents in and around the box contained nothing exciting. Just a lot of copies of land titles from the eighteen hundreds. She checked a few more boxes labeled "Homestead," "Deed transfer applications," and "County assessor documentation." Paisley hadn't found anything out of the ordinary or obviously missing. She returned to the seat at the microfiche, but her brain was hard at work trying to connect the dots on the boxes. Questions just kept popping up in her mind. She turned the camera back toward herself. The wheels were turning.

"So, we have boxes of titles, transfers, and assessors' documents. All stuff dealing with land ownership." She thought for a moment and then jumped up and went back to the shelves. She moved down to the last shelf, which was the only shelf that didn't have a box missing. Her phone chirped with a new message and she slid it from her back pocket to see if it was important. She thought she recognized the name from her live stream but it wasn't someone she knew personally. The direct message was from WhyItHurts. She opened the message.

WhyItHurts - *Did you find what you are looking for?*

Paisley responded.

ParanormalOrNot - *What do you mean?*
WhyItHurts - *In the dusty room you just posted, did you figure it out?*
ParanormalOrNot - *Thanks for checking out the photo, but I don't really know what I am looking for.*
WhyItHurts - *I'm sure you've already thought of this, but there isn't a box missing from the last shelf, which means one of*

two things...

Paisley thought for a minute. The final shelf did not have a box missing, and the box that was out before that was just some old assessor documents, and there didn't seem to be any missing. What could that mean? And who could this person be that was trying to offer unsolicited advice?

ParanormalOrNot - *They either found what they were looking for or they didn't, but I looked in the boxes and there didn't seem to be anything obviously missing. Maybe they didn't find what they wanted and gave up?*

WhyItHurts - *Or they didn't find what they were looking for in that box, but what if they did in another box?*

ParanormalOrNot - *But I checked all the boxes that were out...*

WhyItHurts - *But if you were snooping for something, would you want someone to find it?*

ParanormalOrNot - *No, probably not. What are you getting at?*

WhyItHurts - *So once you found it, what would you do with the box?*

Paisley's head swam with possibilities. Being a real investigator had always been a dream, but she didn't feel like her brain was always capable of making those logical leaps. She felt like this random person online was guiding her in the right direction, but she wasn't exactly sure why. She looked at the boxes.

"I'd put the box back so no one knew which box I was looking for," she said into the empty room. She leaned in close to the shelf, not looking at the boxes, but instead at the dust on the shelf directly in front of the boxes. She scanned each shelf in this fashion. She stopped a few boxes from the end of the third shelf.

"Mother fucker," she said. Paisley's eyes followed her finger as it sketched the lines scraped into the dust and then up the front of the box to where the label sat. It said "Land Sale Documents 1865-2015."

"Hell yes," Paisley whisper shouted, then she sent a direct message to her nearly anonymous helper.

ParanormalOrNot - *What the heck?!? Are you some sort of detective or something? There was a box that was taken down and put back! Thank you so much!*

WhyItHurts - *No problem, glad I could help! Be careful out there.*

ParanormalOrNot - *Thank you! XOXOXO*

Paisley pumped her fist three times and then pulled the box down. The documents in the box appeared to have been rifled through. There were folders labeled by the decade. The contents showed a lot of activity up until around 1910, then a folder missing: the folder covering the period from 1910 through 1919 was gone. Then there wasn't a lot of activity for a long time. The 2000-2009 folder was gone too. Paisley pulled out her phone and took a few pictures of the inside of the box and the gaps where the folders should have been. She put the lid on the box and slid it back into place. Then she walked back over to the desk and sat down facing the camera again.

"Well, first off, thank you so much to my savior Why It Hurts for some expert deductive reasoning and kicking my brain into gear. It appears someone was very interested in who bought what property in a few select decades," she said. "Now, with all that excitement in mind, it may be a little more difficult to search through these old crusty newspapers, but it needs to be done." She paused for a moment. "I need an assistant."

She repositioned the camera to get a wide shot of her doing the research on the massive machine. After getting a few minutes of her searching the microfiche she turned off the camera. She had a feeling this would take a very long time. She found stories dating all the way back to the Civil War. There was a lot about Gerald Lee Harris and the poor employment practices he used. There were stories about land values rising because of the increase in the coal mining business. There were hundreds of headlines about everyday boring things. Like whose pig won in the country fair. Whose chickens won in the county fair. Whose sheep won in the county fair. She longed for a searchable database. She tried Google from her phone, but this town seemed to exist completely offline, except for Hyacinth, who, according to the internet, had not been directly linked to her online persona. Paisley was about ready to give up when she stumbled across a series of stories that caught her eye. She wasn't exactly sure why, but all of the names involved were names that she had heard when talking about the strange happenings around Grey Water Ridge. And even if they didn't matter, it was compelling reading that shined a light on just why people in the town were so pissed off all the time. Turns out that some pretty vile sins were perpetrated by those in power in the early days of the town.

20

The smell of coal was thick as Herk Steiner crossed the loading yard. His coveralls were as black as the boots he wore. He was covered in soot from head to toe. The look of a man who has been down in the mines and can tell you just how hard that labor is. He had been down in number eighty-three when Jesse Stills, a miner he'd chewed ground with for years, came down into the hole steaming mad. Jesse ripped his hard hat off and threw it. The hat banged hard against a coal cart and the noise echoed down the shaft. Herk raised one of his massive hands to try to defuse the situation.

"Now, Jesse, you just calm down and tell me what's going on," Herk said in a level tone.

"That son of a bitch got his hand in our pockets again," Jesse said.

"What are you talking about?"

"I just came from the comp'ny store and they say my pay wasn't even enough to cover what I already owed. And I know that ain't right. I figured it myself and I spent just enough last week to still get three whole dollars back so I can take one them girls that come in on the train from Bixby last week to a show and have some fun." Jesse's hands shook with anger.

"You sure you figured it right?"

"Now you know I ain't the smartest man, but I can count money well enough," Jesse said. "They trying to do us like we was colored."

"It ain't right to mess with a man's money, no matter who you are," Herk said. "Did they give you a reason as to why you were short?"

"Quarters," Jesse said.

"Quarters?"

"Yeah, like if your team doesn't pull enough coal you don't hit your quarter, and if you don't hit the quarter you don't get a full share of the pay," Jesse said.

"Who told you about the quarters?"

"The guy at the comp'ny store. Said we got new weekly quarters that need to be hit before we get a full share."

"Did he say quarter or quota?" Herk asked.

"Well, he said quota, but I think he's one of them guys that came from Boston, so he talks a bit light, if you know what I mean."

Herk thought for a moment. He wished that it would have been quarters, as at least then things just wouldn't make sense. Instead, if the company *was* requiring a weekly quota to be hit before they earned their full share, then this was a bigger problem than someone just mismanaging their money.

Herk was an unofficial union leader, in what they had that resembled a union. A few years earlier Wilbur Bloom had come in and fixed things up, probably saved Gerald Harris's life in the process. Bloom had worked it out so they would get annual raises, bonuses for good months, and time off. Herk loved Bloom for that. His wife had just had a baby boy when Bloom stepped in and he, as a new father, had a lot of added responsibility. Bloom had given him an opportunity to support his growing family. Herk stormed out of the mine without another word.

Wilbur Bloom, after stepping in to single-handedly save Harris and the future of the mining operation, would end up as mayor a short time later. After Gerald Harris realized he was terrible at dealing with people, he asked Bloom to come on as his vice president and handle the labor side of the business. So, in addition to being the mayor of Harris Ridge, he was also the vice president of the Harris Mining Company.

Herk Steiner, who was a large man at about six foot seven inches tall, and nearly three hundred and twenty-five pounds, was an intimidating presence even in the best of moods. But when he was angry, people scattered when they saw him coming. He was easily the biggest man anyone had ever seen go down the mines. So when he barged through the door of the office that Wilbur Bloom used for his role in both his official town position, and his position within Harris Mining, Wilbur nearly jumped out of his seat. Herk had always had a good relationship with Wilbur, but he wasn't about to let anyone take money out of his pocket, or the pockets of his friends.

"What's this I hear about some new percentage for performance?" Herk demanded.

"Well, hey there, Herk, come in," Wilbur said as he stood and motioned toward the chair in front of the desk. Herk stepped in but didn't sit. Instead he walked close enough to force Bloom, who was tall in his own right at six foot four, to look up at him.

"What's going on, Bloom? You told us our wages were set and that they couldn't go down."

"I know, and I'm furious," Wilbur said. I didn't know about it until this morning. It came straight down from Harris, and you know how he is. He doesn't come to me with these things, and then everything ends up in the muck."

"I want to talk to him."

"Well, you know that isn't even an option, Herk, but I'll talk to him. I'm drafting a letter now and I intend to march it over to him as soon as I'm finished. And I can assure you that it is strongly worded."

"Not strong enough," Herk said. "Let me talk to him." Wilbur plopped backward into his chair, blowing out air as he did. He slumped his shoulders and lowered his head.

"I'm sorry, Herk. You guys are down there day in and day out, and I try to take care of you, I do, but I think Harris has finally lost his mind."

"I don't give a donkey's ass if he's lost his mind. We're losing money, and that's all I care about. Either he fixes this, and pays us what he owes, or I pull every guy out of every hole in this state," Herk said, slamming his hand down on the thick cherry wood desk Wilbur sat behind. It shook the room.

"I promise I will do everything I can. Give me a day, and if I can't then I will stand with you as we all walk out of here and let the place grind to a halt." Herk considered this for a long time. He stood with his massive arms across his barrel chest.

"I'm sorry, Wilbur, I am. But I'm pulling everyone until this shit gets straightened out." Herk didn't wait for Wilbur to respond, he just turned and walked out, leaving the door open behind him. He knew that if he closed it, as mad as he was, he would rip the fucking thing off its hinges.

Herk made good on that promise. He pulled every

single man out of every single hole that he could. He sent guys around to every site to tell them that they were stopping work. He promised that any man that didn't come out of the mines, he himself would go down there, and only one of them would ever see daylight again. Between the respect and fear they all had for Herk Steiner, and the anger they all felt toward the corrupt Gerald Harris, it didn't take a lot of convincing to get them to follow.

That night, Herk sat at his supper table with his family. His wife, Abigale, and their sons, Nathan, who was now seven years old, and William, who was 13. They listened as Herk told them about the atrocities that the Harris Mining Company was trying to perpetrate against the miners under his supervision. Little Nathan shook his fist in anger, just as he had seen his dad do a number of times when talking about Harris. After supper, Abigale put Nathan down to bed while Herk sat out on the porch and smoked his pipe. William told him about his day working the small bit of land that they considered their ranch. After Herk had calmed down he went in to join Abigale in their bed and William went to his makeshift bed in the corner of the main room.

Breaking glass woke Herk as something smashed against the side of the cabin. He jumped up and looked out the window. He saw a man on horseback, holding the reins in one hand, a bottle with a rag in the other, and a torch sticking out from under his arm. The rag in the bottle lit and he threw it at the house. Herk saw it coming for the window he was standing in. He could see that fire was already climbing up the side of the house like a demon spider. He ducked away from the window just in time for the bottle to smash through it. The bottle hit the floor and exploded. Flames leapt in every direction, but they were concentrated forward, and they draped over the bed like a blanket. Herk could see Abigale sit up just before watching her disappear in a sheet of liquid fire. He screamed her name and tried to pull her from the bed, but it was too late--she was fully engulfed. He couldn't decipher her screams from his.

Somewhere in the distance, maybe a million miles away, more glass broke.

"Boys!" Herk yelled, and tore out from his room. The cabin was small. There was a main room where William slept, a bedroom that Herk and Abigale shared, and a small nook behind the main room where Nathan slept. As Herk burst through the door he could see that another bottle had busted through the window above the wash basin and exploded on the floor between him and Nathan.

"Pa!" A voice called from the main room. Herk looked over to see William slapping wildly at the flames trying to get to his brother.

"William, get out, now!" Herk yelled.

"But Ma, and Nathan?" William cried.

"Go get help!"

"Poppa?!" Nathan cried from the other side of the room. Herk could see him over the flames. He was standing on his cot. The terror on his face hurt Herk's heart. His family was his life. He pushed the thoughts of his wife, who was burning in the other room, from his mind and lunged forward to jump through the fire to get his boy. Just as he did he heard a voice from the broken window, but he kept moving toward Nathan. That was all that mattered right then.

"Get them back to work, Steiner! Harris won't be bullied," the voice yelled over the sounds of screams and exploding wood as the place came apart around Herk. He saw the bottle out of the corner of his eye.

"No!" he screamed as he launched himself forward toward Nathan. The bottle beat him there by a split second. It ricocheted off of the floor and hopped just before striking the edge of the bed. Everything went white as fire burst from the bottle and covered Herk's field of view. He could hear Nathan scream in pain just before he reached him, wrapping his arms around his son's waist. He drove him back, ignoring the fact that the sleeping pants and shirt he wore were now burning around him. The flames ripped up Herk's back as he landed and pushed the cot away. Nathan was screaming and his nightshirt was nearly gone as it burned up his body toward his face. Herk ripped it off in one quick tear. Nathan's legs were coated in the thick, slippery oil from the bottle, and Herk could hear the sizzle coming off of them. He fought the anger, the fear, and the urge to vomit as he used his hands to try and pat the fire on Nathan's legs out. It was no use, it just spread to his hands. Herk smothered the small fire on his hands in his armpits, ignoring the pain as his chest burned. His clothing fell away from him as he stood, the flames still clinging to parts of his burned body. He scooped Nathan into his arms and tried to smother the fire on his son's legs as he had on his own hands.

He turned and kicked the kindling that was Nathan's bed across the burning room. In two long strides he crossed the lake of fire that was once the main room. He rushed through the open door like a bullet from a gun. The cold night air seemed to reignite the burns covering nearly all of his body. He wasn't sure if Nathan joined him in screaming at that point, or if he already had been. Herk sprinted across the yard, flames whipping out behind him like a bannerman's flag on a battlefield. He kicked open the front gate and dove into the trough they had filled for the horses. He angled himself so that he wouldn't fall on top of Nathan. He thrust the boy forward, submerging him completely, temporarily muting his screams.

Every spring Herk would buy a new horse, and once he even bought three cattle from one of the ranchers who had moved his herd up to Harris Ridge. When he got new livestock he would have to brand them. After the iron was red hot, you'd stick them, and it would make a horrible noise. Then you'd drop the iron in a bucket of water and it would hiss as the water cooled the metal and the steam released from the surface of the water. When Nathan went under the water Herk heard that same sound. After he was sure that the flames were gone he rolled himself fully into the trough with the boy, pushing Nathan's head above the water. The boy was unconscious.

"Nathan!" Herk yelled as he tried to turn Nathan's head toward him. "Wake up, son!"

A hand reached down and dipped under Nathan's arm and pulled him from underneath Herk and out of the trough. Herk looked up and saw William. Just before Herk lost consciousness he heard a small cough.

Herk screamed and sat up. The pain woke him, as it did almost every night. He looked over to see if he had woken Nathan, but the boy slept soundly on the thick bed in the corner. For a moment he thought he was in the old cabin, but the moonlight filling the small room proved otherwise. He turned over in his own bed to check for sure. As every night since the fire took her, Abigale was not there. Herk touched the spot where he wished she would be. He stretched and swung his large, burn-scarred legs over the edge of the bed and put his feet on the wooden floor. It had been a year since the fire. William had got Nathan breathing again, but the boy was burned on over ninety percent of his body. The doctors said it was a miracle that either of them survived. Herk was in the hospital for more than a month while he healed up enough to leave, but Nathan was there for three months. His injuries were much worse. William stayed with a neighbor from the next ranch over.

Herk wasn't sure where they would go when he and Nathan left the hospital, but Wilbur Bloom took care of that. He had personally paid to have a house built on Herk's property. It was much bigger than the house that burned down. It had a bedroom for Herk and for each of the boys, but Nathan couldn't sleep alone in his own room. Herk moved Nathan's bed into his room to calm the boy. It made Herk sleep easier knowing he was in there too. Wilbur had been at the hospital when Herk woke up. When he opened his eyes he screamed, and Wilbur stood over him and reassured him that it was going to be alright. Almost his entire body was in bandages. Wilbur just kept telling him that Nathan was doing better and was going to live. Herk didn't know at the time that Wilbur was exaggerating, and that Nathan was still hanging on to life by a thread, and that thread was unwinding at both ends, but it was exactly what Herk needed to hear.

Wilbur came by to talk to Herk often. Both men agreed that Harris was likely responsible, but Wilbur told him that the day after the fire the miners refused to go back in until they not only got what was promised to them, but got a five percent raise. They also demanded that the Harris Mining Company cover all of Herk and Nathan's medical costs, paid Herk his share for as long as he was out of

153

work, and took care of all of William's needs. Wilbur said that he delivered the demands himself, and that Harris had agreed without ever looking up at him. He said that he just sat and stared into the fire in his fireplace. Herk agreed that he would return to work as long as he was made an official foreman and that they were able to formally unionize. Wilbur agreed and said he would accept nothing less. So that is what they did. Ten months after the fire Herk Steiner went back to work for the man he suspected of killing his wife and nearly killing his son and himself.

Herk crossed the room to where Nathan slept and stood above him, watching as his chest rose and fell. The scars on the boy's face and neck were not as bad as they were on the rest of his body, but they still hurt to look at. Herk could still hear him screaming when the bottle exploded. He stood there for half an hour until the sun came up, and then he gently shook the bed to wake Nathan. The boy rolled over and saw his father towering above him, as he did every morning. The boy smiled as much as his stretched face would allow.

"Good morning, son," Herk said, pulling back the covers.

"Good morning, Poppa," Nathan said back. Herk lifted the boy from the bed and carried him into the kitchen. A chair that would accommodate Nathan stood next to the table. Herk set him down in it and wrapped a leather strap that was fixed to the back of the chair around the boy's chest and buckled it so that he wouldn't fall. Nathan straightened himself in the rig the best he could with his left hand. His right, which was missing all but his index finger and most of his thumb, pressed the strap upward as he shifted. Herk pulled the boy's nightshirt down to cover the jagged scars that marked the place where his legs used to be. Just above the knee on his right leg, and halfway up the thigh on his left.

"After you're done with your breakfast we need to do your studies," Herk said as he started to mix some water with some oats.

"Aww, Pa, do I have to?"

"Of course. You need to grow up and get a good job, and a big brain is the best way to do that. Just look at Wilbur, he's the smartest man I know and he has it made."

"But I plan on working down in the mine when I grow up," Nathan said. Herk turned to look at the damaged boy. When he did he saw that Nathan had a giant smile on his face.

"You're just joshing me, aren't you?" Herk said. The two shared a laugh. It was good to laugh.

Herk worked at the mining company again, but didn't spend a lot of time down in the hole. He spent most of his time in an office in the same building as Wilbur. Just across the hall, in fact. He always imagined a day when Harris would show his face in that building, and he thought that he might beat him to death if he did. They had never caught the person who set fire to the house. Gerald Harris had been questioned but denied having anything at all to do with the fire. So Herk was patient, waiting for the right moment to get Harris.

William worked on a ranch down the road. He was a strong boy, with a big heart, but he wasn't as sharp as Nathan was. He worked long days ranching. While Herk was at work a woman named Velma would stay with Nathan. She claimed to have been hired by Harris Mining Company to look after Nathan so that Herk could return to work, but he was pretty sure that the money she collected came from the overly charitable hands of Wilbur

Bloom. Wilbur had a son that was younger than Nathan. His name was Bernard, and Herk always thought that Wilbur couldn't help but to put himself in Herk's shoes and was glad that it was not Bernard who had nearly been burned to death. The arrangement worked very well for everyone, until the mining peak in the summer of 1892.

Prices for coal soared, and the mine couldn't hire people fast enough. Herk was one of the people in charge of doing that. He had been appointed by Wilbur Bloom himself. Herk managed to staff the mines as fast as they could dig them and profits for the company rose dramatically. Which made it even more surprising when Wilbur came into Herk's office one afternoon to tell him that Harris had ordered the wages for any miner who had not been with the company for more than a year decreased by eight percent. Herk was furious.

"This is horse shit!" Herk yelled. "I'm going to see that cocksucker right now." Wilbur stepped in front of the giant. A dangerous move if they hadn't been such good friends.

"Herk, you can't. He isn't there," Wilbur said. Referring to the office that Harris kept in Louisville.

"Well where the hell is he?"

"He's in New York. He took the train three days ago."

"So that chicken shit ran away to New York before telling us this?"

"Got the telegram this morning," Wilbur said. "Real coward move."

Herk brushed Wilbur aside as if he were nothing more than a curtain hanging in his way and walked out of the office. Wilbur caught him in the hall.

"Where are you going?"

"To the mines."

"For what?" Wilbur asked, though he knew exactly what Herk had planned.

"To pull my men," Herk said without slowing. Wilbur stopped and called after him.

"But what about last time?" he said. He didn't want to bring it up, but he felt he had to. Which is why he stopped, to allow a distance between them just in case Herk snapped. Instead Herk just stopped. He didn't turn to look at Wilbur, he just looked around for a few seconds and then called back.

"If I don't, then last time..." He paused. "If I don't then last time was for nothing." Herk raised his head high and stormed off to grind the company to a halt at the height of production. Wilbur stood for a moment watching the big man go. He smiled.

"Go get 'em, big boy," he said.

With no one left in the mines, and no one there to load the coal cars, all production stopped immediately. After checking that everyone had stopped working, Herk rode quickly back to his house with the intention of gathering the boys and taking them to stay somewhere else. Maybe they would even go camping. He just didn't want to stay at his house in case that coward Harris tried to kill them again.

As he approached the house he could see that his front door was open. Not only was it open, but it hung at an awkward angle. Herk leapt from his horse before it stopped and ran across the small yard and into the house.

"Boys?" he yelled as he entered the house. "Velma?" Herk ran to the kitchen.

Blood dripped from the table and pooled on the old boards beneath it. Lines ran through the blood as it seeped through the cracks between the boards. Velma, who was not a small woman, lay on her back on the table. One eye was fixed on the ceiling above her, the other hung loosely from the collapsed side of her skull. A large rock lay on the floor near the puddle, covered in blood.

"Nathan!" Herk screamed as he ran to the back of the house to find Nathan's bed empty. Herk thought about the door in the kitchen, which had been open. He ran to it, steering clear of the slick red mess on the floor. The house backed up to the woods and he looked helplessly out as the darkness set in the thick trees.

Herk snapped.

Herk stood in the city square without speaking as Wilbur tried to get his attention. The large man was catatonic. His eyes were wide and his jaw was clenched tight, veins rippling up his neck and forehead. Wilbur shook his shoulder. When Wilbur had first approached, a woman said Herk had been standing there like that for the better part of half an hour.

Wilbur stood in front of the man, put his hand behind his head, and pulled his face in line with his own.

"Herk, my friend, we've done it!" Wilbur said. He received no response. "Did you hear me? Harris agreed to everything. He's pulling back the pay decrease and reinstating everyone's wages. We've already sent messengers to notify everyone that they can start work again immediately!"

Herk finally seemed to be registering the words being thrown at him. "Wilbur?"

"And get a load of this, Harris has agreed that all labor decisions from here on out have to go through you and me before terms can be set. What do you think of that?"

Wilbur said, smacking Herk on the arm.

"He took my boy," Herk finally said after Wilbur was done.

"What?"

"Nathan, he's gone," Herk said. "Velma is dead."

"Are you joking?"

"No."

"Have you told the sheriff? We have to get a posse up to look for him," Wilbur said, turning to run down the boardwalk to the Sheriff's office. Herk followed at a lumbering speed.

The Sheriff got up that posse and Wilbur, Herk, William, and nearly a hundred other men searched the woods for Nathan. A mob even rode to Louisville to kick in the door at Gerald Harris's house and found nothing. Harris was still in New York and there was no evidence that anyone had been at the mansion.

Herk searched through the night, and when the time came for the first shift to start work in the mines, they did. There wasn't clear information about what happened next, but Wilbur said that Herk, as he knew him, was gone. That they had gone back to the office to regroup. Wilbur had fallen asleep in a chair in his office and the last time he saw Herk he said he had to go check on the guys. He said that Herk looked calm when he left. Wilbur said that he was woken up nearly an hour later when an explosion rocked the building. It led to a collapse that killed thirty-six men and caused no end of issues for the town.

Herk was arrested and was found dead in his cell the next morning. A witness said that it looked like he had hung himself with a bed sheet.

Gerald Lee Harris never returned to Harris Ridge.

Months later, after the environmental disaster caused by the explosion, and the deaths of all those people, the company's stock prices had dropped to an incredibly low point. To try and save the jobs of everyone there, and in turn save the town, Wilbur Bloom leveraged everything he had to buy the Harris Mining Company outright. The company rebounded under his kind leadership. After the first year the company made an amazing profit and Wilbur donated enough money to the town that they were able to build a new school. At the dedication, Wilbur Bloom unveiled a large stone next to the entrance that announced the Nathan Steiner Primary School.

After the dust from the whole thing had settled, rumors began to fly about what had happened. The consensus was that Harris had burned the Steiner family's house down because he had threatened to stop work and halt production. Maybe he was trying to send a message to the rest of the workers that he wasn't to be messed with. But the death of Velma and the disappearance of the boy became a more legendary tale. A rumor started that someone had seen an ape, one that stood on two legs, running through the woods, carrying something that looked like a human child. No one could ever verify the claims, but everyone had heard at least one version of the story. It was the first recorded story of someone seeing the beast that would be called sasquatch in that region. After the story was published in the newspaper, people began saying that they had seen something similar during the war, or on hunting trips, or late at night wandering the edges of the millions of acres of woodland that stretched across the Appalachian Trail.

Nathan Steiner was never found.

29

Popping sounds, like small firecrackers under a rug,
ripped up Paisley's spine as she leaned back in the chair.
She had been hunched over the microfiche reading the
story of Herk Steiner, Wilbur Bloom, Gerald Lee Harris,
and that poor boy, Nathan Steiner. The follow-up story
said Harris never admitted to having a part in any of it,
and he had an alibi for every night that something
happened at Herk Steiner's house. Of course, it was
assumed that he had just hired some road agent to take
care of it for him. Paisley was so invested in the news
articles that she felt like she was there, watching it all play
out. She was interested in talking to Hyacinth about it. Her
great, great, great, grandfather was a hero and the town
savior. That had to feel pretty cool.

Paisley looked around the dusty room. She wondered
what other secrets this room held. She flipped the camera
on and then spun toward it. She would edit it later to be a
dramatic shot.

"People, balls. There was some crazy stuff that went
down over here. It involves a man burning another man's
wife, his child, and the man himself. Then coming back
and killing the maid when they didn't finish the boy off the

first time. This is some seriously dark stuff. And here I was just looking for the first appearance of this monster from the woods, and it seems to be nothing but a footnote in the town's history."

The machine turned off with a loud thunk as Paisley flipped the ancient switch on the top. At some point someone was going to have to digitize all of that information and make it easier to search. She pulled the thick cover back onto the machine like someone putting some monstrous bird to sleep. She wasn't sure if she would end up back there; she still had a lot of newspaper articles to go through, but she figured she had enough for one day. Her strained eyes, sore back, and aching neck would thank her. She collected her things and headed down to the main floor of the library.

Pilot gave that low woof when she got to the bottom of the stairs. Paisley wasn't even standing where she could see the animal, but apparently Pilot could hear or smell her. She heard movement from the back room and Boyd came out, pushing his glasses back up onto his face.

"So, did you find what you were looking for?" he asked.

"You know, I'm not exactly sure what I'm looking for," she chuckled. "There's just so much."

"Well, let me know if I can be of some service to you. I am the unofficial town historian." Boyd smiled. It was clearly a point of pride for him.

"No kidding? So tell me, Mr. Unofficial Town Historian, what's the deal with this sasquatch stuff?" Boyd's face lit up. He looked ten years younger.

"Oh wow, you came to the right place. I know just about everything there is to know about that," he said.

"Well, do tell!"

"So let me first just start by saying that whether you

believe in the myth of the sasquatch or not, you have to accept that the people here believe in it. They believe so deeply in it that they started a church up in the hills dedicated to that very thing."

"The First Evangelical Assembly of the King's Redeemer," Paisley said.

"Oh, you've heard of them?"

"Yep, I was actually invited out here by their reverend, Hol--" Paisley began, but was cut off.

"Hollis brought you out here?" Boyd asked. His voice had changed from the excited tone of someone willing to help to the scared tone of someone who was ready to crawl under the nearest desk and hide.

"He did," she said. "Is there something wrong with that?"

Boyd looked around as if checking to make sure no one was watching them.

"Listen, if Hollis asked you to come out here, I can't help you," Boyd said. He moved past her, his arm raised in a gesture that she should follow him to the door.

"Wait, why not? Do you have a problem with Hollis?" she asked. "I mean you just said that everyone in town believes in the Bigfoot story. Why would you have a problem with the guy that tells the stories about it?"

"Sasquatch," Boyd said. His voice was serious and trembled. Paisley had seen guys get angry before, and had even dated one who had a serious problem with it, but that wasn't what was going on here. Boyd wasn't mad, he was scared, but he was trying to make it look like mad. "And I didn't say I had a problem with Hollis, I never said that. Never. You better not tell anyone I did." His hand was shaking when he raised it to point at her.

Paisley set her hand gently on his. She lowered his without saying anything. Boyd let her. Once his hand was down she let go of it and moved her hand to his shoulder.

"Listen, Boyd, I'm not trying to get you in any trouble, okay? Trust me, I just really appreciate everything you've already done for me, and anything you may be able to help me with in the future, and I'm not about to repay that by going around town talking ill of you, okay?" Paisley gave his shoulder a reaffirming squeeze. Boyd's body tensed for a second and then relaxed. His shoulders sank and he looked up at Paisley.

"I'm sorry. It's just that I love this job, and I don't want to do anything to mess it up." Boyd glanced over his shoulder, as if to make sure that no one passing on the street could see them talking.

"Does Hollis have the power to cause you to lose your job?" Paisley knew that people loved Hollis, but she just assumed that he was the redneck version of a local celebrity. Boyd stood biting his lower lip. After a second he spoke again.

"I can't talk to you about Hollis, I'm sorry. If he asks I'll tell him that you were here. If he wants to know what you were looking at I'll tell him the very little bit of information that I have, and that is that you were sent by the Sheriff and that you looked at the microfiche. That's it. Okay?" Boyd said. He posed it as a question, but Paisley didn't think her answer mattered. She didn't want to push Boyd, she liked him. It was actually kind of nice to be standing with someone who didn't look like they'd walked right out of a prime time show starring a bunch of supermodels playing regular people. She thought about telling him that she had also gone through some of the boxes, but decided that might send him over the edge in a panic. Paisley figured it might be more prudent to just play her cards close to her chest until she found out more about Hollis's relationship to the Library and why the librarian was so afraid at the mere sound of his name.

"All right, Boyd. Thank you. If Hollis asks I'll tell him that you were a completely respectful public servant, and that you allowed me to use the microfiche, but that you were a steel trap when it came to any other information," she said. "Not the best trait for the unofficial town historian," she added with a wink.

"I'm sorry. If Hollis gives me the thumbs up to talk to you about it, I'm an open book."

Paisley had a hard time accepting that she needed a man's permission to get information that should be public knowledge. She made a mental note to ask Hollis about all of this when she saw him next.

"Well then, I guess that limits any conversation at this point, so I guess I'll be taking my leave," she said.

"Again, I'm sorry." Boyd opened the door and held it for her as she stepped down the stone steps onto the sidewalk. She turned back to look up at him.

"We will talk again, Boyd Gunnerson, I can tell. We're going to be good friends." Paisley's mom, who had been a fierce, independent woman, with a touch of crazy, had told her that every meeting or conversation is a battle and you have to win every battle to get by. Her dad, who was a patient, kind, loving man, told her that her mother was right, but that the contest wasn't to beat the other person, it was to leave them at the end of it with a smile. It made coming back to them next time even easier. She waited to see if Boyd would crack. He did. He smiled a reluctant, but genuine, grin. Paisley turned and gave her dad a mental high five.

30

The diner was busy, as usual for an early afternoon. Some folks were in having a late lunch, others for an early supper. Renee Webb stood looking out the glass front door onto Main Street. She was expecting Hollis to come back. She knew he would be upset at her for the broken glass the day before, but she was just shocked at seeing that whore from Los Angeles, or some other Godforsaken place, touching her Hollis like that. She was running her fingers up and down his arm like she was dreaming it was his pecker. And right there in public where everyone could see. That wasn't what this town was about, and she wasn't going to stand by and let this tramp ruin their good name. She figured Hollis would have come back in to scold her for making such a scene, but after she broke the glass, and Garrett cleaned the mess up, she went back out and took their orders. Hollis ordered his usual, and the bitch ordered a caesar salad. Renee had considered spitting in the salad, but she didn't. She had Garrett do it instead. He had some sort of infection in his gums and she thought that it would be much better if he did it. She had stood in the back and watched as the bitch took the first big bite. Garrett laughed as she did. He had known that both the meals on the table contained his spit, and he thought that Renee didn't notice, but she did. She just didn't really care at that point. She loved Hollis, who didn't? But if he was going to be inviting this kind of filth into their town then he deserved whatever he got.

"Renee?" a woman called from behind her. Renee turned to see Sylvia, another of the diner's waitresses, standing with two full trays of food. "Can you help me drop these off to table three?" Sylvia was older than Renee, nice enough, she thought, but as stupid as the day is long. She grabbed one of the trays and helped deliver the food before the two ladies walked back into the kitchen.

"You hear from Hollis yet?" Sylvia asked as they set the trays down to wait for the line cooks to prep the next order.

"You think he's mad?" Renee asked, knowing what the answer was before she asked the question.

"I don't think he'll care about the glass, but I bet he wasn't too happy with you making a scene like that."

"I didn't do nothin'. It was an accident," Renee said.

"Now, we all know that's bullshit right there. You been doing this crap for how many years and ain't never once dropped so much as a sugar packet on the ground and you expect Hollis to think it was a mistake that you dropped a single glass off your tray and it just so happened to belong to the girl that was touching his arm?"

Renee looked out through the opening that separated the kitchen from the dining room. Sylvia was right. Maybe she wasn't as stupid as Renee thought. She knew Hollis had seen right through her.

A small Latino man set two plates up on the warming shelf and then tapped a bell that was duct taped to the side of the rack.

"Order up, ladies," Jorge Padilla said. Renee went to

167

grab them but Sylvia moved to take them first.

"I got these, hon," she said with a smile. "Thanks, Jorge, fast as always." Jorge just looked up at her and bounced his eyebrows.

"I try, you know," Jorge said.

"Jorge?" Renee said.

"Yeah?" Jorge said, pausing while he was shoveling something around on his griddle.

"You afraid of Hollis?" she asked. Jorge looked off for a moment, his eyes scanning the corner of the room as he sucked air through his teeth.

"No," he finally said.

"Really?"

"Yeah, to be afraid of someone is to wonder what will happen. I don't wonder with Hollis. I know."

"What do you mean?" Renee didn't expect an in-depth answer, but now she was intrigued.

"Hollis is the type of man who has two responses. He will either care for you, or he will hurt you. So as long as I'm on the good side of the line he is good to me. If I step over the line I know what I'm in for. It's like me being afraid of this griddle. It can burn me, but only if I give it a reason to." Renee was impressed at the insight. She was also worried.

"You think I stepped over that line yesterday?" she asked.

"Why don't you ask Garrett?" Jorge said. This wasn't a yes or no answer, but it might as well have been. Garrett didn't always have that scar on his face, and he used to have two working eyes.

"Shit," Renee said.

The batwing doors swung open and Sylvia came in shaking her head. Sylvia wasn't a spring chicken, but she was still young and pretty enough that she drew the eyes of some of the male customers. Her dark auburn hair had a natural curl that always looked good in a ponytail, and she was an expert in applying her makeup. It hid the scars that went along with an addiction to methamphetamine that she had struggled with before the two dealers and cooks in town disappeared mysteriously and she was forced to get clean. Rumors went around that Hollis threatened to personally deal with anyone that tried to bring the filth back into town, so she never had the chance to fall back into the habit.

"Fucking asshole," she said as she dropped the trays on the counter.

"Who?" Renee asked, looking out into the dining room.

"The prick at table four." Renee looked over and spotted a grimy looking man with round-rimmed glasses sitting in the booth alone. Dirt and oil was caked into his skin from his hands to his elbows, the kind you get from not scrubbing after working on a car. Her ex-husband used to get like that if she didn't make him scrub his hands every night when he came home from his job at the body shop.

"What did he do?" Renee asked. Jorge came around and looked through the window with them.

"I sat him and asked if he needed anything. He looked me up and down like I was on the menu and then asked if there was anything younger," Sylvia said. "Then he gave me some shitty little smile like I shouldn't be upset because he was joking. Like that makes it okay."

"Want me to go throw his dirty ass out?" Jorge asked. Everyone knew Jorge had a thing for Sylvia, but Renee didn't think they had done anything about it yet. It was just a matter of time before both of them found themselves drinking at the same place, at the same time, and something would happen. That was the origin story for most of the relationships in Pitt County.

"No, I'll take that table," Renee said as she walked through the doors and headed for table number four.

The man was on the small side, but Renee had known too many mechanics in her life to underestimate both his strength and his temper. He looked up at Renee when she walked up to the table, then he looked around her as if looking for Sylvia. Renee was younger than Sylvia by a few years, but still hadn't seen her twenties in a decade and a half. She thought of herself as a pretty woman. She knew she was no model, but she figured with everyone falling in love with Adele--who she could be a stand in for on camera, if the camera was just slightly out of focus--people would be more accepting of her size. Her self-doubt was all in her head, as if you asked anyone in the county if she was attractive you would be hard pressed to find anyone that said no, but every now and again she would get some shithead from Louisville or Lexington up on a hunting vacation who thought that they were hot stuff because they were from the big city. That type always seemed to think she wasn't good enough. It was something about the town that painted the women there in a negative light to outsiders. Except Hyacinth. Everyone thought that bitch was hot. Even Renee herself.

"I'm what you get, sugar," she said.

"I asked for younger, but..." the man said, looking her up and down.

"You decide yet?" she asked, nodding to the menu is his hands.

"Cheeseburger, well done, no pink, fries, banana milk shake," he said. Then he thrust the menu up at her.

"You can just go ahead and leave that there on the table,"

she said, pointing at the menu holder from which he had taken the one he now held. He looked over and bashfully put the menu back. Renee turned and started to walk back to the kitchen when the man said something under his breath. Renee heard him, but stopped and turned back to ask anyway.

"What was that?" she asked.

"Nothing," the man said.

"No, you said something..." She looked at his shirt; his name was embroidered in red thread, in a white oval, on the dirty blue shirt he wore. "...Courtney." She punctuated his name, knowing that it would bother him that she was throwing a name that could be considered feminine in his face. His body tensed up and he clenched his fists at the sound of his own name. He looked up at her, his eyes firing daggers.

"I said that you could at least acknowledge you got my order," he said, with venom in his voice.

"Oh, I am a professional, honey. I got it," she said.

"Then you should have said something and not just walk away," he said.

"And what would you like me to say?"

"You could have at least said thank you."

"Did you say please?" Renee asked. Courtney seemed temporarily wounded. She had got him with that.

"It's not my job to be nice to you; it is your job to be nice to me," he said.

"My job is to make sure you get your food, correctly, and in an acceptable amount of time. And if you hadn't stopped me with a snide comment your cheeseburger, well done, no pink, would be on the grill, your fries would be in the fryer, and your banana shake would be mixing. But instead you're sitting here giving me attitude because you don't think I'm attractive enough to serve you." Renee's hands were on her hips, but she didn't remember putting them there. Likewise she assumed that her head was moving back and forth on her neck, showing off her entry level of sass. If Courtney knew what was good for him he wouldn't push any farther.

"I just," he started, and then looked down at the table. His hands were still clinched, but she could see he knew he was beat. "Sorry," he said through gritted teeth.

"What's that now?" she asked, wanting to hear it again. He looked up at her. He had so much hate in his eyes, for a brief moment Renee was scared. She saw something in those eyes, something evil.

"I said, I was sorry," he said. Renee took a step back, still feeling like she had won, but now worrying about a second round.

"Okay, hon, thank you. Let me go get this put in for you and it'll be out soon."

Renee walked back to the kitchen. Sylvia and Jorge were both standing outside the batwing doors. Jorge had a large butcher knife, just in case. As Renee approached them she asked quietly, "Is he still looking?"

"He is, and if looks could kill..." Sylvia said. She followed Renee through the doors. Jorge stayed for a moment, drawing Courtney's gaze. The men stared at each other for a moment before Courtney raised his hands slightly in a "what now?" motion. Sylvia reached through the door and grabbed Jorge by the shoulder, pulling him into the kitchen. Jorge never broke eye contact with Courtney until the batwing doors closed behind him.

Once all three of them were in the kitchen Renee knocked a stack of takeout containers across the room.

"What a fucking asshole," she said.

172

"Want me to throw him out?" Jorge asked again.

Renee looked through the window at the man. He was playing on his phone acting like the encounter never happened.

"No, just make him a well-done cheeseburger and fries," she said without taking her eyes off of him.

"What? Are you serious?" Jorge said.

"He wants us to elevate it. He wants us to get mad. Just make his food, and make it well. Make this the best burger he ever ate. Don't give him any reason to justify his behavior." She turned toward Sylvia. "Can you make a banana milkshake, extra whipped cream?"

Both of them just stared at her for a moment. Then without a word they got to work making the food. Renee went out back and had a cigarette. Something else that Hollis had tried to ban from the town, but what he didn't know wouldn't hurt her, and right now she needed something.

When the food was ready, Renee took it out to him. She acted as if the first encounter had gone perfectly and that he was any other customer.

"Here you go, sweetheart, can I get you anything else?" she said with a smile. She set the food in front of him. It looked more picturesque than any meal she had ever served in the diner. Courtney looked at it questionably. He lifted the top bun and examined the food. The lettuce was crisp and perfect, but Courtney used a fork to lift it out of the way to see the rest of the burger. Renee knew he was looking for spit, but he wouldn't find any. She and Garrett may have spit on top of a few burgers, but she hadn't on this one. And she knew that he could look as hard as he wanted and he wouldn't find any, because Jorge always

173

spit in the patty while he was cooking it instead of after it was done. After he had given thorough inspection to the food he looked up at Renee.

"This will be fine," he said. The salt was still in his voice, but it had calmed. Renee stood at the side of the table without saying anything. Courtney started to lift his burger and then set it back down. He sat for a moment, then shook his head and shrugged his shoulders.

"You have to be kidding me," he said to himself, then turned toward Renee. "Thank you," he said with no conviction at all.

"Oh, you are very welcome," she said. "I'll be back over in just a few minutes to make sure everything is perfect, all right?"

Courtney just sat there looking at his plate.

"Great, enjoy," she said and skipped away from his table.

As Renee got close she could see Sylvia and Jorge watching her through the window. When she went through the door Sylvia greeted her with a high five. Jorge did a slow clap. They had won this battle. If only they knew what the war ahead had in store for them.

31

The late afternoon breeze felt wonderful after being in the dusty library for hours. Paisley stood and took a deep breath, inhaling the mountain air. She needed a little time to start putting things together. She wanted to sit alone with some index cards and start writing down everything she knew. In her mind it was like doing a puzzle, which was easier if she had the pieces laid out in front of her. She needed to decide if the twisted history of Grey Water Ridge was important for the story. She needed to determine if Nathan Steiner's disappearance was the first mention of the sasquatch, and when the local church became tied in with the idea of God punishing people through the use of such a creature. Then there was the bigger mystery: if it wasn't a monster in the woods killing women, what, or who, was it? She remembered the hat. There was something about the hat Grover wore. Before her brain could run down that road she was interrupted.

"Forget where you were going?" Hollis's distinctive voice asked. Paisley twitched with surprise and looked at him.

"What?"

"You're just standing out here on the sidewalk like you don't know where to go," Hollis said. He was standing next to his car with his keys in his hand. He must have pulled in when she'd been so lost in her thoughts that she hadn't even noticed. He was parked right next to the yellow Hummer.

"Oh," she said. She looked back at the library and then thought about Boyd. She imagined that he was probably inside looking out at her and being nervous that she was talking to Hollis. She thought about skirting the subject, but then thought about how she wanted to investigate, to get to the bottom of things, and how you did that by charging at them full speed ahead. "I was just in the library," she said.

Hollis took a few steps toward her while he looked up at the building. A small curious smile crossed his face.

"So you met Boyd?" he asked.

"I did, and he seems to be convinced that you don't want him talking to me about town history." She wasn't going to bury the lede. If she just waited for information to fall in her lap she wouldn't get anywhere. Before he could say anything, she asked, "Why is it that everyone in this town seems to be afraid of you?"

A look came over his face that she wasn't exactly ready for. It was one she hadn't seen him wear yet, but she thought she understood it. It was a frustrated and annoyed smile. His head cocked to one side.

"Respect and fear often wear the same mask," he said. "Boyd has a tendency to exaggerate the importance of certain facts when it comes to events, and has often been the cause of a headache or two in that regard. As for the rest of the town, I carry considerable influence. Being one who tries his best to provide for this community, and possessing a good nature, I am often the subject of those who seek to take advantage." The annoyed smile was replaced by the one she was more familiar with. "If there's something you want to know, you are welcome to ask me."

"I just wanted to get an outside perspective about the sasquatch, and Boyd said he was an expert," she said.

"Ah, that he is. He's the unofficial town historian," Hollis said.

"Yeah, he mentioned that," Paisley said. Hollis turned toward the building and cupped his hands around his mouth to yell.

"Boyd!" he hollered at the door. Almost before the name was completely out of his mouth Boyd had come through the door and was bounding down the steps, with Pilot close behind.

"Yeah, Hollis, I'm right here. What do you need?" Boyd's eagerness made Paisley feel a little sad for him.

"Boyd, Miss Mott here has some questions about the sasquatch, and she would like for you to give her some unbiased information about that. Would you be so kind as to sit down and act as an expert in that capacity, please?"

Boyd looked from Hollis to Paisley, and then back to Hollis.

"Of course," Boyd said.

"Thank you, that would be great! Do you mind if we set it up as an interview and I use it for my story? I can put a little title with your name and a thing that says 'Unofficial Town Historian' underneath," Paisley said, asking both of them at the same time.

"Fine with me," Boyd said, but Hollis was not as quick to answer.

"No," he said. "Don't put that."

Boyd's chin dropped slightly.

"Put 'Official Town Historian,'" Hollis said, putting a hand on Boyd's shoulder. The look on Boyd's face was that of appreciation, admiration, and pride.

"Seriously?" Boyd asked Hollis.

"I think you've shown that you are the foremost expert on the town's history, and you've done such a good job with the library that we would be crazy not to honor that with a title," Hollis said. "So give Miss Mott her interview about Sasquatch." Paisley thought she could see a knowing look pass between them.

"Right, about Sasquatch, you got it," Boyd said.

"Fantastic," Paisley said. "Can I come by tomorrow morning?"

Boyd looked to Hollis for an answer. Hollis nodded.

"Any time before the library opens at ten," Boyd said.

"Great, I'll be here. Thank you, Boyd."

"My pleasure."

Hollis clapped his hands together, giving the universal sign that matters were done and that it was time to move on.

"Wonderful, now, I was just heading to the cafe to grab a bite to eat. Miss Mott, would you care to join me?" Hollis bent his arm and extended his elbow in an offering to escort her.

"Well, I would love to get the details about the murder this morning, which I am sure you heard all about?" Paisley said. She wasn't sure that Hollis had heard all about it, but after being called out for that last one she assumed he would be called out in the event that another murder happened. "But, I did promise Hyacinth I would have dinner with her this evening." Paisley had made no such plans, but she had a lot of things that needed to be ordered in her head, and if she was going to do a good job of interviewing Boyd she needed some prep time.

Hollis snapped his arm back in and stood up straight

and tried to look comically offended.

"Well, then, if that's how it will be," he said, turning his face away from her.

"How about lunch after Boyd's interview tomorrow?" she said. Hollis turned back to her.

"I could make myself available if a proper invitation were extended."

"How about after Boyd is done in the interview chair you let me get you on record in an interview too?" The idea of getting everyone with knowledge about the situation on video had just come to her. She didn't know why she hadn't thought of it before, but it made sense. It would be great for the edit, plus it would be a lot easier to comb through people's stories to know which cracks to pick at to find some truth.

"Didn't we do that at the church yesterday?" Hollis asked.

"Well, we talked, but I mean like a real interview. I can prepare some questions and everything. Maybe I can even get the Sheriff, and anyone else that you think would be beneficial, to sit in and do one? We can straighten up the upstairs," Paisley jerked a thumb toward the library, "and I can just shoot all day up there, if that's okay?" The first part of the question was directed at Hollis, but when she asked about upstairs she looked at Boyd. Her goal was to make them both feel included, like she needed both of them to weigh in so that they were more likely to have a favorable reaction.

"You've been upstairs?" Hollis asked. Paisley turned back to him. She thought of the boxes and wondered if Hollis could have been the one looking through them.

"I have," she said.

"It's a mess up there," he said. "Are you sure we

shouldn't set up somewhere else? How about the church?"

Paisley thought about that for a moment, and then decided that it would be a good idea to shoot in multiple locations.

"Why don't I do Boyd's here, and then come by the church after? Then maybe get the Sheriff to let me interview him at his office," she said. Hollis considered that for a moment, then nodded.

"Good idea," he said. "But, you will have lunch with me before we do the interview?"

"I think I could do that," she said. Hollis smiled.

32

On any given day in Grey Water Ridge you would find Sheriff Grover Northfield sitting in his office in the small building that the county had deemed worthy of being the Sheriff's Office. Grey Water was a small town, but it was still the largest town in Pitt County. There were a few smaller towns sprinkled about on this section of the Appalachian Trail, but nothing big enough to warrant the office being anywhere but Grey Water. There wasn't a lot of crime in the county, outside the murders, of course, so most of Grover's time was spent driving his Jeep around the trails looking for people doing things they shouldn't be doing. He would get hunters up there out of season, or campers with fires when the restrictions were on. The Forest Rangers took care of most of that, but he wanted to feel needed.

There were fifteen deputies in Grey Water, and not all of them liked Grover. It may have been his skin color, it may have been what the locals sometimes called "his liberal bias," or it could have just been that he was the youngest sheriff that the town had ever had. They still followed the orders he gave them, but some deputies just didn't seem too thrilled when he gave them. He never cared that they didn't like him--as long as they did their jobs they were all right by him.

Grover felt that the town of Grey Water had started to go downhill over the last few years. He hadn't been there long, but long enough to notice that things were on the decline. People had become more abrasive with each other. More small altercations were being reported. The people of Grey Water had started to feel the weight of the outside world pressing in on them, and they were starting to press back. Grover had been called when one of his deputies responded to a fight between a man who stopped in to the diner one morning for breakfast as he was passing through and two of the old timers who never seemed to leave. The traveler mentioned that it was a nice place, and that he would consider moving up there when he retired. The two men took offense to anyone new coming into town and punched the guy. It wasn't the normal hospitality he had hoped to find in the town, but it was very much the hospitality he himself had received when he'd arrived.

When Grover first moved to the county he had rented a nice cabin up in the hills above the old gristmill. He had the idea that he would live up there alone with his dog, hunt and fish for meat, and use his savings for other necessities. Then he would write the novel that he knew was inside of him. He'd been a lifelong fan of writers like Dean Koontz, Peter Straub, Richard Matheson, and of course, his favorite, Stephen King. He even named his dog, a large Mastiff, not Cujo, as one would think, but Torrance, after the family in *The Shining*. He would normally call Torrance "Torey" for short, but when people were around he would use the full name. It was a touch of pride for him. Grover grew up loving books, and had been an avid reader his whole life. He knew that, if given the chance, he could write an amazing book of his own. So he sold the condo he and Torrance lived in outside Memphis, quit his job as an operations director for a large company that manufactured plastics, and found a cabin that was being rented out by a lake in the hills near the Appalachian Trail. The rental process had been odd and made him question the move. When he called the number on the listing the person who answered said that it was a town library. He would come to learn later that the library often acted in a capacity as a catch-all for whatever light work needed to be done in the town of Grey Water Ridge. In this instance it was the rental of a property owned by H. Bloom Holdings to one Mr. Grover Jefferson Northfield. Grover could have bought a place with the money he had before moving up there, but when you're young and black in America you never really want to plant roots until you see what the soil is like, or at least that's what his grandmother always told him. So he would rent and save his little stockpile of cash.

Being a natural leader, Grover had risen through the ranks after starting as a janitor at a plastics company. After a little help from his parents, a full ride scholarship in college, and some good real estate investments, he was pretty well set when he sold his condo and moved to the hills.

Life up at the cabin was nice, and Torrance liked it up there, but Grover got bored. After nearly a year of starts and stops on a novel about a security guard at a botanical garden who sees ghosts, he finally shelved the project and started thinking about the future.

One day, while Grover and Torrance were in town picking up supplies, they ran in to the town preacher himself. Hollis was standing on the corner of Main Street and saying hello to, and shaking hands with, every single person that walked by. Grover had been one of those people. He had liked Hollis at first, but Torrance didn't seem to. Torrance had a thing about tall people. At least that was what Grover told Hollis, who stood easily seven inches taller than he himself. Hollis had asked Grover if he was enjoying his time in Grey Water Ridge. He had mentioned the failed novel, so Hollis, being the inquisitive type, invited him to have lunch. Over lunch Grover had admitted to Hollis that he was getting a bit stir crazy up at the cabin, so Hollis insisted that he come spend more time in town. Grover started coming down on Friday evenings. The town was pretty active on Friday nights. Sometimes they would move the tables in the diner and have a 50's style sock hop, or a Karaoke night at one of the bars, or a bonfire and barbecue in the field just past Main Street. It took everyone a while to get used to seeing a black man at their events, but since he was often seen with Hollis, everyone just sort of ignored him. He was sure that they were talking about him behind his back, but he doubted anyone would ever really say anything to his face. Even with that he was starting to really love this little town.

A few months after he started making his Friday night trips he met her. She was easily the most beautiful woman Grover had ever seen. It was a bonfire night and he had brought Torrance, and there she was, standing on the other side of the fire, lit only by the flames dancing playfully across her perfectly sculpted face. He had asked Hollis who she was, and Hollis said only that if he was smart he would avoid her. Hollis said she had a lot of baggage and that a nice guy like Grover wouldn't last ten minutes in the orbit of Hyacinth Bloom, but Grover wanted to be the judge of that. Grover recognized the name Bloom as the name on his lease and had asked if there was a relation. Hollis just replied that the Bloom family owns nearly the entire town. He introduced himself to her, and a few days later they had their first official date. He took her out to the lake just down from his cabin. It was far enough off the beaten path that he had never seen anyone else out there. They had a picnic, at which he played his guitar and sang a less than perfect version of a Justin Timberlake song to her. Hyacinth spent a good hour throwing a stick into the water so Torrance could chase it down, splashing around like a whale, and bringing it back. It was the first of many trips to the lake together. Grover started to fall hard for her, and he thought that she was starting to feel the same.

When Hollis found out that they were dating he didn't seem happy about it, but he convinced Grover to move into town. There was a small house just off Main Street, and he could live there for free, if he ran, and won, the election to become Sheriff. The property was owned by the county and was allocated for use by the Sheriff as a perk, since no one really wanted the job in the first place. Grover agreed, thinking that it would be a great way to be closer to Hyacinth, and make a little more money so that he could show her that he wasn't after her money and that he could take care of the two of them if the need ever arose.

When Grover arrived in Grey Water Ridge the people there were depressed but they weren't angry. They felt that their lives had never been fair, and the fact that an outsider came in and became Sheriff didn't make anyone too happy. It was an elected position, so he never fully understood why they voted for him if they didn't want him. He assumed that it was Hollis's doing. Hollis had been the one who nominated him for Sheriff in the first place. He had told him that the introduction of the town's first black resident would be much more effective if that resident was in a deserved position of power. Grover admittedly liked the whole *Blazing Saddles* aspect of it.

Now there he was, with Torrance asleep in the corner on his giant pillow, while he sat staring at a large cork board with a map of the county stretched across it. A grouping of red push pins was stuck into the board, each representing one of the murdered girls from the last few months. Grover wondered where he might have to put the next one. He looked over at Torrance, who raised his head and blinked the sleep from his large dark eyes when Grover spoke.

"Look at the mess I've gotten myself into would ya'?" The dog answered with a hard exhale as he dropped his large head back onto his pillow. "A big mess indeed."

33

Hollis walked into the diner with that same smile on his face. He wished that Paisley would have joined him for lunch, but he had the next day to look forward to. She would interview him and he would get his chance to tell her about the sasquatch. Boyd would surely tell her what little there was to tell in regard to how far back the sightings go, but only Hollis was qualified to speak to why it was happening.

The smile on his face soon faded when he walked in to see Renee yelling at a dirty little man in one of the booths on the far side of the restaurant. A broken plate lay fifteen feet away, and a few leftover french fries and part of a burger marked its path from the table. Sylvia stood near the doors to the kitchen, holding Jorge back, who had a large knife in his hand. Clearly something was developing.

"Jorge, just call the Sheriff," Sylvia was saying to Jorge as Hollis entered the scene. He raised his hand and then slowly lowered it, and as if he was turning down the volume on the situation, both Jorge and Sylvia stopped yelling and relaxed. Hollis walked toward the table where the dirty man was yelling at Renee and she at him.

"What seems to be the problem here?" Hollis asked as he

put a supportive hand on Renee's shoulder.

Renee tensed at the touch as she clearly hadn't heard Hollis come in. When she realized it was him she relaxed and Hollis could see the emotion that she had been hiding come to the surface. Before, it had been all anger, but at the sight of him she looked like she might cry. Before Renee could tell her side the little man started barking.

"This bitch brought me undercoo--" he started before Hollis stopped him with another simple raise of his hand.

"Stop," he said in a stern voice. "Now, I'm happy to hear you out, but I will not abide by you talking to Miss Webb in that fashion. She's a hard working woman, who has served this town for years, and deserves the respect you would give your own mother."

"I hate my mother," the dirty man said.

"Well, then, she deserves the respect you would give *my* mother," Hollis said, tilting his head down to glare at the man.

The man rethought what he was going to say.

"My burger wasn't well done, and I tried to send it back and she wouldn't take it," he said.

Hollis stepped between Renee and the man.

"Well, Courtney," he said pointing at the name on the shirt, "if the burger was undercooked then the person deserving of your umbrage is not Miss Webb, but instead that angry-looking man back there wielding that large butcher knife." Hollis cocked a thumb toward Jorge, who in turn snarled at Courtney. "And umbrage alone isn't an excuse to scream at anyone, and it certainly isn't cause to throw a plate." Hollis looked at the trail of food and the broken plate. "Which I assume you did, since last time I was in here the plates didn't have legs, am I right?" He asked this last while looking at Renee and holding up his hand in honest inquiry.

"They did not," Renee answered.

"They did not," Hollis repeated to Courtney, who looked angry but intimidated by the much larger man, "which means the former must be true. Correct?" Hollis waited for Courtney to answer.

"I said that it was undercooked and she wouldn't believe me. She said that I was just trying to get out of the check," Courtney said, all his words coming out in a burst.

"Renee?" Hollis said without shifting his gaze from Courtney. "Reach me what's left of that burger patty, would you please?" Hollis said, slipping into a colloquial phrase used by the folks in the hills and hollows of the Appalachian South. He did this often with outsiders when he wanted them to feel out of their element and remind them that they might as well be in a foreign country.

Renee walked over and used a napkin to pick up the two or three bites of meat that were left of the burger. She brought them back to Hollis. Hollis crouched down on his haunches next to the table, it put his face just a little lower than Courtney's so he had to look upward at him, but he forced Courtney, who had his head down, to meet his gaze. When Renee offered the napkin Hollis just took the meat out and looked at it, grease dripping down his fingers. He inspected it the way someone would inspect a Rubik's Cube to try and figure out their next rotation. After a few moments of quiet inspection he looked over at Renee.

"Is this all that's left of it?" he asked.

"That's all of it," she answered, not pointing out the conclusion that had obviously been drawn, instead letting Hollis make the point he was trying to make.

"This is it," he held the meat up to Courtney. "You ate it

all but a bite or two, which means it couldn't have been that bad. And I don't see a single sliver of pink anywhere in there."

"I ate the pink," Courtney said. "I wasn't going to complain, because she was being such a..." Courtney stopped himself when Hollis turned his head to look at him sideways, knowing what he was about to say. "Because she was being rude. So I ate it. Then when I mentioned it to her, just so that they knew and no one else got raw hamburger, she got in my face about it."

"Now, Courtney, I have known this woman my entire life, and she is stern, but she is not rude unless provoked, so I am willing to go out on a limb here and say that you may have done something that upset the relative ease that this establishment normally enjoys. Am I right?" Hollis asked, not entirely rhetorically.

"I just asked about the burger," Courtney said.

Hollis turned his head to look at Renee. He didn't say anything.

"He made some inappropriate comments to Sylvia and me," she said.

Hollis rotated on his heels, turning his whole hunkering body, to look at Sylvia. She nodded. He rotated back. He raised an eyebrow at Courtney.

"I made a joke and they took it seriously," Courtney said.

Hollis stood, towering over the sitting man and looking down at him. He dropped the meat on the table.

"Now, I recognize everyone that lives and works in this county, and I don't recognize you, which means you aren't from here. So are you just passing through or do you have business?"

Courtney didn't answer, he just looked down at the table, but away from the beef that sat right in front of him.

190

"I'm going to take that as you were just passing through. And I would like you to do that as expeditiously as possible. So what I am going to do is step back so you can stand up. You are going to apologize to these wonderful young ladies, and then you are going to keep on passing through. I'll go ahead and pay for your meal, as I am about to have a delicious burger myself, and they can just put it on my check. That sound like a plan?" Hollis asked. Courtney didn't look up.

"Whatever," he said, and started to slide out of the booth, but he had to stop as Hollis had not yet moved. Courtney looked up at Hollis. "I said fine."

"No, you said whatever," Hollis said.

"Fine, okay, I'll say sorry and go," Courtney said, throwing his hands in the air in mock surrender.

Hollis stepped back and gave him a wide berth. Renee did the same. Courtney stood and brushed crumbs off of his dirty shirt as if it was a fancy suit.

"I'm sorry," he said as he walked toward the door. Jorge stepped in front of Sylvia as he went by. Hollis would not have been surprised if the scrappy little Mexican took a swipe at him with that knife as he did.

"Oh, and Courtney?" Hollis called after him as he opened the door. Courtney looked back at him. "Do not come back to Grey Water Ridge, ever."

Courtney pushed the door the rest of the way open. It banged at the end of the arm on top of the door and Courtney stomped down onto the sidewalk. He pivoted and gave an angry finger to Hollis through the window and then stormed off out of sight. A moment later a black hatchback peeled out and went up Main Street.

Hollis sat down. He had a cheeseburger, rare, with coleslaw, the way you do in the South. And at the end of

191

the meal, as usual, no check was brought.

34

Paisley came down the stairs but there was no smell of coffee, there was no bacon, there was no Hyacinth. Paisley had waited up for her, but when she hadn't come home by ten o'clock Paisley had texted her and learned that Hyacinth would be out late with Grover. He was upset about the latest death and wanted to go up to his cabin, so she went with him. Paisley had asked Hyacinth during her text messaging the night before if she would ask Grover about doing the interview, and he had agreed. So she would meet him right after interviewing Hollis. Paisley was feeling pretty good about how things were coming together.

She found her way around the kitchen well enough to make her own coffee. As she did, she found an appreciation for the design of the kitchen that helped her understand the depth of Hyacinth Bloom. When you looked at the things in the kitchen, while you were standing there, they seemed oddly placed. Like a vintage breadbox that was pulled out from the wall and turned slightly. It made no practical sense that it be that way, but if you stood on the other side of the kitchen, and looked across to see what a camera would see, it lined up perfectly and stood out, looking normal as could be. The bowls and mugs were on shelves far away from the dishwasher because there were no doors on those cabinets, whereas if they were in the cupboard with the plates, near the dishwasher where you could easily put them away, you wouldn't be able to see them, and they made for a great backdrop. Paisley found it all brilliant, but it also made her feel like she was standing on a set--and she was, to a degree. What if Hyacinth herself was like the kitchen. What if everything she showed was exactly what she wanted people to see? What if everything she had told Paisley was a lie? What if she wasn't with her cowboy-hat-wearing Sheriff boyfriend up at his cabin.

The cup of coffee Paisley had poured herself fell from her hand. That hat. She *knew* she had seen it before. It was the same type of hat the person who broke her drone and then threw it down at her was wearing. She remembered Hyacinth acting a little strange when she saw the person on the tape. The hair prickled on the back of her neck. She wiped up the coffee and tossed the paper towels and broken cup into the garbage but the whole time she was thinking about what questions to ask the Sheriff now, or if it was even a good idea to talk to him at all.

The library was locked when she arrived, and knocking on the glass of the door produced a few soft barks from behind it. Boyd answered a moment later; he was wearing a button-up, short sleeve, mustard-colored shirt, a brown tie with matching mustard stripes, and brown slacks. His hair was parted straight down the middle, and he had traded his boxy, hip glasses for a pair that were much larger and looked like the ones Paisley's eighty-year-old pharmacist wore. Paisley laughed when she saw him. She hoped to God that this was a joke, because she would die if he was honestly dressed up and he wasn't trying to look like Dwight Shrute from *The Office*. Boyd struck a pose.

"Get it?" was the first thing he said. "I hope so, or your laughing might hurt my feelings."

"This is the best thing ever. I love that show," she said.

"I would have gone with the Jim Halpert look, but I didn't think it was obvious enough. Then there was the old Ron Swanson look, but I couldn't grow a mustache fast enough."

"Oh my God, I love *Parks and Rec* too!" She laughed again. "Are you really going to wear that during the interview? You realize I'm recording this to put it on the internet, right?"

"Yep. I want the world to know that librarians are the coolest people on Earth. People think we're just quiet and reserved, but we're so much more. We have depth."

"Well, I love it," Paisley said.

She carried in her camera bag and Boyd took the box she had brought with her. The box had two shop lights she had picked up from the small hardware store, and two white bed sheets she had borrowed from Hyacinth's linen closet. They set up on the second floor. Paisley set up the lights on either side of a chair in the middle of the room. When she set up the camera, got the microphone ready, and sat Boyd in the chair, it looked very professional. She was pleased with herself.

"Are you ready?" she asked.

Boyd nodded. Sweat had formed on his brow.

"I'm going to just ask some questions. You don't have to do an introduction because I'm going to put a title card underneath, all right?"

"Don't forget that I'm the Official Town Historian as

195

well as the Curator and Head Librarian," Boyd said. "Also, it wouldn't hurt with the ladies if you mentioned that I'm the county's *Battlestar Galactica* trivia champion three years running." There was a pause as Paisley considered this.

"Really?"

"False," Boyd said in his best Dwight Shrute voice. Paisley laughed.

"Okay, I'll make sure to mention all of that. Now, how long have you lived in Grey Water Ridge?"

"I was born and raised here. So I've been here for 28 years."

"And when did you start your study of the town's history?"

"When I was about twelve."

"Why so early?"

"My father would tell me stories when I was a kid. I loved them. We would sit up all night sometimes and he would tell me things about growing up in Grey Water, and about the time before that. So after he died I grew obsessed with two things: stories--like in TV, movies, and books-- and the town's history," Boyd looked down away from the camera.

"I'm very sorry to hear about your father," Paisley said. "It was nice that you took up his passion after his passing."

"Thank you. I love books, but movies and TV are my favorite--but the video store we had here in town closed a while back. People up here just don't care much for that type of entertainment. I worked there for a few years when I was a teenager, but when it went under I came to work here."

"How long were you here before making head librarian?"

"A few years. My mom ran the place before me, which is why it was so easy to get the job."

"Did she retire?"

Boyd bit his bottom lip. His eyes shifted.

"No, they just didn't have enough to pay two people anymore, so she quit and went to work at the diner so that I could stay. She knew I wouldn't be happy anywhere else in town. And after Dad died she was always afraid I'd leave Grey Water the first chance I got. A lot of the young ones do, it's why the town is in the position it's in." Right after he finished his sentence he sucked air in as if he was trying to pull the words back in.

"What do you mean the position it's in?" Paisley asked.

"I shouldn't be talking about that. After all, you're here to hear about the sasquatch!" Boyd raised his hand in the air like a knight.

"Is something wrong with the town? Off the record."

Boyd seemed nervous. He looked at the camera. Paisley reached over and switched it off. He looked up at the microphone pointed at him.

"It's going through the camera, so it isn't on either. I promise," she said. "Boyd, what's going on here?"

"The town is going broke. Everyone in it is broke." He paused. "Well, not everyone."

"Hyacinth Bloom," Paisley said. It wasn't a question, but she didn't want him to have to say it. He seemed uncomfortable naming names.

"Not just her."

"Is there someone else here that has that kind of money?"

The color had left Boyd's face. His hands squeezed the seat of his chair.

"Can we talk about the sasquatch, please?" he asked. The sweat had begun to run down his forehead. "I just got the title, I don't want to lose it. Please?"

Paisley thought for a moment and turned the camera

197

back on.

"Boyd, can you tell me about the sasquatch that's been seen in this area?" Paisley didn't want to drop the new topic that Boyd had unintentionally opened up, but she knew pushing him would get her nowhere. She would get him talking, then see if she could get the answers she wanted from him after his tongue was a little looser.

"The first reported sighting was in the 1880's. A boy was taken and someone claimed that they saw a sasquatch running into the woods with him," Boyd said.

"Nathan Steiner."

Boyd looked surprised that she would know that name. "That's right, Nathan Steiner."

"Is it true that the town founder, Gerald Harris, was also a suspect in that disappearance?"

"Well, yes, Gerald Lee Harris was questioned, but his alibi was very solid," Boyd said. "He was in New York at the time of the kidnapping, so he was never arrested or charged with anything and any other involvement was purely speculation." The color had come back into Boyd's face, and the conversation seemed to bring him to life. Paisley thought that having an intelligent conversation about something he was passionate about would help.

"So do you, as the Official Town Historian, have an opinion on whether the attack on Herk Steiner, that left his wife Abigale dead, and his youngest son without his legs, was carried out or commissioned by Gerald Harris?"

"Well, some say that--" Boyd caught himself. He looked sideways at Paisley. "Now that has nothing to do with Sasquatch. Are you trying to get me in trouble?"

Paisley smiled. "Of course not."

"Well, then, I'd rather not talk about that part of the history, and I would like to stick to Sasquatch, thank you,"

Boyd said.

"Okay," Paisley said. She was even more annoyed now. "Do you think that there is a mythical creature roaming the Great Smoky Mountains killing hookers and drug fiends?" After she asked the question she wished she could have it back. She hoped it didn't sound as condescending as it felt, but judging by the look on Boyd's face it likely did. "I'm sorry," she said.

Boyd took a moment and recovered. His brow was furrowed, but he didn't seem as insulted as Paisley thought he should.

"It may seem like a joke to the outside world, but a large part of our county's history, and Grey Water Ridge particularly, involves that so-called mythical creature. Nearly every resident who's been here more than a few years has a story about him." Boyd had sat up straight and his shoulders were back.

"Really?" Paisley asked. She had to be very careful not to be insulting again. So she tried to soften her tone as much as she could: interested without sounding skeptical.

"Yes, really. People have seen it cross the road in front of their cars at night. They've seen it at a distance on a picnic, while hiking, or just looking out their back windows out into the woods. I'm no cryptozoologist but if I had to wager a bet, I would put every cent I have on the fact that a sasquatch really is wandering the hills here. Now, I can't say that he's killed anyone, but I do believe he's up there."

"I heard that the hands of the victims had been ripped off--is that something that a sasquatch could do?" Paisley asked.

"Again, I'm not an expert in what a sasquatch could or could not do, but I would guess that something that big could do whatever it wanted."

"What else can you tell me about the history of the sasquatch as it pertains to the town of Grey Water?"

"Well, I can tell you that with the number of sightings we've had from tourists just passing through, I'm surprised that we don't have more people coming up here to try and spot him." Boyd chuckled at the idea. "I can just see someone setting up a business taking tours up to the hills to see if they can spot him."

"Have you seen an increase in tourism since word got out?"

"Well, word really hasn't gotten out. The tourists that have seen him are all older. So it isn't like they're going on the Facebook or the Twitter to talk all about it."

"But you would think that with all the murders it would be a big story," Paisley said.

"You'd think that, but no one really cares much about us crazy hillbillies. They'd just prefer not to ever hear from, or about, us."

Paisley thought about what she could ask Boyd to bring him back around to her side. She thought about the questions she'd prepared for Hollis and for the Sheriff.

"What about the Sheriff?" she asked.

"Grover Northfield? What about him?"

"Does he believe the sasquatch killed those girls?"

"Well, that's two different questions right there," Boyd pointed out. Does he believe in Sasquatch, and does he think that it was a sasquatch that killed them girls?"

"Well, does he believe in Sasquatch?"

"Yes, he does. I know that for a fact, as he told me that he was up by the lake in the hills above the gristmill and he said he had seen it plucking fish out of the lake with its bare hands. He said that it heard him from all the way across the lake, probably half a mile, and it ran. Most people don't know that he rented a cabin up behind that lake when he first came to the county, but before he ran for sheriff he came down to live in town so that he could get elected easier."

Paisley knew she had to ask the next question fast--if she allowed for any break in the conversation Boyd would have enough time to think, and if he did that he might stop talking. So she lined her questions up and prepared to fire.

"So does he believe that the sasquatch killed the girls?" she asked.

"Well, if he doesn't think they did, he sure hopes they did," Boyd said.

Paisley fired the obvious follow-up question. "Why would he hope so?"

"Because if it wasn't the sasquatch then his best deputy, and my best friend, Rowan, is the prime suspect," Boyd said. "Rowan has been on the run since the fifth or sixth girl disappeared and someone said he saw him with the girl in his pickup right before she died."

"Who saw him?" Paisley asked, not even giving a moment for him to breathe.

"Well, Hollis was the one who called the Sheriff," Boyd said. Right after he said it he stood up as if he had spilled hot coffee in his lap. Paisley stood up quickly too, more from being startled by Boyd standing so quickly. For a moment she worried he was going to come at her.

"Hey, you can't ask that," he said, which didn't even make sense. "You have to erase that, now." He reached for the camera. Paisley stepped in front of it and put her hand up. She didn't touch him, but if he took another step forward her hand would be in his chest. He looked down at her hand and then up in her face. She did not look like she was playing around. Boyd looked at the camera as if it was a million miles out of his reach.

Pilot had come up the stairs at the sound of the commotion and was looking at Boyd with worried eyes. The dog came over and put her long nose into his open hand. Boyd looked down at her and it seemed to calm him instantly. He plopped backward into the chair and began to stroke the massive dog's head.

"You tricked me," Boyd said, not looking up at Paisley but instead focusing on the dog.

"Is there something wrong with Hollis calling the Sheriff's office to make a report after the girl died?" she asked.

Boyd looked at her.

"I'm not supposed to talk about Hollis and his business. I'm allowed to talk about the history of the sasquatch, that's it," he said. "And I'm done doing that, so I would appreciate it if you would pack up your things and head on out. I've got to get this place open."

Paisley started taking down the sheets and lights, but left the camera running. Boyd didn't get up the whole time. He just sat petting the dog. Once Paisley had finished with the lighting equipment she started toward the camera.

"Please don't use that last part," Boyd said.

Paisley stopped and looked at him. He looked so sad. He looked like a child who had let his father down and didn't want him to find out. Paisley guessed that was exactly how he felt.

"I won't, I promise. I just want to get a good story out of this, and hopefully find some information that will help Sheriff Northfield solve this whole thing if I can." Paisley put a hand on his shoulder. "You're doing a great job here. Your dad would be proud."

Boyd didn't look up but Paisley could hear him sniffle.

She carried her stuff down the stairs. It was much harder carrying the box and her bag without Boyd's help, but she had Pilot as her escort as she walked out the door into the morning sun. The door closed and locked behind her.

35

The town of Grey Water Ridge was quiet to begin with,
but when Paisley pulled up to the church for her interview
with Hollis, the silence seemed to roll off the hills like
waves. The red door to the church stood open, and Hollis
leaned against the frame. He wore long, black shoes and a
white linen button-up shirt with the sleeves rolled to the
elbows and tucked in to his black slacks. He took a large
bite out of an apple as Paisley parked and got out.

"I thought we were supposed to be having lunch
together," she said, motioning toward the apple.

Hollis ignored the question.

"You know the apple in the book of Genesis, the one Eve
takes from the forbidden tree and gives to Adam?" Hollis
asked, holding up the apple as if it was one and the same.

"I know there was one," Paisley responded.

"Genesis chapter three, verse one. Now the serpent was
more crafty than any of the wild animals the Lord God
made. He said to the woman, 'Did God really say you
must not eat from any tree in the garden?'" Hollis said.

"What?" Paisley asked.

"Genesis three three, but God did say 'You must not eat
fruit from the tree that is in the middle of the garden, and

you must not touch it, or you will die.'" Hollis walked down the steps to where Paisley now stood holding her equipment. There was something about him. Something crazy, but brilliant. Normally a man spitting bible verses would be a major turn off, but it showed a deep love for something. He stopped directly in front of her. He looked down at her and their eyes locked. Hollis's eyes were deep pools of knowledge that she wanted to swim in. He was so close that when he spoke again she could feel his deep, bass-rich voice in her bones.

"Genesis three five, 'For God knows that when you eat of it your eyes will be opened, and you will be like God, knowing good...'" he paused, "'...and evil.'" He snapped off another bite of the apple. He chewed and Paisley watched as his jaw clenched and flexed, his lips moving rhythmically in and out as he chewed. He swallowed. Without realizing it she had lifted herself onto her tip toes and was so close to his downturned face that when he licked his lips his tongue was inches from her mouth. She had the urge to pull him down to her.

"Then what?" she whispered.

"The apple wasn't an apple at all," he said. Paisley could hear the apple hit the ground near her feet. "It was Eve herself that was the forbidden fruit."

"Oh," Paisley squeaked.

"She took some and ate it. She also gave some to her husband, and he ate it. Then the eyes of both of them were opened, and they realized they were naked," Hollis said in a low whisper that drifted from his mouth, wet and sweet with apple, into hers which was thirsty and dry. The back of his fingers brushed her cheek and her knees quivered. His hand moved back and those long fingers slid into her hair and cupped near the top of her neck. He pulled her in and she could taste the apple. It was the most delicious kiss she had ever shared. His lips were soft and sticky and she could feel them part slowly. Her eager tongue slipped quickly into his mouth, reveling in the taste. His tongue slipped over the top of hers, dousing her in the flavor of the apple.

36

Hollis sat in the back pew, his shirt now untucked, with one arm stretched across the backrest. Paisley lay against his chest, her jeans laying in a pile in the center aisle next to the pew. She felt immensely satisfied, in a way she had not in a very long time, but she also had a pang of guilt. Hollis was a religious figure--was this allowed? If it was, she was certain this was not the venue for it. They sat without talking, his muscular chest rising and falling and her breath matching his tempo. She reached out and touched the back of the pew in front of her. There were letters, old and worn, in the wood. She skimmed her fingers across them.

"Someone had the nerve to carve letters into a pew in church?" she asked, breaking the silence and the mounting tension.

"Yeah, I did," Hollis said. "Turns out this is the third time I've done something I shouldn't have in this pew," he said with a laugh. She joined him.

"Third time?" Paisley asked, sitting up and turning around to look at him. She felt guilty, but that didn't mean she was okay with being the second woman he had done this with.

Hollis reached up and touched the first two letters with

the index and middle finger on his left hand.

"I did these two when I was nine or ten, and these when I was seventeen or so," he said, and touched the second set of letters. "It actually started all of this." He waved a hand around toward the empty church.

"What do you mean?"

"Don't you think if you want to ask questions like that you should turn your camera on?"

Paisley smiled. She got up, put her pants on, and went back out to grab the camera gear she had left sitting at the bottom of the stairs. Hollis followed and assisted.

The set up didn't take long. There was enough sunlight from the windows that her lights weren't needed. Instead she just hung a sheet over the window next to where Hollis would be and it lit him perfectly. He was sitting sideways in the same pew they had made love in. One foot sat on the ground and the other was pulled up on the pew, putting his knee up, and Hollis rested his forearm on it, the tattoos showing prominently. He ran a hand through his thick black hair and smiled.

"Ready when you are, Pickle," he said.

Paisley hit record on the camera.

"Reverend, tell us about why you wanted to go into ministry," she asked, still trying to switch gears into the professional side of herself.

"You mean when did I have my calling?" he asked.

"Yeah, if that's what it was," she said.

"When I was ten years old I carved my initial, an H, and my brother's initial, a C, for Cecil, into the pew here." Hollis put his hand on the pew in front of him.

"Why?"

"I thought that if our names, or at least part of them,

were here, we would be protected, or that maybe God would listen to our prayers." Hollis's eyes stared through the pew and back in time.

"What were you praying for?" It wasn't one of the questions Paisley had planned to ask, but like the interview with Boyd, she felt like something else was just under the surface and she wanted to get to the bottom of it.

"Back then?" Hollis asked rhetorically. "I was praying for my mom to come back home."

Paisley felt that maybe she was being invasive now, but that line hit her hard. She let Hollis continue.

"She left my dad. He was a poor preacher. She wanted us to go stay with her in town, but we didn't want to leave our dad out at the cabin alone. That cabin has been in our family for more than a hundred years. And, we had the woods and the lake. After a while we would spend weekends with my mom and her new husband. We would go over for a month or so in the summer, or we would all take a trip. Mom got lost in her new relationship; she had a new family and she sort of forgot that Cecil and I existed for a while..." Hollis's voice trailed off. He shook the cobwebs from his head and looked back up at Paisley.

"You okay?" she asked.

"Sorry, I don't talk about my mother often. You want to know about the sasquatch though," he said.

"No, it's okay, really," Paisley assured him. But she could see by the change in his eyes that it was time to get down to business, and not the business they had already gotten down to, but the kind she was hoping would make for a heck of a story.

"After carving our initials into the pew, my brother and I went camping in the woods behind our father's house."

Hollis told her the story of seeing the beast in the woods

that night. He told her about running from it and about his father sitting at the table when he and Cecil got home. He told her about his father explaining that God would send punishment for the wicked. He told her that from that day forward he believed the sasquatch that roamed the hills in this region was sent by God and he had been preaching it since he returned to reopen the church when he was seventeen. He was purposefully coy, like he enjoyed the mystery of it all.

"So, you told me the other day that you are certain it's the sasquatch that's killing the women in the woods, correct?" Paisley asked. She knew he was, but for the audience's sake she asked again.

"Yes, and as of yesterday morning we have another victim," Hollis said gravely.

"I heard. What can you tell me about it? Was it the same..." she searched for a way to put it without eliminating options. "Thing?"

Hollis gave her a little smile, recognizing the technique.

"If you are asking if it appears that it was the beast, then yes, it certainly looked that way. With the wound patterns, the amount of destruction, and the target, we have reason to believe that it's part of the pattern."

"What do you mean? Who was she?"

"She was a young woman who was reported missing from Lexington. She was an exotic dancer, or something of that nature. She was last seen with her boyfriend, and it seems they decided to come up and camp on the trail, and that didn't turn out well for them. Apparently his car was found the next county over, but the boyfriend is still missing."

"Would this, if the boyfriend is found dead, be the first time that a male was killed by the thing?"

"Well, I'm sure, since you spoke to Boyd Gunnerson, our Official Town Historian, you know the first confirmed death by the beast was a young boy?"

"Nathan Steiner?" Paisley said. Hollis's brow went rigid briefly. "I was told that a body was never found and that it was a single witness that reported seeing the monster. That's hardly conclusive evidence, wouldn't you agree?"

Hollis's eyebrows relaxed and sank. He looked at her like he was disappointed, or maybe insulted.

"Well, yes, but there were other signs that were found to support the conclusion," he said.

"I see. So there were no other suspects in the Steiner case?"

"What you are getting at?"

"Well, I'm just trying to collect information, and Boyd told me that he was instructed not to provide any," Paisley said.

"Well, there was evidence in that case that is not common knowledge," Hollis said.

"And the current string of murders--there is more evidence than in that case?" Paisley asked. Hollis looked mad now.

"Yes, much more," he said.

"Which is why my investigation shows that there isn't a suspect at this time?" Paisley knew that this was a touchy subject and that she shouldn't press this hard, especially after what they had done. She didn't want it to seem like she was taking advantage of him in that way. She was ready to back off, but the condescending tone in his voice made her give that a second thought.

"Is it an investigation if you just wander around and let people fill your mind with pointless nonsense?" Hollis said.

Paisley sat up straight in her chair. She was prepared for

things to go south and have to do the heavy lifting in the conversation, but she wasn't ready for him to insult her.

"What about the deputy that's under investigation?" Paisley said.

"What? How do you know about that?" he asked, his brow now properly furrowed. He stood as if she had accused him of the murders.

"Let's just say I was just wandering around and I let it pointlessly fill my mind," she snapped. Hollis looked like he was approaching rage. Paisley let the camera run.

Hollis stepped out of the pew and walked back toward the door. Then he began pacing at the front of the church. Paisley was aware that Hollis stood between her and the only door to the place. The day had taken a strange twist. She hadn't planned on sleeping with him, and she hadn't planned on trying to corner him, and now he was mad.

"I'm sorry," she said. "I didn't mean to upset you. It's just that I want to be thorough. I want this story to be right."

Hollis stopped his pacing and he turned to her.

"I'm not angry," he said. "I'm just thinking. I think best when I stand, and when I walk. Call it a side effect of the job."

"What are you thinking about?"

Hollis stopped pacing and walked toward where Paisley sat near the camera. It was a slow deliberate walk. Paisley tensed.

"Have you spoken to Hyacinth about this?" he asked.

"You mean the murders?"

"I mean the deputy on the run."

"I haven't had the chance." Paisley wondered why Hyacinth's opinion on the matter would be important, other than because she was dating the Sheriff.

"I suggest that before you speak on that particular

subject again, you talk to her. You ask her to tell you everything there is to know about Deputy Rowan Bloom." The weight of the name dropped from Hollis's lips and landed like a suitcase full of books on the floor in front of her.

Paisley said nothing. She remembered seeing holes in the decor of the house. Pictures missing where there had clearly been a photo before. Rooms that looked like they had been recently occupied but with no proof that anyone had been there. She tried to speak but didn't know what to say.

"Hyacinth has been very guarded about that information, and I suggest speaking with her before you say something you may regret," Hollis said.

Paisley just looked up at him in shock. She reached over and shut the camera off.

"So, can I expect to see you here Sunday morning for our service?" Hollis asked.

She had planned on attending the service. It was an understanding that the service would be recorded and word about that had spread through town. People weren't happy with it, but once they heard that it was Hollis's call they had all fallen in line. Hollis tilted the camera, looked at where the record light would normally be, and found it satisfactorily turned off. He nodded. Then he leaned down and kissed Paisley gently on her forehead.

"Let's meet at my house next time," he said, and then turned and walked toward the door.

His house. Paisley thought about that. In all of the conversations and in all of her thinking about Hollis, she had not realized that he probably didn't actually live in the church. She watched him as he opened the door and the bright light, which had been attacking the building from the side, poured in like an invading force through the front. It cast Hollis as a silhouette. The long shadow slithered out behind him as he walked down the steps, and he and the shadow merged into one and then vanished. Paisley felt lied to and taken advantage of. She had the urge to just drive herself back to the train station in Hyacinth's yellow Hummer, leave the keys in it, and text Hyacinth when she got there to tell her where they could find it.

37

The sheriff's station wasn't anything special. It was a small ranch-style house at the end of Main Street. Paisley noticed that, of the few official vehicles outside, Grover's Jeep was not among them. She was glad that she noticed this and decided to leave all of her equipment in the Hummer.

She walked through the front entrance and was met almost immediately by a chest-high desk. The desk closed off the front of the house and created a bit of a lobby. There were three plastic chairs, a desk with a woman of about sixty in a sheriff's uniform behind it, and a heavy-looking door that clearly led back behind the desk and provided entry into the rest of the building.

"Can I help you with something, sweetheart?" the older woman asked. Paisley looked around to see if she could see Grover. Beyond the wall that was the desk, she could see a few deputies milling about, but Grover was nowhere to be seen. Paisley could see a conference room and what appeared to be a large office, with the lights off. "Excuse me?" the lady said again. Paisley snapped to.

"I'm sorry, I'm looking for Grover Northfield. I have an appointment with him," Paisley said.

"Oh," the lady said, and looked down at a paper in front of her. She looked back up and judged Paisley. "Well, Miss Mott, I do have you scheduled here, but *Sheriff* Northfield is out, and he asked that I pass on his considerable regrets that he cannot make your appointment," she said, emphasizing her boss's title.

Paisley guessed there were two camps in this town. You were either team Hollis or team Grover, and whichever person you chose walked on water in your eyes. This lady seemed to worship at the altar of the good sheriff.

"Did he say where he was going?"

The woman leaned back abruptly as if Paisley had just asked if she passed gas.

"I'm very sorry, Miss Mott, but the Sheriff is not required to share his whereabouts with every person who strolls in off the street."

"I just thought that maybe if he was somewhere, and wasn't too busy, I could just interview him on the job. It would actually make for some pretty good footage."

The lady looked at Paisley as if she were insane.

"No," she said, "that isn't going to happen. I'm sorry."

Paisley smiled and took another look around the office to see if anyone was going to step forward and be helpful. They didn't. She smiled at the clerk.

"Thank you, I really appreciate your time," she said.

"Yeah," the clerk replied.

With that Paisley turned and left the claustrophobic-feeling lobby.

Paisley hoped that Grover was currently sitting in Hyacinth's kitchen. She hoped that because then she could rip both of them a new one, on camera if she could manage it.

38

It wasn't hard for Courtney to locate Raven Bloom once that bitch, Mott, said the name of it on her live stream. He had been cyber stalking Hyacinth long enough to track her house down. There wasn't a lot online, outside of the standard social media sites, about Hyacinth or her family. But Courtney thought that he would find out everything he needed to know about her soon enough. He had just enough time before the asshole at the diner tossed him out to hone in on exactly where the house was.

After driving up to the open gate of Raven Bloom, he turned his Ford Focus around and drove back down the mountain to the first pull off and swung the car in. It was as good a place as any to stash his car while doing what needed to be done. The sun was setting and the trees had blocked what was left, casting the car into darkness when it was pulled up against the far side of the small clearing. He slid out from behind the wheel and as he did so a sound caught his ear. The familiar sound of a car engine came from up the hill, and a second later the trees a few hundred feet from the pull off lit up. Courtney slammed the door and ran around the car to duck out of sight. The headlights moved across the trees, but he never saw them flash under the car, so he felt confident that he was far enough back that he wasn't seen. That was good. He had work to do. He worried that the car he heard was Hyacinth leaving since her house was the only thing up the road. If it was it wasn't a huge problem. He would just wait. He would hide in that big, obnoxious, arrogant house and wait for her to come home, and then he would get to show her who she had laughed at online. It's a lot harder to block someone when they have their hands around your fucking throat.

Courtney opened the hatch and pulled out a pair of thin black leather gloves. He slipped them on before pulling out the small hard case hidden under the floor in the back where the spare tire should be. He slid his hand across the front of the case and moaned as if this was a sensual moment. He flipped the latches and opened the case. His wet lips stretched into a grin as he looked at the gun that he had spent more than a month's salary on.

He had bought the gun at a trade show. He'd heard that was the easiest way to get the one he wanted and not have to explain to anyone why he wanted it. The one he'd picked was a Glock 17, 9 millimeter. He had paid so much for it because the vendor who sold it specialized in turning semi-automatic weapons into fully automatic ones. He had also bought four extended magazines for the gun, each holding twenty-four rounds. He had nearly a hundred rounds of ammunition, and if he reloaded fast enough, he could blaze through all of it in less than fifteen seconds. He had an extra box of ammo under the seat, but he figured that if all went well he wouldn't have to fire a single shot. Though he may want to anyway. Maybe he would shoot the vlogging bitch, just to test out what the Glock could do, and then use his hands on Hyacinth. That seemed like a solid plan to him.

He stuffed the gun into the waistband of his dirty jeans, closed the hatch of his car, and started up the road toward Raven Bloom.

The house seemed dark as he sneaked up to the front steps. He figured he would try the front door first, and if it was locked he would either sneak around until he found an easy way in or he would just break a window. He considered ringing the doorbell and just kicking it in when she answered, but what if she didn't actually live alone? Or what if the bitch was with her? He wasn't going to take a chance of getting caught or killed before he got what he felt he deserved--an hour alone with Hyacinth Bloom. After that he didn't care. He thought that maybe if all went well up at Raven Bloom maybe he would go down and visit that cunt at the diner. If he was really lucky the tall faggot would be there too. With as unlucky as he thought his life had been, he hoped that this was the chance when the planets aligned and he got everything he wanted. When he reached the top of the stairs and crept toward the door he thought that maybe, just maybe, they had.

The door was closed, but he tried the handle and found it was unlocked. Courtney hesitated--maybe someone was home and just liked sitting around with the lights off. He pulled the Glock and raised it, pointing it at the door. If it moved he wouldn't even wait to see who it was, he would just start shooting. He was too nervous to make decisions right then. The door didn't move. Courtney leaned forward and used the fingertips of his free hand to carefully push the door open. A high-pitched creak came from the door as he pushed, so he stopped. The opening was wide enough for him to slip his narrow frame through without having to push any farther. He stepped through, first with one foot, tapping the toe of his shoe gently on the marble floor to see how much noise it would make, before shifting his weight and swinging his other leg in behind him.

He stood in the foyer in awe. He had seen it before on the live stream, and parts of it in pictures, but it was a little overwhelming in person. The large black marble raven in the center of the room caused him to flinch backward and he bumped the door, the sound of it clicking closed echoing through the house. He choked up on the gun, standing, listening for any movement reacting to the sound of the door closing, but no noise came. The house was silent.

A light broke the darkness and invited him farther into the house. He walked toward it, first gently setting his heel on the floor and rocking forward onto his toes, one step after the other. Like a kid playing hide and seek, he crept toward the kitchen.

Courtney peeked around the corner into the kitchen. He held the gun low and leaned in like the cops on TV and then whipped the gun up, clearing the room. There was no one there. The kitchen was empty. He had seen that kitchen so many times, and it looked exactly as he remembered it. He pulled his phone from his pocket with his free hand and flipped open his Instagram app. The last post from Hyacinth was earlier that day. She was sitting on the corner of a giant four-poster bed. She was wearing a white tank top and, it looked like, nothing else. Her hair fell down around her face. She had one leg on either side of one post and had her crotch pushed up against it, hiding the presence of any underwear. She leaned to her left around one side of the post. She had a hand lifted to her face and had her index finger resting on her lip. Courtney reached down with his gun hand and adjusted his crotch.

His head snapped upward and looked around. The realization struck him that that photo, as well as hundreds of others that she had taken, were taken right there in this house. He could visit the spots right now. He listened. The house was silent still.

"Hello?" he called out. There was no response. He smiled. He would find her room and lay in wait.

It took him nearly fifteen minutes of opening and closing doors before he found the room he was looking for.

Hyacinth's bedroom was twice the size of Courtney's living room and dining room put together. It didn't resemble a normal room, however. In each photo everything looked cohesive and perfect. Standing in the oddly familiar room it looked very different. Each area was set up like a television or movie set. Everything pushed together with like furniture and decor. The white tufted chair she often took pictures of herself in, sipping coffee and staring out the window in the morning, actually faced a very full tree that would still let a lot of light in, but did not make for a very interesting view. Instead, the view that she always posted of was on the other side of the room, near a bunch of light pink furniture, all of which was set up to look like a small seating area where people would get together. Courtney remembered those pictures too. She had posted the area with multiple champagne glasses strewn about, a few small plates placed around on the table with unfinished treats littering them, and there had been a small board game set up in the middle of the table. The caption claimed that she was tired from a long game night with friends. In the photo, which judging by the height and angle was taken by a taller man, Hyacinth was curled up on a loveseat, a homemade-looking knit blanket pulled up over her as she slept. Courtney walked over to the seating area and looked at the tripod set up there. He stood on his tiptoes and looked in the direction it pointed. It had been set up. The whole picture was fake. He guessed that she had staged the whole thing. Did she even have any friends?

Courtney mentally checked off places he had seen photos of her, then cross-referenced them with her Instagram account. After he had spotted a few he went back to the latest picture of her that morning. He crossed the room to the bed and stood where it appeared it had been taken. A chair had been pulled over and placed in front of the bed. Courtney sat down on the chair and held the phone up. The picture was a match. She had set the camera on that chair when she took the photo. Courtney almost felt sorry for her. She must be so lonely. Maybe she would be grateful to him for coming. She probably needed a man. He stared at the photo and then used two fingers to zoom in on the place where her crotch pushed up against the pole. He smiled and stood. He crossed the few feet to the bed and leaned against the post. The gun made a depression as he set it on the ultra-soft bed. He pressed against the post and could already feel himself getting hard. He ran his hand down the inside of the post, coming to rest where she would have been. He set the phone on the bed so he could see the picture but keep his hands free. He knelt next to the bed, pressing his face to the post, and inhaled deeply. The sound of his fly unzipping was loud in the quiet house, but he was too focused on his pleasure to notice.

Courtney left the mess on the floor. It was a badge of honor. He knew Hyacinth wouldn't notice it since it was mostly in the white fur carpet that sat at the foot of her bed, and what had gotten onto the hardwood floor was under her bed and wouldn't be noticeable without close inspection. And if he was lucky he would hear her come in, and he would sneak out of the closet once she was in bed and go to her. She wouldn't have time to notice the small dried pools of fluid on the floor before climbing into bed, probably naked. And when he went to her she would be thankful that someone saw through her ruse and noticed how lonely she was. She would beg him to take her, and he would. And if she didn't, and she tried to scream, well, then he would choke the life out of the slut until she died. And he would fuck her, before, during, or after, possibly all three. To him it didn't matter.

There were three closets in the room, and from the looks of them, one was used often and had the standard clothes that one would wear daily, one had dress clothes, and the third, and the largest of the three, was more of a storage room packed with furniture. This last, he assumed, was furniture she used for staging her pathetic little life. This is where he would wait. He turned off the light in the bedroom and used the light on his phone to navigate back to the closet. Once inside he closed the door, removed the plastic on a small black leather couch, and lay down with the gun resting on his chest. Within minutes he was asleep. The adrenaline had worn off, and after pleasing himself he was ready for a quick nap. He was a fairly light sleeper. He might not hear her when she came into the house, but he was sure he would when she turned on the light in the room and started banging around in there.

39

The door was unlocked when Paisley returned to the house. That was a normal Hyacinth thing to do--she thought she was invincible up here deep in the mountains. Hyacinth wasn't home, but the cars were there, so Paisley assumed she had left with Grover. There was something off though. A familiar smell hung in the air like a kite in an updraft. It was one Paisley recognized from her youth. She would sit with her dad while he worked on their cars, and after a while he would smell like musk and grease. The sense memory hit her and she looked around the kitchen. Nothing was out of the ordinary, but she couldn't shake the feeling that something was wrong. She hadn't been close enough to Grover to smell him, but she was pretty sure that what she was smelling was not Grover, but instead someone else. She called Hyacinth, but it went directly to voicemail.

She listened, but the house was silent. She checked the library, but it was empty. She knocked softly on the secret door, not remembering which book opened it, but there was no answer. Then she checked the living room, where Hyacinth liked to sit and watch movies, but it was dark as well. As she went she turned on lights, making the house brighter, but not feeling any less cavernous. Paisley climbed the stairs to the second floor; the only other place she knew where Hyacinth liked to spend any time in the giant house was in her bedroom. The door was closed, and it looked like the light was off. She knocked.

If Hyacinth was asleep, maybe it was hard for her to hear a knock on the door, since her bed was on the other side of the massive room. She knocked again, harder this time. The loud sound, even though it came from her, startled her. She flinched when it reverberated down the halls, but she did hear something. A noise from inside the room. She pressed her ear closer to the door.

"Hyacinth?" She kept her voice low, afraid to make too much noise, the way children do when they're afraid of the dark and worried about alerting ghosts and monsters to their presence. There was another faint noise. She knocked again, lighter this time so as not to wake the dead. All was quiet. Her hand lay gently on the doorknob and she turned it softly until the deafening click of the latch retracting caused her to tense. She froze for a moment, listening, but there was nothing. She pushed the door in a few inches and pressed her face into the opening. The smell of musk and grease were stronger as the air in the room swirled out around her face. She coughed at the unpleasant smell. It was dark, but the moonlight shone through and she could make out the shadows of all of the furniture. She looked around as her eyes adjusted. Her breath was cinched in her chest as she looked at the bed to see if Hyacinth was in it, but other than the pillows lined against her headboard, her bed was flat. A noise came from the corner of the room. It was slight, and slow, and quiet, but she recognized it: a latch clicked. A sliver of black framed the door around one of Hyacinth's closets, and Paisley watched as the line on the right began to widen, and the moonlight swept across the opening door. Paisley fought a scream. Something dark slipped from the shadow of the closet, the silhouette immediately recognizable--it was a gun.

Cold washed over Paisley when she saw it. With every second that passed she was losing any advantage she might have. She slid her hand into the room and waited, watching the shadow grow as the closet birthed a form. First the gun, then an arm, and as soon as a head began to emerge from the black blob she made her move. She flipped her hand upward and all hell broke loose.

The lights were blinding even to Paisley, who had only been in the dark for a moment, but they hit the figure in the corner like a sucker punch from a lover. It was not Hyacinth, or Grover, but a dirty little man, with slick hair, carrying a gun. He screamed in shock and fell back against the wall. Paisley could see what was going to happen next and acted. She jumped backward just in time for the bullets that began to shred the walls to miss her. Holes appeared in the plaster of the hallway as Paisley darted for the stairs. The man's shrill voice tore through the air like ripped fabric. He was coming after her.

Paisley hit the stairs running and took them three or four at a time. She was acutely aware that the spiral stairs would make her a perfect target for the gunman as soon as he came through the bedroom door, so when she was eight steps from the bottom she grabbed the rail and flung herself over. She could see the man out of the corner of her eye. She dropped to the marble floor below as bullets ripped the wooden banister to nothing more than kindling above her head.

"God damn you, whore!" the man yelled. Paisley could hear him taking to the stairs himself. She was at a crossroads. If she went for the front door and the man made it halfway down the stairs, he would have a clean shot. If she went for the kitchen and the back of the house, and if he knew anything about the layout, he could cut her off before getting to the back door by going the other way and have a clean shot there. She saw the scenarios play out in her head. She looked up at the hallway that was her final option. She ran for it. She made the corner before bullets started peppering the wall and the door at the corner.

Paisley skidded into the bright light of the library and stopped, looking back. She only had a few seconds before he would come around the corner. She started pulling books wildly.

"Which fucking book was it?" she cried as she pulled. He was getting closer. His feet falling hard on the marble floor in the wide hall betrayed his location. Then she saw it. She should have known. A royal blue book, with gold filigree, sat just above eye level. The spine read *Beauty and the Beast*. Paisley grabbed it and pulled just as the man came flying around the corner, gun raised. She heard the thunk of rounds punching into books as the door swung outward, blocking him from her view. She jumped behind the door and the force from the shots clacking against it pushed it against her. Paisley rolled inward, pulling the door shut behind her. As soon as the door was closed the gunshots were muffled like they were fired under thick blankets.

Hyacinth had told her that this was an office, but that it doubled as a panic room. She was joking when she said it, but that didn't stop Paisley from noticing the large metal latch that dropped from the wall and could be put across the door, essentially sealing it. She slammed it down hard. The gunshots had stopped. She wondered if he was pulling books down from the shelf trying to find the right one. She must have been right as the door attempted to swing open but was stopped by the steel bar across the back. Paisley could hear the man's muffled yelling through the thick door.

"Fuck you, bitch! You're going to fucking die!" he screamed. Then there was something that sounded like applause as the man unloaded his magazine into the door. Paisley stumbled backward and bumped into a desk. She leaned against it, scattering a stack of files that had been placed there. She could hear the man yelling. Tears welled in her eyes. She pulled her cell phone from her pocket. She had three bars of service. Thank God for Hyacinth for making sure that, even in her secret hideout, she would have cell service. She hit the emergency call button on the phone. As the phone rang on the other end of the line she listened but couldn't hear the little man outside the door. A voice came on the line. Paisley's first reaction was of recognition. The voice was that of the lady at the front desk at the sheriff's office.

"Pitt County Emergency Services, what is your emergency?" the voice said.

"I'm at Raven Bloom, and there's a man here with a gun trying to kill me!" Paisley sounded a lot calmer than she felt. She lifted her leg to slide onto the desk and sit. The files she had knocked over fell to the floor and she looked down, watching them fall. She knew immediately what they were when she saw the dates printed on the tabs. The first said "1910-1919," and she guessed the other was "2000-2009." The folders hit the floor and spilled their ample contents. She knew if she looked at them they would be the missing land sale records and deeds. The voice on the other end of the phone was saying something but Paisley didn't hear her.

"I'm sorry, what did you say?" Paisley asked.

"Are you hurt? Is there anyone else in the house? Is the shooter still on site?" Paisley answered the questions, and within minutes she heard the sirens. They sounded like they were far away, but she knew they were just outside the house. The dispatcher relayed information about her location to the officers on the grounds, and once they had cleared the house, she confirmed it was safe, and Paisley opened the door.

40

Grover showed up ten minutes after the house had been cleared. Paisley was sitting in the kitchen. A few deputies milled about collecting evidence. Grover came down the hall toward the kitchen nearly at a run. He burst into the room and looked around. His eyes glanced right past Paisley.

"She isn't here," Paisley said.

Grover's head swung back toward her.

"What?" he said.

"Hyacinth. She isn't here. Was she not with you?" Paisley stood up. Her heart was now in her throat.

"Why would she be with me?" he asked. Before Paisley could answer he was turning and heading off to search the house. A deputy came around the corner and Grover grabbed him. "Did you find her?"

"Who?" the deputy asked.

"Hyacinth, is she here?" Grover shouted.

"No, Sheriff, it was just her," the deputy said, raising a hand in Paisley's direction. "We checked every single room."

"Dammit." Grover turned back to Paisley. "Who was it? Who was in the house? Did you see him?"

"No, it was dark. He was short, and dirty. Oh, he had on some sort of like mechanic's shirt, the kind with the little name tag sewed on. I couldn't see what it said, though."

"Mechanic's shirt?" Grover asked.

"Hey, Sheriff," the deputy he had grabbed said. Grover spun to look back at him. "It kind of sounds like it might have been the guy from the diner yesterday."

"The guy Hollis ran off?"

"Yeah, they said he was short and greasy. Courtney, I think his name was. Drives a blue Focus I think."

"Did someone see the vehicle?" Grover asked, switching effortlessly from boyfriend mode to Sheriff mode.

"Yeah, he tore out of there after Hollis yelled at him, and Renee got a look at the car. Said it was the same type that Jeanine from over at the general store drives, just a different color. And we know Jeanine drives that tan Focus because we had to tow it a few months back because she kept parking the damn thing in front of the city building because she was protesting all the parking tickets we kept giving her for leaving her car double parked when she got her hair done on Sundays." By the time the deputy finished talking, Grover looked like he was thinking of hitting the young man.

"A simple 'yes' would have sufficed, Deputy, but thank you," Grover said. "Did anyone get the tag number?"

"Unfortunately, no."

"Shit. Did you put a BOLO out on it yet?"

"Not yet," the deputy said. "I'll do it now."

"Right now," Grover said. The deputy picked up his radio and started the call. Grover turned his radio down to avoid the feedback.

"The car wasn't here," Paisley said. Grover looked at her. "What?"

"The car, the Focus, it wasn't here. When I got here I checked to see if Hyacinth was here. Her truck was out front like normal, all the other cars were in the garage, but there weren't any extra cars. So he wasn't parked here."

Grover stepped closer. "Maybe he got here after you pulled up?"

"No, I was walking the house and looking for Hyacinth. I would have heard him come in. He was hiding in her room when I went in."

Grover looked like he had been shoved. "He was in her room?"

"He was. She wasn't in there. He was waiting for her." Paisley hoped that giving him just the facts would keep him in Sheriff mode, where he needed to be, and not slip back into boyfriend mode.

"We have to find her," Grover said.

"Sheriff," Paisley said. It was taking every bit of her focus to not let the anxiety eat her alive. He looked back up at her, his eyes going soft. "The car. It wasn't here. That means he parked it somewhere and hiked up here. Now, I'm not from around here, but I've driven the road a few times. And I've noticed that the nearest actual parking spot is a few miles from here."

"But there *is* a pull out," Grover said. He was the Sheriff again.

"Exactly."

Grover turned and sprinted for the door. He shouted into the radio as he ran. He was saying something about closing off the road leading up to the house, and she was pretty sure that he was calling for all the roads out of town to be closed as well. A moment later she could hear his Jeep fire up and the rocks from the gravel drive kicking up and hitting the house. Paisley flinched as the sound was too similar to the sound of the gunfire that had threatened her not long before.

The car was found in the pull off just half a mile from the house, tucked up against the trees. The passenger side door was open, and it looked like someone had been trying to get away quickly as a box of bullets lay opened and a quarter of the box was laying on the ground near the door leading into the woods. Grover started a manhunt right away. He called over to Lexington to see if they could get some air support, but they were too busy to make it out right away. Running the plates on the car led them to the shooter's name and address. His name was Courtney Teere, and he lived just seventy miles from Grey Water Ridge. The local police kicked his door in within three hours of the shooting, but he was gone.

Crime scene investigators at Raven Bloom found evidence of semen on the floor and bed in Hyacinth's room, but there was no sign that Hyacinth was involved. Her phone was gone, but her keys, purse, and everything else she would have taken with her were still there. It was like she just vanished with no sign of a struggle.

Grover kept three deputies at the house while the rest of them, himself included, searched the woods for Courtney. Paisley wasn't keen on staying at the house, but her options were pretty limited by the fact that there wasn't anywhere else in town to go, and she didn't want to leave town with Hyacinth missing. There were two small motels in town, but Grover said they would be too hard to secure and keep her safe. So she stayed at Raven Bloom.

41

The sound of Christmas music wafted on the air as Paisley sat down to read the files. She tried to do it without music, but the quiet made her nervous. She could hear the deputies walking around and talking from the guest room, and she could hear the occasional groan from the house as if it was adjusting to the new holes that were now pock-marked around the place. She had put on a radio station but everything made her feel anxious. So she played a Christmas music station on her phone, even though it was still a few months early. She tucked her legs under herself on the bed and spread the files out in front of her.

It didn't take long for her to see a pattern in the folders. Most of them were land deeds, title transfers, or purchase statements, each containing a county map showing the different parcels of land. There was an early document that outlined the sale of the property containing Wilbur Bloom's failed gristmill to the Harris Mining Company. The sale seemed like a high price, but the thing that struck her as odd was that it was just after he took over the company. It seemed a little suspicious that he would buy his own property, but it didn't seem like the dirtiest thing that happened surrounding that time.

The documents from 1910-1919 showed that the town was bustling and booming. Hundreds of different families purchased property in that time. It was a rush for the coal industry, but it wouldn't have been the largest rush, so why was this folder important?

Then she saw it, the title to a large parcel. It belonged to a W. Bloom, and it had been paid for in cash. He'd bought two hundred acres that surrounded a lake up in the hills--it was the lake she had been flying the drone near. It belonged to the Bloom family, and according to the records, a cabin had been built up there. She pulled out her phone and opened her map app. The satellite view of the area was just a mass of trees, but using the old map to locate landmarks, and then zooming in on her phone, she could see that there was still something up there. She didn't know the condition of the place, but she could see in the satellite image there were ruts leading up to the cabin, so someone had been going up there. As she scrolled across the map she realized that the cabin would have sat up on the hill that overlooked the road and the open space where she had parked the Hummer. There hadn't been a road going from where she parked, so she knew there must have been another road up, and she was determined to find it.

The files from 2000-2009 were both more interesting, and less. There were an equal, if not greater, number of land transfers, but they were all going to the same place. A single entity bought up the entire town: the Harris Mining Company had purchased nearly every single parcel of land in the county. All but four. There was one property owned by a man named Delano Christopher Bruss. The property had been in his family since the late 1800's. Looking at the map Paisley could see that it was a large parcel past Main Street. If she was correct then Delano was the old toothless man that spat at her when she was driving with Hollis the day she arrived in Grey Water Ridge.

The other three parcels not purchased by the Harris Mining Company belonged to H. Grimm. She couldn't be certain it was Hollis, but since one of them was the property the church sat on, she was pretty sure that was the case. Two of the three properties belonging to Hollis had been deeded to him by his father, but the third had been purchased by Hollis just two years prior. It was a property on Main Street, and with a little help from her trusty map app, she was able to see the house was a cute little ranch, neatly kept and seemingly perfect for Hollis. The third property was a cabin on the very edge of town, backing up against the woods. It was surely the cabin Hollis grew up in, and it had been built, according to the files, in the late 1800's, replacing an existing structure on the property.

The Harris Mining Company had owned most of the town in 2009, which the files officially covered, but a handful of newer documents had been shoved into the folder. They were title transfer papers granting ownership of all properties, minus Raven Bloom and the cabin by the lake, from the Harris Mining Company to H. Bloom.

Paisley dropped the papers onto the bed and looked around the room. She needed to talk to someone about what she had found, but other than the deputies down the hall there was no one. So, she did what she always did now when she needed to talk--she pulled out her phone and live streamed.

"Guys, you are not going to believe the fucking day I've had. Someone tried to fucking shoot me today! And Hyacinth is missing. The Sheriff thinks that the guy who tried to shoot me, some asshole named Courtney, was here looking for Hyacinth, and that he has something to do with her disappearance. So now they have me locked in this house with badged babysitters all over the place. I don't think Hyacinth was here. I think she was gone before he got here. Why else would he have been hiding? And then I find these files that were taken from the library," she waved the papers in front of the camera, "and they say that the whole damn town belongs to H. Fucking Bloom. That's right, Hyacinth owns every single house and building in this town." Paisley shuffled through the papers and looked at them again. "Except a few. Hollis owns a few, and then some old guy. Maybe she's out to get them all? I don't get her angle. And why, if she owns everything else, does her father's company still own the house she lives in and some lakeside cabin?" She looked to see if anyone was commenting. There were a few, but she grabbed on to one person's specifically.

WhyItHurts - *I don't have all the info, but it sounds like someone is trying to hide some high level shit here.*

"Right?" Paisley said to some person sitting behind their keyboard somewhere. "But where do I begin?"

WhyItHurts - *Well you should listen to law enforcement and stay where they can keep an eye on you.*

"I can't just sit here and do nothing. Something is going on here and I need to get to the bottom of it. Either Hyacinth is in on some crazy plot to overthrow the town, or her brother is ripping women apart and leaving them in the woods, or there really is some fucked up ape man in the woods killing people. Either way, I've got to get to the bottom of this."

237

WhyItHurts - *Where would she go if she wasn't there?*

Paisley thought for a moment. Where had Hyacinth gone?

"Grover's cabin!" Paisley said. "Which, according to the deeds, her father's company now owns. They went up there yesterday. And that's where the drone was thrown from." She paused to think.

WhyItHurts - *Keep going. You seem to be on a roll.*

"So if I saw a man with a cowboy hat, that looked like Grover's, near the cabin where he and Hyacinth have been sneaking away to, then there's a very good chance that they're up there. But Grover didn't seem to have a clue where she was, unless he was acting."

WhyItHurts - *Would her brother have any reason to hurt her?*

"I don't know, we never talked about him. But it sounds like that's the place to go for answers." Paisley thought about the fact that, even though no one up here seemed to use the internet, broadcasting her plans live might be a bad idea. She really didn't feel like Hyacinth could be a part of all of this, but if anyone in the town was going to watch her live stream it would be her. "I think I'm just going to sit here until things start to look a little more clear. Thanks for listening, everyone. I'll check back in soon. Mott out!" She threw up a peace sign and then clicked off the live stream.

42

In the morning, Paisley opened the door from her room and tiptoed down the stairs. She had waited for half an hour before making her move. She had been sitting and listening for the deputies, but from the sound of it, they were all asleep. When she got to the bottom of the stairs she could hear one in the kitchen, but she was careful to open the squeaky door slowly, and he didn't hear her sneak out. By the time she fired up the Hummer's giant engine it was too late to stop her, and she drove between the gates and headed for the cabin. She had to see if Hyacinth was there. She hoped she was safe, because she had really begun to like Hyacinth, but she was also upset that there seemed to be so much that Paisley didn't know. How much was Hyacinth required to tell someone she had known for less than a week, though? Paisley tried to focus on the positive as she pointed the Hummer to the back side of the mountain, where she thought the trail to the cabin must come out.

Her instincts about the trail were correct, though she passed the narrow off to the trail the first time. The drive up to the mountain was a little bit of a trek, and she was thankful to have the big four-wheel drive to get there. On the way up the trail Paisley passed a small turn off that looked like it had only been used a few times in the past few years, but she noticed that some of the branches looked recently broken, so it was plausible that someone had been up that way lately. She kept driving toward where she hoped the cabin would be.

It was an old, tired-looking cabin. According to the records it was more than a hundred and twenty years old, and it showed its age. Its white boards had been painted over countless times, their latex skin sagging in spots where the wood hadn't been sanded before the new coat was applied. Evidence of some boards being replaced stood out as they weren't as warped as the others. Paisley backed the Hummer up as close to the door as she could get it. A quick getaway might be necessary, and she wanted to be prepared if it was. There weren't any other vehicles around, but that didn't mean that no one was there, and she was keenly aware that someone could be watching her.

She turned off the Hummer, opened the door, and slipped out. She didn't close the door all the way. If she came out here running at full speed she didn't want to have to fuss with a door handle. Her cell phone peeked up from the pocket of the red flannel shirt she wore. Before leaving the house she had sent a message to WhyItHurts with a link to a private page on her website. The page was just a file page that would automatically update anything she recorded as soon as she had signal. So, if anything were to happen to her, WhyItHurts could download the footage and send it to the proper authority. She just had to hope that if something happened to her that her phone would make it back to somewhere with service. If nothing happened to her, at least she would have some footage of this escapade to cut into the vlog.

It was quiet up here. Down near town was peaceful, but up here was serene.

The old floor boards squealed when she stepped on the porch and it made her jump. This was the second time in less than twelve hours that she stood on the outside of a door not knowing what could be on the other side waiting to kill her. She knocked on the door. She knocked again. There was no answer.

The door had small, dirty glass panes that were nearly impossible to see through, but she could see well enough to guess that no one was in the cabin unless they were ducked down out of sight. Paisley tried the door, and was both surprised and unsurprised that it was locked. She looked around to make sure no one was within ear shot. When she felt sure there wasn't, she picked up a decent sized rock and broke one of the small panes of glass, then reached through to unlock the door.

Inside, the cabin had the same old charm that the outside had, but it was surprisingly clean. A bedroll lay on the plank floor, and next to it sat a small oil lantern and small stack of books. The stack contained a few history books, a few biographies, and a small collection of puzzle books. Someone had been living there. Had Rowan been hiding out up here since they accused him of the murders? Did he murder those girls? If he did, was it wise for her to be up here alone? And where was Hyacinth? Paisley had come thinking that Hyacinth might be hiding out here, but there was no sign of her.

"I may have made a big mistake," she said to the future audience of the vlog, or to the crime scene technician charged with watching the footage of her possible grisly murder. The cabin appeared to be a bust. It was obvious that someone, presumably Rowan, had been staying up here, but no one was here now, and maybe that was a good thing. She would report her findings to the authorities, if she found one she could trust. Coming up here didn't get her any closer to finding Hyacinth, though. She headed back to the Hummer and started back down the mountain.

Multiple properties seemed to be a part of this, and Paisley needed to figure out how they were connected.

Paisley slammed on the brakes, and dust from the tires surrounded the vehicle.

"The gristmill!" She pulled the phone from her pocket and held the camera up. "The gristmill. What if Hyacinth is in on this and trying to hide the documents that show the properties she owns? Or, what if she isn't in on it and was investigating these properties?" Paisley sat for a moment. "Fuck. I don't remember where it was." She thought for a moment trying to remember. Then it hit her. She remembered something about Wilbur Bloom building it at the head of the river above the coal mines so that the dust wouldn't get into the water before it ran through the mill. Paisley shut off the camera and turned on the map. She traced the river from the mining company up the mountain. It was hard to follow in spots as it narrowed in places or the trees were too thick to see through. Then she saw something. A light brown dot sticking out over the river. She zoomed in and could make out the trademark water wheel of a gristmill.

"Gotcha!" Paisley said. She zoomed in even more looking for a road leading up to the building, but couldn't see one. She was just going to have to go and look.

43

The gristmill wasn't nearly as hard to find on the map as Paisley thought it would be. It wasn't close to town, at least not by road standards. It would have been just a few short miles up the river, but with the way the mountain roads wound around up there it took a while to reach it. She found a spot where someone had driven off the road and through the trees, tearing open a scar of a pathway that looked long since healed. She wasn't a tracker by any stretch of the imagination, but she had traversed a lot of woods in her day, and she knew freshly broken branches and recently flattened shrubbery when she saw it. It was less than a week since someone had been up there. She angled the Hummer toward the tracks, set it into four-wheel drive, and pushed her way into the thicket.

Paisley winced at the screeching sounds as the branches dug lines into the canary yellow paint. If Hyacinth was alive Paisley would have a lot of explaining to do. She had already dented and scratched the hood. Now it was going to look like she'd pissed off Freddy Kruger and he took his claws to the side of her truck.

The gristmill was about two and a half miles off of the road and the trail lead her right to it. Whoever had come out here recently was going to the same place she was. Part of her expected to see a vehicle there when she came through the trees and laid eyes on the impressive building. It was smaller than Paisley thought it would be, but still a feat of ingenuity, especially knowing when it was built. Part of the old water wheel clung to the side of the building and hung out over the river, but the bottom portion looked like it had been worn away some time ago when the gears finally locked up and the wheel stopped turning. Other than the roof being bleached by more than a century of sun and rain, the place looked pretty good. She set her phone to record again and then got out of the truck.

The door to the building was old and the hinges had given way, but someone had stood the door back in its frame. Paisley lifted it and walked into the building. The small room smelled of moss, mildew, old wood, and something else that didn't fit. Paisley couldn't put her finger on it.

In the center of the room stood two large, flat, circular stones, one on top of the other, with a pole going through the middle. An easy spot for bone, instead of grain, to be turned to grist. Paisley shuttered.

The light in the room was dim, but there were enough windows, and holes in the roof, that it wasn't too hard to see that the place was covered in dust and old leaves. Except it wasn't completely covered. There was one small area that looked like it had been swept, or as if something had pushed some of the debris into a pile in the corner. Paisley crossed the creaky floor to the dark corner.

As she approached the spot it became obvious that the area was not just clear, but also clean. Recognition slowly crept into her consciousness and her veins tingled with ice water as the flesh on her arms begin to stipple with bumps.

The smell in the building was bleach. A foreign smell in the context of the situation. She stepped back from the spot, staring at it as she went as if it might somehow leap at her. One foot went back and found nothing but air as she stepped backward into a hole in the floor. Paisley crashed hard as the back of her thighs hit the far side of the two-foot hole. She tried to grab at the floor to stop herself from falling in, but she couldn't get purchase before being swallowed whole. She landed awkwardly and rolled to her side. It was dark, damp, and smelled like hell. She laid on her back and looked up at the small square seven feet above her. Unless she could find something to stand on, she wasn't going to be able to pull herself out.

A small square of light cut into the darkness just a few feet from where Paisley lay. The smell of bleach was overpowering even with her shirt pulled up over her nose. She sat up and found the flashlight on her phone. When the small LED turned on it lit a small circle around her. She pointed the light at the square of daylight and could see that it was a small black gate. She began to move toward it.

Spiders had strung easily eighty years of webs back and forth across the hole, and the flashlight beam bounced off of them like tinsel on a Christmas tree. The light moved onto a mound covered in a potato sack in the corner. Paisley froze as horrible visions of Hyacinth lying under that sack flooded her mind. The thing under the sack had the rough shape of a body, though it would have to be a small one.

"Hyacinth?" Paisley asked the potato sack. She knew deep down that it couldn't be her since the sack looked as if it had at least a few decades worth of dirt on it, but she had to know for sure. She rolled to her knees and crawled toward the sack, her arm stretched as far as it could go so she could keep her distance. She hooked a finger into the frayed edge of the burlap and pulled. As she pulled the light bounced and Paisley's eyes went with it, being afraid to look into the darkness. Something deep in the corner, away from the gate, reflected the faintest light back toward her. Before she could fully accept what she saw, she felt the sack give way and fall. She turned the light back toward it.

When Paisley was a child she had seen a movie where a man pulled the bricks out of a wall to expose the skeletal remains of a person who had been buried alive. That image stuck with her through the years, and in that moment she relived the terror she'd experienced when seeing that skeleton for the first time. There, in the corner of the hole, was a body--or most of a body. It looked, from the size of it, like it was a child. The skin was gone and tatters of a bed shirt hung around its bony shoulders. Vacant eye sockets gazed out at her as its mouth hung by the final threads of tendons long decayed in an eternal scream. It was missing one of its arms below the elbow, and both of its legs above the knee.

Paisley jerked away and began scrambling to the gate. Thankfully the rusty metal didn't put up a fight when she rolled forward and planted both feet directly into the center of it. It let out a squeal as it swung open on a rusty and broken hinge. Within seconds Paisley was out of the hole.

Nathan Steiner. He hadn't been taken by a sasquatch. He likely hadn't been taken by Gerald Lee Harris. This building had been in the Bloom family since Wilbur Bloom himself built it, before Nathan's disappearance. Paisley felt like she was going to be sick. She looked around the forest. She hadn't found what she was looking for, but she'd found something. She was looking for her friend and instead found a boy who had been missing for more than a century. And if the family had lied about the sasquatch then, they might be lying about the creature's involvement now.

Paisley ran back to the Hummer. Her ankle was still sore from rolling it by the lake, and now her legs burned from scraping them against the lip of the hole when she fell. That was what she focused on as she ran. She tried not to think of the young boy's body under the gristmill, or the bodies that had been found in the hills above it.

44

Grover was waiting at Raven Bloom when Paisley got back. He stood with his arms folded across his chest while she parked. She looked up at Grover and he shook his head, but never broke eye contact. For a minute she thought that maybe she should just start the car, throw it in reverse, and get the fuck out of Grey Water Ridge. If Grover was involved in the killings, even just in that he knew about Rowan hiding at the cabin, and did nothing, then her life would be in danger, and not just from the psycho with the gun. Courtney was the least of her concerns at the moment. He had every law enforcement officer in the county looking for him. This was either the safest place she could be, with Grover and all of the deputies, or the most dangerous. Grover continued to stare at her through the windshield, until another deputy came out of the front door and stood next to him. Grover turned and said something to him and the deputy nodded and went back in. It was unlikely, she thought, that he would do anything with the other deputies present. So, with her heart beating so hard she was afraid someone would hear it, she opened the door and slid out of the Hummer.

Before she could make it to the steps Grover had come

down to meet her. He said nothing, he just put his hand out, palm up.

"What?" Paisley asked.

"Keys," Grover said.

"What?" she asked again.

"The keys, Miss Mott. I've got someone killing women and stringing them in trees, a man who hides in women's bedrooms with a gun running loose, and my girlfriend is M.I.A., so I can't have you disappearing without telling anyone where you're going." Grover seemed genuinely concerned, and for a moment Paisley felt bad for giving them the slip.

"I'm sorry, but--" Paisley was cut off by a ringing cell phone. Grover pulled his phone out with the hand that wasn't demanding keys.

"Shit," he said as he answered the call. "Hello?"

Paisley couldn't make out what the voice on the other end was saying, but it was a man. Grover thrust his hand firmly at Paisley. She considered it, and then dropped the key onto his palm. She was putting a lot of faith in him right now. If he was in on the killings then she might have just resigned herself to being the next victim.

"Are you kidding me?" Grover said into the phone. The look on his face was worried and surprised. He had been looking at the key in his hand and then the voice said something and Grover's eyes shot back up to Paisley's. "Yeah, I think you may be correct. She's standing right here. I'll be there in a bit, don't touch anything." Grover hung up.

"Who was that?" Paisley asked.

"Where were you?"

"Why?" Paisley suspected that he knew exactly where she had been.

249

The deputy that Grover had talked to on the porch came back out. He had a cup of coffee and he was walking toward them, trying not to spill it. Holding it out in front of himself as if he was presenting a gift, the deputy approached and extended it to Paisley.

"Here you go, miss."

"For me?" Paisley had assumed Grover had instructed him to bring coffee for himself.

"Yup," the deputy said. "It's black, because I didn't know how you took it."

Paisley took the cup. Grover looked at the deputy.

"Please see that Miss Mott stays here, and that she is safe," Grover said, then he looked back at her. "It isn't safe out there."

"No problem, boss."

"Thank you." Grover started to walk toward his Jeep, then stopped. His head lowered and he turned back toward Paisley who was taking an exploratory sip of the coffee. He stepped toward her so when he spoke quietly she could hear him.

"Did she say anything to you? Was there anyone else here? Anything that might help me find her?" There was a pain in his eyes.

"No, she was supposed to be here," Paisley said. Grover looked at the ground. His thumb and forefinger pinched the bridge of his nose. He took a deep breath and turned back toward the Jeep without looking back at her.

"Go inside and stay away from the windows. And try not to break any." Grover said as he walked away. Paisley thought about telling him about Nathan Steiner, but decided that it could wait.

Paisley did go into the house, but she didn't stay there. She stepped inside, finished her cup of coffee, and told the deputy that she was going to go up and shower. Then she slipped out the back door, went to the garage, broke open the flimsy key box holding the spare keys, and took the one for the luxury sedan. It was a little less conspicuous than the Hummer, so maybe it would take a while before anyone noticed she was gone. She managed to drive out of Raven Bloom without the deputy chasing her down. She headed for the one place she thought she might be safe, even as angry as she was with him. She went to find the preacher.

Paisley drove to the church but it was empty. She cruised down Main Street looking for the Plymouth, but it wasn't there. The third stop was a winner. She had saved the address from the records, so she knew where he lived, and her map app took her directly to the place. It looked exactly as it had in the street view. It was a small, well-cared-for house. She drove past it, then circled, coming up the alley behind the house. She found a spot hidden from the street by a fence, so the car couldn't be seen. She knew that if Grover really wanted to find her, there wouldn't be a long list of places he would check before coming to Hollis's house, but she wanted to make it as complicated as possible.

45

There wasn't a doorbell on the tiny house. Instead there was an old brass door knocker that would look more at home on an old ship than on someone's house. She rapped the knocker twice, then looked around to see if anyone was watching. She didn't see anyone, but that didn't mean they weren't there. The door opened, and Hollis stood in front of her, a surprised look on his face. He was wearing a black button-up shirt with the sleeves rolled to just below the elbow. It was even more slimming than the white one he normally wore, and he reminded her of Jack Skellington.

"Paisley?"

"Hey, um, can I come in?" she said, glancing around again to see if anyone was there.

"Of course," he said, and stepped back, raising his long, tattooed arm and welcoming her in. He glanced around to see if anyone was watching, then he closed the door.

Hollis's house was very minimalistic, which seemed fitting given his occupation. In the living room there was a modest, gray, flannel couch, a wooden coffee table that looked like someone with some decent carpentry skills had made it themselves, and a small desk in the corner with a closed laptop and a lamp on it. Next to the desk was a short bookcase. Volumes that looked to be from every decade for the last hundred years filled the shelves. The walls were mostly bare except for a cross on the one opposite the couch. On the coffee table sat a half-full glass of water and an open Bible.

Hollis walked past Paisley and gathered up the Bible and the glass of water. He slid the Bible into a slot on the bookshelf, downed the glass of water in a single drink, and then disappeared around a corner.

"Is everything okay?" he asked. Paisley could hear the glass set into a sink, and then he was back. "Paisley?" he asked again. She watched him closely. He moved so fluidly for such a tall man.

"I just didn't know where else to go," she said.

"Is everything okay?"

"You heard about the shooting?" she asked.

"What shooting?" He stepped closer and put his hands on his hips. "Is everyone okay?"

"It was at Hyacinth's house. When I got home last night someone was there waiting. He was in Hyacinth's room."

"Oh my...one of Grover's deputies came by to ask if Hyacinth was here, but I told him I hadn't seen her. He didn't mention anything about a shooting." He crossed his arms over his chest. "Is everyone okay?"

"You haven't heard about this?" With as small of a town as it was, Paisley had a hard time thinking that he hadn't been told, especially with his position in the community.

"I turn my phone off on Saturdays, and I don't normally leave the house. I have to prepare for my sermon. So I come home Friday evening and turn off the phone until after service on Sunday. Everyone knows not to ever bother me on Saturday." He paused. "Is everyone okay?"

"Hyacinth is missing."

"What do you mean, 'missing?'"

"The crazy guy, Courtney, I think his name was," Paisley said, but Hollis cut her off. He grabbed her arm. It probably wasn't meant to hurt, but she suspected that he didn't realize how strong his hands were.

"Courtney?" he asked. She pulled back, and he let go. He looked at his hand like it had been operating on its own.

"Yeah, they said his name was Courtney, some creep from out of town," she said. "Do you know him?"

"We've met."

"He was hiding in Hyacinth's room, but she wasn't there. I scared him when I got back to the house. I was looking for her and he was in the closet. He tried to shoot me but I hid in the panic room."

"In the library," Hollis said absently.

"Yeah, you know about that?" Hollis nodded.

"Was Grover there?" he asked.

"He came by later, then he went searching for Hyacinth."

"Did he say anything about her missing? Does he have any leads? Where was he going to look?"

"I don't know, but he did get a call right before I left that sounded suspicious," Paisley said. Hollis tilted his head, which reminded Paisley of what a dog does when it hears something.

"What do you mean, 'suspicious?'" he asked.

"It seemed cryptic, and then he had to leave all of a sudden, but I think it was--" Paisley stopped herself. She had suspected that the call came from Rowan, and if that was the case then Grover knew he was up there, and there was a good chance that Hyacinth did too. She wasn't sure if the three of them were in on this whole thing together. She didn't know if the call was about the cabin or the gristmill. If it was about the gristmill, and they knew about

Nathan Steiner's body, she didn't yet know the implications of the town knowing that the mighty Bloom family had a secret. And she didn't know what they would do to keep that secret. She wasn't sure if she should mention it to Hollis either. She knew he and Hyacinth were close, or at least they had been, but she wasn't sure what the history there was. She decided that it wasn't the time to tell him. Maybe that time wouldn't come. Maybe he would just have to wait until she finished her documentary, or whatever it would end up being, and find out with the rest of the world. Maybe it would be best if she were far away from Grey Water Ridge before mentioning to anyone that the town's savior may have also been a child murderer.

"Did he say where he was going?" Hollis asked.

"Do you think he knows where Hyacinth is?" Paisley asked, neglecting his question.

"I don't know. Maybe she's just holed up somewhere? Maybe she got wind of the guy out to kill her and she went into hiding. She has been known to disappear for a day or two at a time in the past. I wouldn't worry too much about her yet."

"Seriously?"

"Yeah, we're all surprised that she stuck around this long. So when she disappears for a few days no one bats an eye." Hollis put his hand on her shoulder.

"But she isn't answering her phone," Paisley said.

"Would it make you feel better if I went out and looked for her?" Hollis asked.

Paisley considered that. Hollis would know the ins and outs of the town better than anyone else. And he knew Hyacinth pretty well, so maybe he would know where to look. But the fact that none of her cars were missing made her worry.

"I could come with you?"

Hollis shook his head. "If you really do have someone out there looking to hurt you, we shouldn't have you out in public," he said. Paisley supposed this was safer, but she didn't like the idea of sitting alone while Hyacinth was out there, even if she was in on something that she shouldn't be.

"I guess so," she said, wringing her hands.

"Did you bring your camera and everything?"

"It's in the car down the alley."

"The Hummer?"

"No, I thought that would stand out too much."

"Smart girl," Hollis said, and gave her a wink. "Give me the keys and I'll go get your gear. Then you can stay here and work on your story while I go see if I can find Hyacinth."

Paisley thought about that. It was the reason she was there. She had made a deal with herself that everything would serve the vlog, and she had begun to let that go.

"Okay, thank you," she said. "It's the Lexus down the alley."

"I'm pretty sure I could find the only car that's worth more than the gas in the tank in this whole town," Hollis said. Paisley smiled awkwardly.

Hollis went out the back door and she watched as he casually walked down the alley. He returned a few minutes later with her camera bag.

Paisley began getting her gear set up while Hollis went into his room to get ready to go look for Hyacinth. He wasn't gone long, but when he came out Paisley had moved the couch across the room to underneath the cross

256

on the wall, and then moved a lamp so that it served as a key light for her setup. Hollis stopped and looked at the room.

"You know, it doesn't look bad this way," he said.

"I'll move it back when I'm done. I hope that's okay?"

"Move whatever you need. My home is your home."

"Thank you. Are you sure you don't mind me staying here while you're gone?"

"No," he said. "I really do think it's better this way. There's fixins for sandwiches in the kitchen, bread in the bread box, and meat and cheese in the fridge. I don't have any soda or alcohol, I'm sorry."

"That's okay, thank you."

Hollis opened the door and Paisley stopped him.

"Will you be back before I leave?" she asked. Hollis turned and gave her a skeptical but protective look.

"And where would you go?" he asked.

"I don't know, back to Hyacinth's for the night?"

"Paisley, you are here because you were afraid to go back there. I don't think it's a good idea for you to leave."

"I can go to one of the hotels," she said.

"You are staying here. When you get tired, if I'm not back, just sleep in the bedroom." He pointed to the door that he had come out of.

There was a pause, as Paisley didn't know how to respond. She wasn't sure if that was an invitation to something more. With what they had done in the church the day before it wouldn't be unheard of. He must have seen the thought process.

"I'll sleep here on the couch, or there," he said, pointing to where the couch was before Paisley moved it.

"I'll put it back," she said.

"Thank you," he said. "I have service in the morning, so

I'll be rising early."

"Do you think it's still safe for me to come?"

Hollis's lips curled in and he looked down.

"I think it should be okay. If you're afraid of someone from out of town, they likely won't know to look for you up at the church. If someone from town has something in store for you, then they will know not to try anything with me around, especially at the church."

"Okay, so then I'm going," Paisley said.

"Fantastic."

There was another moment of quiet, and then he walked out and closed the door behind him. There was no goodbye--Paisley thought it might be because it felt like the situation was such that a lot of goodbyes could be permanent if people weren't careful right now.

When midnight rolled around and Hollis had not returned, Paisley decided to take him up on the offer. She couldn't keep her eyes open. She wasn't used to this sort of excitement. She had sat down and recorded some commentary for the vlog. She had recounted the entire story up to that point. She wasn't sure if it would be the narrative of the documentary or if it would just serve to remind her of the steps when it was all over. But she felt better for doing it. She had her headphones on and was going over footage, so she was blissfully unaware of what was happening just down the street. She would find out in the morning, but for one more night she was free from the burden of that particular tragedy.

46

The smell of books made Boyd happy. His three favorite things about working in the library were the smell of the books, being able to read all day, and the fact that he could bring Pilot to work with him. He turned off the lights and made sure the back door was locked before checking the windows. It was part of his routine of closing the library down every night. Pilot followed closely behind, making sure that he got everything. If he skipped a step she would wuff her low bark and he would go back. He would test her sometimes to make sure that she was paying attention. He had completed his closing duties, and walked to the front door. Pilot looked at him, knowing what came next. He would either tell her to come and she would, and they would walk home, or he would tell her to lie down, and she would go to her bed so that he could go next door to the cafe and have dinner. If only one of them would have known the weight of the decision on this particular night.

"Go lay down," Boyd told her. Her large head lowered and she turned toward her bed. Boyd could hear her step onto the large pillow, circle, and then plop. "Be good," he hollered as he opened the front door. She responded with a shallow bark--whether it was agreement or disdain, he was unsure.

***

The smell of bacon made Sylvia happy, but she had stopped eating it. Ever since she had left the job at the library to work in the diner she had lost some weight, she felt healthier, and she knew that it was because she was moving all day long instead of sitting behind the circulation desk next door. She scooped up a tray with three plates on it: two were bacon cheeseburgers and one was Jorge's famous meatloaf. She threw Jorge a wink as she took the tray. She backed through the batwing doors and out into the noise of a packed dining room. Saturday night was the busiest night at the diner every week, but this week it was even busier because everyone came out to gossip, and this was the place to do it. They had to talk about the new body that was found this week, and the gunman up at Raven Bloom. Sylvia knew that tips that night were going to be bigger than normal. When people got the dirt on what was going on they felt powerful, and when they felt powerful they tipped well. Every table was full and every stool at the counter was occupied. A few people stood near the front door waiting for the first available table. The place was packed. Sylvia thought that it could just be the busiest night she had ever seen, but they were keeping up. She set the three plates down, asked if the table needed anything else, and spun back toward the kitchen to grab the next order. They were rock and rolling.

***

The smell of car grease and sweat momentarily

distracted Grover as he walked by the dinner and glanced in the window. The place was packed. There were people waiting for tables. He hadn't eaten that day, and he was tempted to stop in and grab a burger to go. He could eat it while debriefing at his office. He didn't often eat when stressed, but he felt like he could continue on without either sleep or food, but not both. If he ate he could continue the search, at least for a little while longer. He paused for a moment, but decided he didn't want to waste valuable time waiting for a burger. He walked back toward the sheriff's office. Later, he thought to himself that he wished he had turned around when he heard Boyd come out of the library, but he hadn't. He didn't want to get stuck talking to someone that might not provide any information on Hyacinth's whereabouts. He didn't turn around for fifty-eight more seconds. And by then it was too late.

***

Footfalls echoing off the buildings around him let Courtney know that the cop hadn't seen him cowering between the cars. He must have been looking toward the diner instead. The footsteps got farther away, and Courtney knew that he had a shot. He stepped out from behind the car and reached under his jacket. The feel of the pistol's grip in his hand made him feel powerful. His fingers tightened around it, but before he could pull it out the door of the building next to him opened and he heard the slight bark of a dog. He pushed the gun back into his inner pocket and pretended to be looking for his wallet. A scrawny man stood at the door, but hadn't seen him yet. Courtney turned and cut between the cars, hoping it looked as if he was going back to his car to look for his missing wallet. He stopped at the end of the row and waited.

A cacophony spilled from the diner and out onto the street as the scrawny guy pulled the glass door open. The sounds of silverware hitting plates, glasses being set on tables, and people talking over each other filled the otherwise quiet night. It sounded like every other dining establishment that was filled with people. Courtney turned back and started walking toward the diner. The scrawny man saw him and held the door.

"Evening," the man said.

Courtney said nothing. He just walked in and looked around. The place was busier than he thought it would be, which was just fine by him. There were people standing at the front, waiting for tables. He stepped up to the sign instructing patrons to wait to be seated. The scrawny man just walked right by him and peeked over the doors leading into the kitchen. That's when Courtney saw her. It was Renee, the bitch that had talked shit to him. He could pull now and get her, but he wanted to see if the tall son of a bitch who told him to leave was there first. He didn't want that piece of shit getting away. He stepped to the side, behind a group of people, so Renee couldn't see him. He scanned the dining room but he didn't see the tall man.

"Hey Boyd," Renee said to the scrawny man. Then she turned and yelled back into the kitchen, "Sylvia, your son is here." Renee stood there listening to someone say something. She was holding a few plates without trays. She turned back toward Boyd. "She said just wait for a seat at the counter," Renee said, relaying the message from the kitchen. Boyd glanced over the patrons at the counter and then walked back and leaned against the rail next to the seating sign. He was now directly in front of Courtney.

"How many for you tonight?" a voice said to Courtney. He flinched at the surprise. "I'm sorry," the voice said.

Courtney looked up to see a young woman, maybe twenty, wearing a similar uniform to the waitresses, but hers was impeccably clean. She was holding a small notepad that had names written and then crossed off on it.

"What?" Courtney said.

"Is it just you joining us for dinner tonight?" the woman asked.

Before Courtney could respond, two things happened. The first was that Renee had just recognized him, making eye contact and looking angry. The second was that the other waitress he had seen before, the skinny one, had just come from the kitchen and was talking to Boyd as she walked by carrying a tray of food. As she passed Boyd she also noticed Courtney--who made the decision to go. The next few seconds played out in slow motion for him.

His hand slipped under his jacket and found the handle of the gun. Sylvia's eyes went wide, and a small scream started to rise. Boyd turned when he saw the look on his mother's face, and his gaze quickly moved to the gun that was now rising.

The first six bullets sent chips of tile flying from the floor like miniature geysers. The seventh bullet struck Renee in the shin, punching a small black hole in her leg, her pantyhose retracting from the hole. The bullet hit the bone just beneath the skin and sent a spider web of fractures up and down Renee's shinbone. The bullet popped out the back of her calf, tumbling from the impact of the bone and lodging itself in the floor, producing a similar but smaller geyser as it did. The next bullet hit Renee in the meat of her thigh and went right through; the next hit her right hip, shattering it and ricocheting, causing more damage before exiting her right butt cheek. That bullet cut through the chair of a woman who had just started to turn her head at the sound of the scream, driving into the woman's spine. She was paralyzed for the split second she remained alive. The next bullet ripped through Renee's abdomen, and since there was no bone to slow the bullet, it went right through and struck the paralyzed woman in the back of the head. The next two bullets went into Renee's chest, one through a lung and the other just above her heart. The next hit her in the neck and the next in her chin. The last bullet to hit Renee was the one that caught her just below the left eye. It collapsed her cheek, causing her eye to roll forward. The bullet's trajectory altered slightly from hitting the bone and angled upward, breaking through the top of her skull and coming to rest in the ceiling about ten feet behind her.

Courtney released the trigger for a moment as he watched Renee's body, riddled with holes, fall to the floor as others began to scatter. Tables turned over, dishes broke, and all hell broke loose as the packed diners tried to move in every direction at once. Courtney saw Boyd leap forward, away from him, and grab his mother. Boyd was the only one close enough at the time Courtney started shooting that could have grabbed him, but it was clear that his first thought was to get in front of his mother.

One of the guys waiting at the front started to move toward Courtney. The gun swung toward the moving man and began spitting rounds before Courtney finished aiming it, hitting a number of people along the way. The man's head snapped back as a bullet tore his head off from the brow up. Courtney smiled as he swung the gun back the other direction, watching people drop as the bullets entered the surging crowd. Then there was a click and the slide on the Glock froze in its back position. Courtney saw that he wasn't the only person who knew the sound meant he was out of ammunition in his current magazine--a man who had been ducked down behind a booth reached for his waist. Courtney clicked the magazine release and the spent magazine dropped to the floor even as Courtney began swinging the gun toward the man. It was a showdown now. A race to see if Courtney could get the new magazine seated before this cowboy drew and fired.

It was close. The man had pulled his gun and was just starting to aim when the sound of metal on metal signaled that Courtney's ammo was in. The slide jerked forward and the room was again filled with the thunder of automatic gunfire. The shots were wild but accurate enough for two of them to find the wannabe gunslinger. The man flew backward and the gun clattered to the ground and disappeared under a table in the corner. The crowd surged again, pushing toward the back door. Courtney stepped around the rail and leveled the gun at the mound of people.

Pain shot down the side of his face as Boyd smashed a plate into the side of his head. Courtney managed to squeeze off a few shots into the crowd and saw a few people drop before he stumbled sideways. Boyd attacked again, grabbing at the gun as it swung toward him. Courtney pulled the trigger as Boyd grabbed his arm, just below a faded tattoo of a ghost. A series of red dots appeared across Boyd's chest, accompanied by the sound of the bullets hitting the back wall behind him. Boyd's face was first surprised and then went slack as he fell forward. His fingers went limp and slid off of Courtney's arm as he went down.

Movement caught Courtney's eyes as Sylvia disappeared through the batwing doors. She was screaming Boyd's name as she clambered across the floor on all fours. Courtney stepped over Boyd, throwing a few quick shots into the crowd without looking. He stopped at the doors and glanced in. Then he pushed the doors open and stepped through.

The kitchen appeared to have been evacuated. The light from an unseen door shined off a wall in the back. The noise from the dining room still filled the area as the people pushed through the back door, but it was quieter in the kitchen. If Courtney ran through the kitchen, he could cut off the flow of people as they ran out the back of the building. He turned that way to do just that, but then he heard her. A sniffle. A whimper. He turned back just in time to see the meat tenderizer as Sylvia swung it at him. He managed to get his left arm up and take the brunt of the attack, but he felt bone crack. The woman drew back to swing again, and Courtney raised the gun and pointed it at her stomach. She froze.

"Sorry, bitch," Courtney said. His finger tightened around the trigger, but his shot went wide as searing pain ripped at his shoulder. He screamed and turned. The short Mexican who had been holding the butcher knife when Courtney was thrown out was standing there, holding that very same knife--this time, however, dark spots of blood dripped from it. Courtney began raising the gun but dropped it as the meat tenderizer came down on the side of his head. There was a thunk and a crack as Sylvia put all of her might into the swing. Courtney heard his skull split from the inside. It sounded like jumping on a wet branch. Then everything went dark.

47

The next morning, Paisley woke to the smell of bacon and coffee. Before her eyes opened she smiled. She had thought it was all a dream: the shooting at Raven Bloom, Hyacinth missing, Nathan Steiner's body. For a brief happy second, when she opened her eyes she believed she would be in the giant bedroom at Hyacinth's house.

The room was small and, save for the narrow bed and a handmade wooden wardrobe, empty. The single window allowed the light to pour in through the sheer curtain that hung in front of it from a wooden dowel.

Paisley rose and got dressed. The home's only bathroom was across the hall, and when she went in she could feel the dissipating humidity from what must have been Hollis's morning shower, though she was surprised that she didn't hear him. She washed her face, did her business, and went out to follow the breakfast smells.

Hollis stood at the stove over a thick cast iron skillet which was currently sizzling both bacon and eggs. He was dressed in his typical black slacks and white shirt, but both appeared to have been freshly pressed.

"Hey there," he said, dumping half the eggs and bacon onto one plate and the remainder onto another. His voice was sullen. Paisley's first thought was that he had found Hyacinth, and the news was not good.

"Did you find her?" Paisley would have liked to carry on with the morning pretending that everything was okay, but she needed to know if Hyacinth was safe first. Hollis's shoulders sank as he set the skillet on a cool burner on the stove. He puffed out a breath and put his hands on his hips without looking at her. "What is it?"

Hollis reached into his pocket and pulled out a cell phone and held it out to Paisley.

"Hyacinth's phone!" Paisley grabbed it and held it close to her chest. "Where is she?"

"We don't know. I found that south of Raven Bloom. It looks like she may have been out for a walk when she disappeared."

"Does Grover know?" Paisley had hoped that he wasn't in on it, but she couldn't write him off yet since he might be one of the only people who could find her.

"He was searching the area, too. There were other signs she had been there, but I didn't give him the phone." Hollis's chin sank to his chest. "I don't know if he's ready to see what's on it yet."

Paisley pulled the phone away from her chest and looked at the black screen. She could see her own reflection in it, crying.

"What's on it?" Paisley asked, not sure if she really wanted to know.

"Look at the last picture she took," Hollis said, still not looking at her.

Paisley took a deep breath and woke the phone up. The phone wasn't locked. Paisley played back all the times she had seen Hyacinth turn on her phone, and she couldn't remember if she used the fingerprint scanner or not, but she never remembered seeing her enter a pass code. The screen displayed all of the normal apps with a picture of the sunrise from her bedroom window as her background. Paisley clicked on the gallery button. She hadn't realized she was holding her breath until she gasped when the image came up.

The angle was low, like the person who took the picture was on the ground. The sky was black as ink, contrasted by the bright flash of the camera's LED. All sides of the picture were dark, and the trees of the forest crept into the edges like ghosts. And there, in the center of the photo, out of focus but present, stood a tall figure. It was hard to make out exactly what it was, but the shape looked very humanoid. The focus made it very hard to tell if it was covered in fur or just wrapped in brown and red cloth. A bear has short legs and wide hips, but this had long legs and broad shoulders, like a person. It appeared to be coming forward toward the camera, and it had a hand raising to reach out.

"Oh my God," Paisley blurted. The tears poured from her eyes now. Hollis stepped forward to take the phone, but Paisley pulled away and turned, not taking her eyes off of it. "We have to go out there. We have to go look."

"We can't."

"We have to. We need to get a search party together and go find her."

"We can't," Hollis said again.

"Why?"

Hollis's face told Paisley that something was seriously wrong.

"What is it?" she asked, afraid to hear the answer.

"There isn't a search party, because all of Grover's people, and everyone else, are dealing with something else," he said.

"What do you mean, something else? What could be more important than this?"

"There was a another shooting last night. At the diner. It was the same guy that shot at you."

Paisley froze. "Was anyone hurt?" she asked.

"Yeah, a lot of people. Eighteen confirmed dead, twice as many hurt, and a handful in critical condition."

"Oh God. Did they get him?"

"Yeah, he's dead," Hollis said.

"God dammit."

"I have to go. People will be scared and my sermon will be more important now." Hollis put his hands on Paisley's shoulders, then leaned forward and kissed her forehead. "I can take your camera, set it up, and record the service, if you want?"

"What?" she said, pulling away from him. "I'm not staying here. I'm coming with you. I'll set up my own damn camera, thank you."

Paisley walked over and snatched up her camera bag. She wasn't about to sit and wallow. There was too much shit going on for her to sit back and be a passive observer. She looked back over her shoulder at Hollis.

"Come on," she said. "Take me to church."

46

Murmured tones blanketed the congregation like a plague of locusts. Women in their Sunday hats whispering about the girl in the woods above the gristmill, about the shooting, and about Hyacinth. Men speculating as to whether the girl in the woods had been "abused" or not before she'd been killed. The reports said no, but the men thought it was likely. From the voices that Paisley could hear it seemed that half the room thought Hyacinth had been taken by the shooter, which Paisley knew was not entirely impossible, but that it wasn't likely. He could have run into her when he ran into the woods, but that didn't explain the picture. The other half of the room seemed to think that the sasquatch had her. Paisley was starting to worry that this might be the case.

The red door to the small white building banged open and light pushed in like an unwelcome lover. The light made the thin silhouette that Hollis created even thinner. To those who turned to look--and it was the majority--he looked like a scarecrow who had lost his stuffing with his arms raised like the image of Christ on the cross. Hollis walked forward with his arms still jutting out to his sides, his hands hanging at the wrists as if the pins holding them in place had broken loose. His boot heels drummed a steady beat that the congregation followed as he walked between the pews toward the front of the rundown church. Paisley looked up at him when he went by, but he was focused on the front and didn't notice her in the back pew. When he reached the pulpit he stopped. With his arms still raised, he spun on his heels to face the crowd.

"The first came out red," Hollis began, in the typical over-the-top way only a preacher can do. He raised his hands into the air and looked up as if waiting for God to hand down some tribute to him. He paused for a moment and then continued. "All his body hairy, like a cloak." Hollis lowered his gaze from the ceiling and set it upon the packed house who had come to worship at his word. There wasn't a single open seat, and a few people stood at the back of the room.

Paisley had followed Hollis up to the church in Hyacinth's car, as Hollis had said he always had business on Sundays after the service. She had set up the camera in the corner of the room and turned it on before everyone arrived. She thought it would make for a nice time lapse sequence as the church pews filled. She had her pick of the seats and chose the one where Hollis had sat when she interviewed him the first time. The letters carved into the pew in front of her caught her eye, and she remembered Hollis running his fingers across them. He had said they were his way of protecting his brother. She traced the letters the same way. The first H, then the C, followed by the second, newer, H. She paused on the last letter, the capital R.

Hollis's arms again went to his sides, this time palms up. "So they called his name Esau," he whispered, just loud enough to creep into the ears of everyone in the congregation. There were gasps, and one woman screamed. An older woman seemed to faint for a brief moment. Hollis peered around the room. His head hung low and his eyes gleamed from under his sharp brow like a hawk. He stood there, palms up, for more than a minute in silence just looking around the room. Tension built as the crowd of awkward onlookers began sneaking glances around at each other, and that was when Hollis ceased his moment. When a good amount of heads were turned he swung his arms forward and clapped his hands together hard. The sound cracked like a man's rib under a tractor. A collective scream ripped from the congregation. Paisley flinched in her seat. Hollis's grin widened.

"Genesis twenty-five: twenty-five. The good book itself mentions his existence. It speaks of the devil that wanders our woods and kills our loved ones," Hollis said, his voice rising at the end. One man in the back gave a barely audible agreement of amen. "We are reminded to heed his word or suffer those that he has damned," a pause for dramatic effect. "Esau had a brother, Jacob, and what does the good book say of Jacob?" Another dramatic pause. "He was a quiet man, who slept in tents." Pause. "A normal, God loving and *fearing* man. A good man. A man we would welcome into our home and share our daily meals with. But what of Jacob's brother Esau? What became of the boy who was born covered in fur of the enemy's red?" Pause. "We find out in genesis twenty-five twenty-seven, where it is written: 'When the boys grew up, Esau was a skillful hunter, a man of the fields.' A man of the fields, a hunter." Hollis stopped and seemed to switch into a lower gear. He made eye contact for the briefest of moments with Paisley, and she thought he looked like a different person.

"It looks like our pews are a little more fruitful than they were just last week," he said, gesturing at the nearly full room. "Am I to assume this is to be attributed to the horrific shooting that occurred last night?" Murmurs crept through the crowd. "Or one of the whores who found herself being judged in the woods? Is it about the disappearance of one who lives among us, but doesn't walk with us or break bread with us?"

Paisley felt a heat growing inside of her. He didn't talk about Hyacinth as a friend, he spoke about her as if she wasn't part of the town and that she was somehow less than everyone in the room. Her hands clenched into fists.

Hollis looked around the room at the shameful nods of his flock. When he spoke, his voice was angry, its shrill pitch echoing off the old boards and windows and attacking the congregation like a murder of crows.

"Is that what this house of holy protection has become to you? An insurance policy against His wrath?" Not a soul dared bring their eyes above the back of the pew in front of them. Hollis bent sharply at his waist and leaned in to a plump woman's face in the front row. He was close enough that he could smell her. He breathed deep.

"Is that what this is, Miss Reed?" Hollis asked. "Is this church your hiding place from the things that hunt the non-believers?" A tear crept from the woman's eye and traced a line down a wrinkle on her face. "What do you have to confess, Miss Reed?" The heavy woman shook her head lightly. "Miss Reed," he said, taking her hand, "the Lord loves you. He wants only good things for you, but without our full honesty he cannot give us our salvation." He put his free hand on the back of her thick neck. "Now, what can the Lord absolve you from?"

"I can't," she said through a constant stream of tears. "Please, I don't want to."

Hollis pulled her toward him. His narrow face nearly touching hers. "Confess."

"I don't want to," she cried.

"Confess and let Him heal you," he said.

"But I can't."

Hollis looked over the woman's wet face, then gently kissed her forehead in the way a mother would kiss a child's. Then, with a speed that caught the congregation off guard, he leapt to his feet and slapped the woman hard across the face. Paisley was horrified but she was frozen with shock.

"Confess!" he screamed. Before she had time to utter a word, be it a confession or a plea, he slapped her again. And again. No one moved. The red of broken capillaries started to peek from under her pale skin. "Confess, Miss Reed, and allow me to do my work so that He may do his." Hollis pointed toward the sky. He said this in a conversational tone that would be more at home in a conversation about using the proper type of caulk for your shitty old tub than in one of salvation and damnation.

"I had impure thoughts," Miss Reed muttered, just loud enough for Hollis to hear.

"About who?"

"It was no one," Miss Reed answered. He slapped her again. Paisley gasped, but no one heard.

"Lies in the house of the Lord? Miss Reed, if it were my place to collect for the great redeemer I would take the paring knife from my supper kit and run it right up your fat belly to that mound you call a chin and dig that liar's heart right out of your chest for your sins." Hollis paused and lifted her face to look at him. "Now, tell us who you thought of and what you thought."

"What?" she gasped. "I couldn't."

Hollis raised his hand again to strike. Miss Reed recoiled and threw her hands up. Paisley stood and was about to shout for him to stop, but then the woman spoke.

"It was Mr. Moore, from the deli in Grovton," she said in a burst.

"And what are you and Mr. Moore, from the deli in Grovton, doing in these impure thoughts?" Hollis stood and turned his back to Miss Reed.

"I'd rather not say, please," she pleaded.

"Did it have to do with..." he paused and looked slyly over his shoulder with a grin, "his meat," he said with a wink to an onlooking member of the flock.

"Yes, it did, I touched it," she admitted before burying her head in her hands and sobbing. Hollis turned to her. He put both of his hands on her shoulders, bent, and kissed the crown of her head.

"With the power given to me by our Lord and savior, I forgive thee for thy sins," Hollis said. "No penance is needed, save for a little bit extra as the plate goes around, for the lies in His house, of course."

Hollis stood again and addressed the congregation. His eyes met Paisley's. He stared at her as he spoke.

"There was another girl found, and those of us who are enlightened know who put her in the woods. It was him. The beast. The collector. Esau." He paused, the congregation hanging on his words. "Sasquatch." Paisley sat back down without a word.

The congregation responded with a practiced "Amen."

"Who amongst us has seen the beast in the hills who serves to balance the ledger for the Lord?" Hollis asked the crowd. A few muddled voices murmured. "Come on, let me see those hands." A few hands went up reluctantly.

"Don't be ashamed, for I, God's servant, have seen him

as well," Hollis said, placing his hand on his chest. "He's a terrifying beast who cares not for the laws of man, but who takes what He, the Lord, our God, tells him to."

Paisley sat numb for the rest of the service. Hollis talked but she couldn't hear him. She felt so betrayed. She thought she knew this man, but now she felt like she had been deceived.

When the offering plate came by Paisley didn't even touch it. It had only been down the row she sat in, yet it was already full of cash and checks. She stared at it as the man next to her, a skinny man wearing coveralls and an old green suit jacket, held it out to her. She looked at it as if she had no idea what it was, until a man who was standing next to her in the aisle reached down and took it, then handed it to the first person in the next row. He shot back a look of disgust at Paisley. The look broke the trance she felt she was in and she stood up. No one took notice of her. Hollis stood at the front saying a prayer with his head down, so he didn't see her walk over to the camera and turn it off. When she snapped the tripod closed he finally looked up, as did half the congregation.

"Miss Mott?" Hollis said. Paisley didn't respond. She grabbed her bag and with the camera still on the tripod she headed for the door. Hollis stood and started moving down the aisle toward her. She stopped and pointed at him with the hand holding her camera bag.

"Don't you come anywhere near me," she said. Hollis stopped in his tracks. She turned and threw the door open and stormed out into the bright morning. She could hear the chatter from the congregation as she walked down the steps.

Paisley tossed all of the gear into the trunk, got behind the wheel, and roared out of the church parking lot, tossing dirt and stones into the air. She didn't know exactly where she was going, but she knew she didn't want to be there. How could she be so stupid? Hollis Grimm was just another opportunistic asshole. Paisley's hands tightened around the wheel as tears pooled at the corners of her eyes.

Everything went through her head like a film reel set to high. She thought about the town and how quickly they could turn on one of their own. No one seemed concerned with Hyacinth's disappearance. How could they care so little about someone who owned everything in the entire town? According to the papers Paisley had found, H. Bloom took over all of the properties that Hyacinth's father had purchased during his time running the Harris Mining Company, and since Hyacinth was the only H. Bloom, it would appear that she owned it all. It looked like she owned the houses, the buildings, and most of the businesses in them. But why didn't she talk about that? Why did it seem like she was an outcast? And why didn't her father buy the three properties that were in the name of H. Grimm and the one in the name of D. Bruss? She would have liked to ask Hollis that question, but since she couldn't she figured there was only one other logical next stop.

She drove toward Main Street, and then past it. She turned the car onto the long dirt drive of the man she had seen sitting in front of the crippled little house the day she had arrived in Grey Water Ridge. She thought the car might be worth more than the house, everything in it, and the property combined. The man who had spat in her general direction sat in the same chair, wearing the same clothing, and likely the same dirt, as the day she first saw him. She wondered if he had moved. If he ever moved.

49

Dirt filled every available crevice on the property, including the old man's. Everything in Grey Water looked dirty, but everything else at least looked like someone had run a broom or cloth across it at some point. This property, however, did not. Before coming up to the house Paisley had set her tripod up on the front seat to record the whole exchange, and had her phone recording the audio from her pocket. She got out and approached the man.

"Mr. Bruss?" Paisley approached slowly. He sat in a chair on the pallet wood porch. His head didn't move as his single eye traced her up and down. She wasn't sure if he was eying her in a sexual manner, or if he was just sizing her up. A large gob of yellow spit launched from somewhere between his gray and white, overgrown mustache and the dirty beard that hung down his wire-haired chest. The spit landed with a plop on the dirt drive near Paisley's feet. She stopped. "Delano Bruss?"

"Wha-ye-wan?" the old man said. His thick Southern accent was more hill folk than townie. It came out all in one word.

"What I want is to speak with Mr. Delano Bruss...is that you?"

279

"Fak-ot," he said.

"Fuck off?" Paisley asked.

"Aye yup. Fak-ot," he said, confirming her translation.

"Sir, I don't mean to bother you at all, I'm just trying to put some pieces together for a story and I was hoping you could help me, please?" Paisley said.

The man's yellow-and-red eye worked over her again. She decided that it wasn't a sexual thing since he looked so angry while doing it.

"I have money and can pay you for your time," she said.

The old man laughed hard, causing him to cough and then spit the largest wad of phlegm Paisley had ever seen.

"Nah-wot-I-b-niddin-ja-mun-fer?" he asked. He spit the remaining phlegm at her feet. She determined that he was asking what he needed her money for.

"Well, you could start by buying some manners," she said. She figured if he was anything like the old men she had known before then he would enjoy a little spirit.

The man laughed and slapped his knee.

"Nah-wot-I-b-niddin-da-manners-fer?" he laughed.

"Mr. Bruss, I am here to ask you one simple question, and then I will be out of your hair."

The old man tilted his head in interest.

"I've been doing some research about the town and its history, and I have a feeling that something is going on here, and that it has to do with the Bloom family," she said. The man's ears perked at this. "It is my assumption that you don't like that family very much, which would be why you didn't sell your property to the Harris Mining Company. My question to you, sir, is why?"

"Hey-cit-mah-gra-ba," the man said as he looked in the other direction, as if recalling an unpleasant memory.

"I'm sorry?" Paisley asked, not picking up the meaning.

Bruss looked at her.

"Meh-gran-sin," he said again and paused for recognition. Paisley nodded.

"Your grandson?"

"Yea, he-cit-em."

"He cut him? Bloom cut your grandson?"

Bruss drug a long dirty thumbnail down from his forehead, over his eye, stopping near the corner of his mouth.

"Cit-em-bah," he said.

"He cut your grandson's face and that was why you were only one of two people that refused to sell?" Paisley asked.

The man sat back in his chair and stroked his beard with one gnarled hand and with the other he held up a single finger.

"Ja-won," he said. Then he tapped himself on the chest with that finger. "Ja-won," he repeated.

"Just one?"

"Ja-won," he agreed. "On-won-nit-sill."

"What do you mean? The registry shows that Hollis Grimm didn't sell either." This produced a longer and harder laugh than before. He slapped his knee, he hooted, and he even howled at the end before coughing up another gob of yellow and white gunk.

"I-din-sill-cas-Bloom-mer-da-her-in-leaf-dim-chillins. Din-nah-sill-ka-cit-mah-ba," he said.

"Murder?" Paisley asked. "Did Bloom murder someone?" The man laughed again.

"Mer, mer, mer," the man said, pointing at the empty ring finger on his left hand.

"Oh! He married someone. Who did Bloom marry?" she asked.

"Dit-her, Grimm." That whore, Grimm--that was easy

enough to understand. Then it all hit her. Information flooded Paisley's head as the hair on her arm stood up.

"Wait, when Bloom married the woman, did he adopt her children?"

"Aye yup. Aft-der-da-die."

Hollis had said that his mother left his father when he and his brother were young and married someone else. She remembered the letters on the pew. There was an H, a C, another H, and an R. She had assumed both H's were for Hollis, but that wasn't right. It was all of Hollis's siblings. It was Hollis, Cecil, Hyacinth, and Rowan.

"Holy shit," she said. "That's why she called him Holly." The old man just looked at her. "So H. Bloom isn't Hyacinth, it's Hollis. Hollis Bloom, isn't it?"

"Aye yup, sum-bit-cit-mah-ba," the man said. He snarled at the thought, showing off the tiny tower of yellow and brown that was his remaining tooth.

"Wait, Hollis cut your grandson?"

"Cit-em-fer-pit-es-han-in-de-offerin," he said.

"The offering plate at the church?"

"Aye-yup. Cit-em-good," Bruss said, then dragged his nail down his face again, this time slowly.

"Holy shit," Paisley said to herself again, putting the information together in her head. "He's got her." Then to the man: "Thank you so much."

"Aye yup," he said.

Paisley leaned forward and kissed the grimy old man on his forehead. He didn't move as she did it, but when she came away he was grinning from ear to ear. She turned and ran to the car. If she was correct, Hyacinth was still alive, but wouldn't be for long.

50

Raven Bloom was empty when Paisley got back. She had hoped Grover would be there. When he wasn't she called the Sheriff's office.

"Pitt County Sheriff's Office," the voice on the other end of the line said. Paisley could tell that it was the same woman who had been rude to her when she went in.

"I need to speak with Sheriff Northfield right away, please," Paisley said.

"What is this regarding?" the dispatcher asked.

"It's an emergency, please, I need to speak with him right now."

"I'm very sorry, but we're in the middle of an investigation and he's not available to take any calls that are not critical, so if you'd like to leave a message I'll see that he gets it."

Paisley could feel the anger growing in her stomach. She also felt the anxiety rising.

"This is critical," she said. "This is Paisley Mott, and I believe I know where Hyacinth Bloom is, and she is in grave danger."

The other end of the line was silent for a moment.

"And where do you think she is?" the dispatcher asked.

"I think that Hollis Grimm has her."

Paisley wasn't certain, but it sounded like the woman laughed.

"If Ms. Bloom is with Hollis then she is perfectly safe. I can't imagine a safer place to be," the dispatcher said.

"Please just get the Sheriff," Paisley said.

"Ma'am, the Sheriff is very busy right now. He's out conducting an investigation, but I will pass on your message when he returns. Now, is there anything else I can help you with this afternoon?" Her voice was condescending, and it made Paisley want to vomit with anger.

"Listen, just call him on the radio and tell him that Paisley is at Raven Bloom and she needs him to come here right away."

"I will make sure he gets the message when he gets back."

"Call him," Paisley demanded.

"Ma'am, I don't take orders from you, so if there is nothing else?"

"There is one more thing," Paisley said. After a beat of silence she said, "Go fuck yourself," and clicked the end call button.

Paisley leaned against the counter and slid down to the ground. She could feel the anxiety starting to cripple her. The confidence she normally used to put the camera in front of her face and get through this didn't seem to want to respond to her calls. Her breath quickened. She wasn't about to go running off into the woods to save someone when she didn't know exactly where she was going. And what would she do when she got there? Hollis was twice her size and made of muscle. She could improvise a weapon or two. There were kitchen knives she could swipe. She had also seen a few fireplaces in the mansion, so she was sure there was a poker she could take. She prided herself on being independent, but she also prided herself on not being the type of person who was arrogant enough to do something stupid just because she couldn't accept that she couldn't do everything herself. She felt trapped. Helpless. Paisley laid down on the floor, the tears beginning to well up in her eyes. She needed to talk to Grover but the dispatcher was no help and she didn't know his direct number.

Paisley sat bolt upright. The tears still sat on her cheeks, but her eyes were bright and sharp. She leapt to her feet and ran to the counter where she had dropped her bags. She pulled Hyacinth's cell phone out and grinned. She pressed the home button but the phone wouldn't respond. Paisley yanked her charger out and plugged it in and the phone came to life. She felt a split second of horror when she thought that she would see the lock screen and still wouldn't be able to get in. Then she remembered Hollis showing her the picture on the phone. If it had been locked before, how had Hollis gotten in? The thought caused a pinch of pain in Paisley's gut. It meant that Hollis had used Hyacinth's fingerprint to unlock the phone and then change the settings so that he could access the camera and the photos. She just hoped that Hyacinth was alive when he did it. She exhaled as the phone opened to the home screen.

The recent contacts, Paisley assumed, would be the fastest way to find Grover's number, and it was. It was her last call. She hit the small green phone icon next to his name and the phone began to ring. It was answered almost immediately.

"Hyacinth?" Grover yelled into the phone. "Oh God,

where are you? Are you okay?"

"Grover?" Paisley said.

"Hello?" Grover said on the other end of the line. It was not the voice he was expecting.

"Grover, this is Paisley. Paisley Mott?" she said.

"Paisley?" Grover said. The disappointment and sadness in his voice broke Paisley's heart. "Why do you have Hyacinth's phone?"

"Listen, I'll explain all of that, but right now I think I know where Hyacinth is and I think she is in trouble."

"Where is she?"

"Where are you?"

"I'm at the diner, there was a shooting last night. Where's Hyacinth?" he pleaded.

"I'll be right there, don't leave," Paisley said. As she was ending the call she could hear him asking again where Hyacinth was. It would only take a few minutes to get to the diner. Main Street was at the bottom of the hill Raven Bloom sat on. She turned for her bag and something caught her eyes. It was the keys to the Hummer. Grover must have left them when they realized she had just taken a different car.

51

Paisley tore down the road as fast as she could safely navigate the winding roads in the large SUV. She had driven back roads her entire life, so the speed at which she slalomed down the hill was impressive. She made it down in no time. As she sped past Delano Bruss's house he waved his gnarled hand at the speeding truck to say hello. When she roared up Main Street she could see Grover in the street waiting for her. The tires squealed as she slammed on the brakes, coming to a stop right in front of him. She half expected him to scream at her for the reckless driving.

"Where is she?" Grover asked as she rolled down the window.

"Get in," she said.

"What?"

"Get in, she's at Hollis's father's cabin but I don't know exactly where that is. Do you?"

"What do you mean she's at Hollis's father's cabin?"

"Just get in, I can explain on the way," Paisley said again. Grover stepped back. His brows sank in thought. "Okay," she continued, "I think Hollis is killing the women and saying it's Bigfoot so tourists will come."

This snapped Grover out of his thought. "What?"

"I can't prove it, but I think Hyacinth is next," she said.

"I know it isn't a sasquatch, but I don't think Hollis would kill Hyacinth. There are things you don't know about them," he said.

"Yeah, that Hyacinth is his half sister, I got that much. I know about Rowan too, and that you think it's him." Grover looked hurt by that.

"I never suspected Rowan. He's one of my best friends and when he said he didn't do it I believed him," Grover said.

"Listen, I know it's hard to believe, but I watched the footage I recorded when Hollis took me to see that body after I got here. It was hard, but I wanted to see if there was anything I could show. I couldn't see the body, but I could see that Hollis took something from the mud next to it."

"What do you mean he took something?"

"I couldn't zoom in close enough, but it looked like it could have been a watch," she said.

"A watch?" Grover asked, surprised. "The pin," He said to himself.

"What pin?" Paisley asked.

"We found half of a broken watch pin at the murder scene, and the other half of the same pin where the girl was abducted. We assumed the pin broke during the struggle and half the pin fell out, then the other half fell out at the murder site. But we never found a watch. We assumed the murderer found it and took it."

"His wrist!" Paisley said. She was mad at herself for not putting it together sooner. She had seen Hollis take the watch from the mud, but at the time she would never have considered that it was his watch. Now she remembered the white ring around his wrist at the end of his tattoo. "We have to go, now."

"No, I have to go, you have to stay right here," Grover demanded.

"I have to come with you," she said, but Grover was already climbing into his Jeep. Paisley pulled the Hummer up behind him so that he couldn't back up. Grover opened his door.

"Move, now!" he yelled. Paisley turned the Hummer's ignition off and pulled the keys out. She was not going to be told what she was and wasn't doing. She got out and marched up to the door of the Jeep.

"I figured this out. You have to let me come with you," she said. Grover stepped out of the Jeep.

"That isn't how this works. This isn't the movies. You are staying right here. Now move that vehicle or I'm going to arrest you for obstruction of justice," Grover said.

"I'm coming with you." Paisley held up the keys so Grover could see them. Grover looked around. A few people had stopped to watch what was going on. He looked at the sidewalk that had been closed off in front of the diner after the shooting. Then he looked back at Paisley.

"No," Grover said. Paisley was shocked with the speed at which he moved as he snatched the keys from her hand. "I am not going to allow you to put yourself in danger for a story," he said, and threw the keys down the street. They hit the pavement and slid under a car.

"This isn't about the fucking story, it's about my fucking friend," she said, and shoved him. Grover didn't move with the shove. He just lifted his finger and put it in her face.

"This isn't a game, and I can't do my job if I'm worrying about protecting you too." Grover turned back toward his

Jeep and climbed in.

Paisley realized what he was going to do before he even started the Jeep. She ran to the door and pulled it open.

"Wait," she said.

"What?"

"Take this." Paisley pulled Hyacinth's cell phone from her bag. It was attached to a small portable charger, which Paisley pulled free. She thrust the cell phone toward him. Grover looked at the phone and then back at Paisley.

"Why?" he asked.

"It's hers," she said. She could tell Grover didn't understand, but he nodded at her and put the phone in his shirt pocket. Then he pulled the door closed, put the Jeep in drive, and tore out over the sidewalk. He went half a block up, scattering a few people who had gathered at the caution tape, then swung the Jeep into the street, the engine whining as he sped away.

52

The wind ripped through the leaves as Grover drove up the narrow path toward the property. The trees on either side of the path showed damage, letting Grover know someone had been up that way recently. He himself had been up this way a time or two in his stint as Sheriff, but it was just in getting to know the land. He had seen Hollis's father's cabin. He knew who it belonged to, and he even wondered why it hadn't been torn down. It was a ramshackle pile of wood and scrap that could barely be called a structure. Boards had been nailed over the broken windows at some point over the last decade, and the door had a hasp latch on it with a padlock holding it closed. Grover remembered wondering what there was to protect in the place. And he was pretty certain that you could just push the door off its hinges anyway, and then it would just be left hanging from that lock. Hollis had told him once that he worried that hunters might try and set up camp in there and accidentally burn the place down using the old wood stove. Grover thought that they might be doing Hollis a favor if they did.

The Jeep rolled into the clearing and Grover parked it behind the small red truck that Hollis sometimes drove to haul wood. The wind was loud enough that he wasn't worried about being heard. He slid the gun from his holster for the second time in two days, and only the third time in his career. The night before he had heard the shots coming from the diner, but by the time he got there the shooting was done. He had run through the door and found Sylvia holding the lifeless body of her son, Boyd, people trying to stop the bleeding of countless victims, and Jorge, the diner's cook, sitting with a bloody knife over the man they identified as the killer. The man had a few stab wounds and a broken arm, and the side of his head had been caved in with a meat tenderizer. Grover had just stood there with his gun in his hand, not knowing what to do. Ambulances had come from a few counties around and took victims away. A lot of people had died. He'd felt helpless. So he was damn sure that if Hollis really was killing women, and he had Hyacinth in there, Grover wasn't going to let anything happen to her. If that meant shooting that righteous motherfucker, then so be it.

Cracking noises came from the trees as the wind pressed older, weaker branches past their breaking point. Grover walked up to the cabin. He leaned down, peeking under one of the boards that had been haphazardly nailed to the window frame. It was dark inside, but a small line of light from another board placed askew allowed him to make out a form in the middle of the room. Someone was in there. He couldn't see who, but whoever it was wasn't moving. Grover waited to see if anyone else was in there, but he saw no one. The truck was there, so Hollis had to be around somewhere, but Grover also noticed that the lock was on the door, which locked from the outside, so without checking the back to be sure, he felt confident in assuming that Hollis was not there. He knocked on the board, hoping that if it was Hyacinth in there, she was still alive. The figure inside jerked at the sound.

"Hyacinth?" Grover said, his voice getting lost in the wind. "Hyacinth!" he shouted. The figure jerked again, its movement restrained. Grover pulled a small flashlight from his duty belt, turned it on, and pressed the beam into the slot under the board. A dusty line of light streaked through the murk revealing the room and its single occupant. A woman, who Grover was nearly certain was his girlfriend, was chained to two logs that had been attached to form a cross. She was hung in a crucifix position with the chains binding her arms, legs, torso, waist, and neck. A burlap sack was pulled down over her head and bunched under the chain around her neck. She struggled against the chains but she was unable to move.

"Hyacinth!" Grover yelled again. The burlap sack stopped shaking and seemed to turn toward the sound of his voice. He wasn't sure if she was saying something because the wind had become almost deafening. "I'm coming!"

Grover turned and ran to the door. The lock hung on the hasp, but a swift kick near the latch broke the door to pieces. One small bit hung from the lock, but the majority of the door flew inward, assisted by the wind. The air blew in, creating a tornado of dust in the nearly empty room, forcing Grover to turn and cover his face. He marched forward toward the crucifix in the middle of the room. Grover pulled the burlap sack free and his heart leapt as he saw that it was Hyacinth, and that she was alive. The chain was wrapped around her head and pulled through her mouth. Grover saw her teeth on the metal, the pain and tears in her eyes, and he had to fight the urge to fall to his knees. He had to get her down. She was staring into his eyes, begging him to help her.

"I'm here now, everything's going to be okay." As Grover started to move to see where the chain was connected he saw her head raise quickly. He looked up at her to see that her eyes were wide like the headlights of an oncoming truck. He spun just in time to see what she was looking at.

Hollis was sprinting toward the cabin, coming directly at him. He was still at least twenty-five feet from the door, but he was moving quickly and he was holding something. Something large. It was an axe. Grover reached for his gun, but it was too late. He saw Hollis's arm fly forward and he watched in slow motion as the bright red axe head dipped, disappeared, and then reappeared at the top of its arc. Grover had time to marvel at just how amazing the throw was before the head hit him high in the center of his chest and stuck. He could feel his ribs break in the front and back as the blast transferred through him. The force drove him straight back. He felt his body crash into Hyacinth, and he could hear her muffled scream. His body ricocheted off the crucifix and he spun sideways. He could feel the axe handle hit the ground first, like it was an added appendage. The world went dark as the warm blood began to flow. Whatever was to happen to Hyacinth next, Grover Northfield would have no say.

53

Hollis had been pulling his tools from the shed on the hill when he thought he heard a car door over the wind. The shed was built far enough away from the cabin that if you didn't know it was there, deep in the thick of the trees, you wouldn't find it. He left most of the tools and headed up the hill to get a better look. He watched from the tree line as Grover kicked the door in. Hollis knew that he needed to wait until he was sure that Grover wouldn't hear him coming. Grover had a gun in his hand and Hollis was under no illusion that he could get within throwing distance for his axe before Grover could swing that gun around and put him down. So he waited. He had been out cutting wood, which was part of his routine when he killed the girls. He would catch them and chain them to the cross in his cabin. There he would leave them for a few days. He would weaken them. He would preach to them about their wicked ways. Then, once God told him it was time, he would take them off the cross and out into the woods to be sacrificed. It normally meant ripping them apart with his bare hands, which he enjoyed. He had been looking forward to killing his sister for a very long time.

Hollis watched as Grover kicked the door. He knew at

that moment that there was no going back. That Grover had to die. He had seen too much. Hollis moved quickly from the trees and broke out in a flat run toward the cabin. He could see Grover put the gun in its holster and pull the sack from Hyacinth's head. He was almost in range. He lifted the axe into position. The wind was howling, but the weight of the axe, and how hard he could throw it, would negate almost all of the wind's redirection. Hyacinth's eyes flipped up and met his. There was a moment of recognition on her face. He watched as she bit against the chain, helpless to warn the love of her life that he was coming. Grover turned, but Hollis knew he wasn't close enough yet. He managed three more long strides before the gun was out of its holster. Hollis threw his arm forward and watched as the axe took a nearly flat trajectory and hit Grover squarely in the chest and stuck the same way it did when he would throw it at trees and stumps. The force blew Grover backward and he could see him bounce off the cross and fall sideways. He reached the door a second later. Hyacinth was pulling hard against the chains. Tears poured down her face as she looked from Grover's motionless body lying in the growing pool of blood, and then back to Hollis. She was trying to scream something.

"Now, you can't blame me for that, Hi, he shouldn't have been up here," Hollis said, using the nickname for her they had grown up with. He was Holly, Cecil was CeCe, Hyacinth was Hi, and the youngest of them, Rowan, was Ro. When Hollis was a teenager, and Hyacinth and Rowan were kids, he would greet the two of them together by saying "HiRo" in a terrible Chinese accent. He thought it was hilarious. Hyacinth pulled against her chains, but it was useless. She had been hanging there for nearly two full days without food or water, and what little sleep she got was just when she passed out from the pain of being hung there by chains. Hollis felt that the chains were a bit much, but rope would leave fibers, and he wasn't about to have his entire mission derailed by something you should know by watching the first season of any cop procedural. The chains left bruises, but they would blend in with the bruises that Hollis would leave with his hands as he beat her. At the end of it the marks left by the chains ended up looking like they were squeezed by a massive, powerful hand. The hand of a sasquatch.

Hollis looked back out the door at the driveway. Grover's Jeep sat there, a beacon of law enforcement. He needed a plan for that, and he thought he had one. Hollis had been the one that started the rumor that Rowan had been seen with one of the victims before she died. He needed something to take the focus off of himself after Grover had spoken with a trucker who had dropped the girl off at a rest stop. The trucker had said he saw a tall, well-built man following the girl. It was Hollis, but Rowan looked enough like his half brother that when he started the rumor it took quickly enough. After all, Rowan had left Grey Water to go to college. In the town's eyes, when he came back, he might as well have been an outsider.

Hollis's plan now would be to take Hyacinth out to the woods, kill her as planned, and then place an anonymous call in to the sheriff's office the next county over. That should get all the deputies out there dealing with the murder and not looking for Grover. He wasn't positive that Grover didn't tell anyone where he was going, but since he came alone, he had to trust that he hadn't and that he would have time to deal with everything. Once he was done with Hyacinth and had the deputies distracted, he would drive the Sheriff's jeep up to the old Bloom Cabin, where he knew Rowan had been hiding, and drop off Grover's Jeep and body. He knew Rowan was unarmed up there, other than a baseball bat. Hollis had been up to see him a few times. He knew that during the day Rowan would be down fishing at the lake, so it would be fairly easy to set him up. He would need to stab Grover with a fishing knife and mutilate the body a bit so that it didn't look like it was an axe that had nearly split him in two, but that wasn't a problem. He might even throw the body off the cliff by the cabin, the way Rowan had thrown Paisley's stupid drone. Or perhaps toss the body in the lake and let the deputies search for it after finding the Jeep and Rowan at the hideout. The one thing he couldn't do was allow it to look like Rowan was in fact killing the women. Which wouldn't be a problem after he was either arrested or killed by the deputies. It would be easy enough to paint Rowan as the jealous underling of the black outsider. He would say that Rowan despised the fact that someone from outside was protecting the town when he was born and raised in Pitt County. Or that he had killed Grover because he suspected him in the death of his only sister, Hyacinth. There were a number of ways Hollis could play it, and with his influence in the town he could get those people to believe anything. But first, he had a sister to murder.

Hollis pushed Grover's body out of the way, and it slid across the wood floor on the slick, bloody pool surrounding it. He looked at Grover. He thought they could have been friends, or even brothers in law, if things had worked out differently. He nudged him with his foot, then noticed something. A white corner sticking out of Grover's shirt pocket, just above where the axe protruded from his chest. Hollis had seen it before, just that morning. It was Hyacinth's phone. He wasn't sure how Grover ended up with it, but he would need it if his story was going to hold up. He reached down and plucked the phone from the pocket.

A padlock held the chains together at the back of the crucifix, but before unlocking it he pulled the chain around Hyacinth's neck. He pulled it upward and back, so that it wouldn't break her windpipe, only suppress the arteries supplying the blood to her brain. He wanted to knock her out, not kill her--yet.

Once she was out he undid the chain that held her to the cross. He had done this enough times to have established a solid procedure. He would undo the chain that held his victims up, and then pull the ones around the arms, legs, and torso back and clip them together with the lock, effectively hog tying them. He carried Hyacinth like a heavy suitcase out to the truck and slung her limp body over the side and into the bed. Then he walked back down the hill to collect the rest of his tools, as well as the small bundle of firewood he would drop on the tarp he used to cover the body in the truck. If anyone saw him driving through town it would just look like he was out gathering firewood.

He put the wood and a few tools into an old blue tarp, made a makeshift bindle, and then hauled them back up the hill. Hollis spread the tarp over Hyacinth's unconscious body as well as the red and brown fur ghillie suit that was balled up next to her, then tossed a few pieces of wood around to hold the tarp down in the whipping wind. Afraid it might not do the job, he grabbed a few large rocks and set them around the edges to be sure that it wouldn't fly up at an inopportune time and expose his secret beneath.

He stood in the back of the truck, his clothes beating in

the wind, looking down at his hard work. It looked just like every truck that you would see driving around Grey Water Ridge. It helped that the sun was almost down and that it would be dark by the time he got down the hill into town. He began to turn when the back window of the truck exploded behind him. Hollis instinctively leapt out of the truck and landed next to the tools that he had yet to put into the bed. There had been a gunshot, but Hollis couldn't tell where it came from. The wind masked the sound of footsteps, so he wasn't sure if the shooter was approaching or holding their ground. He looked under the truck to see if he could see anyone moving. He couldn't see anything, which meant that the shooter was either in the cabin, or on the wooden porch, just out of his low perspective. He took a breath and popped his head up to look over the bed of the truck. And there, on the porch, aiming Grover's gun at him, was Paisley fucking Mott.

54

Paisley stood with the gun leveled at the back of the truck. She wasn't going to shoot now and risk hitting Hyacinth. Her aim wasn't terrible, but she had just missed Hollis as he was standing still, and she didn't trust herself to take the shot when she saw his head pop up from behind the truck.

"Come on out, asshole," she yelled over the wind.

"No. No, I don't think I will," Hollis yelled back. She saw him look down into the bed of the truck. She had hoped he wouldn't realize that Hyacinth was the only reason she wasn't blowing holes through the thin metal of the truck bed to try and hit him. "Put down the gun, Paisley."

"And what? You'll let us go? Ha! You must think I'm an idiot."

"No, you know I can't do that. But I will make it quick and painless. You'll be part of my masterpiece," he shouted.

"Fuck you!" she yelled. Hollis's head dipped back down behind the truck. Before she could yell at him to get back where she could see him, his head popped up again.

"Okay, I'll come out, but you need to put the gun down," he yelled.

"Not a chance, asshole," she yelled back. The wind pressed into her face and it felt like someone trying to smother her with an invisible pillow. She squinted her eyes to protect them.

"All right, I'm coming out, but don't shoot," Hollis yelled. Before she could respond she saw his hand piston back and then swing forward. She only had a split second to register what was happening, but once she saw the hatchet flying toward her she didn't think, she just threw herself backward through the open door. Wood splinters fluttered off into the wind as the hatchet buried itself into the door frame right behind where Paisley had been standing.

"You mother fucker," she yelled, and pushed herself to her feet. She slammed herself against the door frame and swung outward with the gun pushed out in front of her. She expected Hollis to be running at her, but instead she didn't see him at all. She ducked low and looked under the truck, but didn't see his feet.

Wind pushed at her as she rounded the truck, swinging the gun as she had seen on so many cop shows and movies. He was gone. She scanned the trees and the clearing, but didn't see him. She reached into the truck and pulled the tarp up. She watched Hyacinth closely to see if her chest was rising and falling. It was shallow, but it was there. Paisley refocused her attention on Hollis. She looked up into the sky, and she knew where he had gone. She jumped down from the truck and ran through the clearing behind the cabin.

Paisley moved through the trees as quietly as she could. The trees were thick there, so the wind was a little quieter and she wasn't sure if Hollis had seen her following him.

With the sun setting it was already dark in the woods and Paisley's eyes took a moment to adjust. When they did she could see a small point of orange light ahead. It was the infant flame of a new campfire. Paisley approached cautiously.

There was a small clearing where the fire burned lightly. A few small pieces of wood had been dropped into a stone circle that, judging by the amount of dead leaves and pine needles everywhere, hadn't been used in a long time. She stood just outside the fire's dim light and looked around.

"I know you're here," she said into the clearing.

Pain flashed as a small log crashed down across her outstretched arms, sending the gun flying into the dark. Paisley fell backward and tried to crawl away, but he was already on her. The pain in her arms was screaming, but she could tell they weren't broken, so she punched at him as he tried to grab her.

"Get the fuck off me, you piece of shit!" she screamed. Hollis leaned away as she kicked at him. The first kick hit high on his thigh, causing him to rock back, but the second hit nothing at all, and he plucked her foot out of the air by the ankle. "Let go!"

Hollis dragged her toward the fire, which had grown considerably over the last few seconds. Hollis whipped her around by the leg and her back hit the stones surrounding the fire pit. He stood over her now, looking down at her, his head cocked to one side.

"Why couldn't you just leave well enough alone, Pickle?"

"Don't call me that," she said, and kicked out at him. He batted her foot away as if it was a gnat.

"You are ruining my big plan, and it would have made you a star. You fucked it up. You almost fucked it all up," he said.

Paisley tried to crawl backward but she was trapped between him and the fire. She could feel her back growing hot.

"You killed those girls," she said. It wasn't news to him, but she had hoped that hearing it would throw him off his game. She was wrong.

"I did. For the Lord," he said.

"Don't try to blame God for your crazy-ass fetishes," she said. Hollis inched closer, she pushed harder against the rocks.

"They are not fetishes. I gain no pleasure at all from it. I simply do what Esau cannot," he said.

"Oh, now you blame it on Bigfoot," she said.

"Esau, not Bigfoot. Do not disrespect him," Hollis said, stepping closer.

"You're a monster. Those girls didn't deserve to die."

"Women can be selfish, irresponsible creatures. Sometimes they need to be punished," he said, kicking dirt in her direction.

"You're fucking insane," she said. The heat on her neck made her worry that any closer and her hair was going to catch fire.

"No, I'm totally sane. And had you done your part the world would have understood exactly what's at stake in all of this."

"You weren't trying to help people. You were trying to get me to amplify your signal. You wanted me to show the world that you were preaching about this monster in the woods so that you could drive tourism up." Paisley leaned forward. She wanted it to look like she was being confident and aggressive, but really she just wanted to put some distance between her and the fire. Hollis seemed taken slightly aback by the revelation that someone knew his plan. "Oh, yeah, I figured all that out. You own everything in this town. You bought it all up thinking that you would make this shithole town the next big tourist trap. What did you have planned? Bigfoot World or some shit?" She leaned even closer.

Hollis took a half step back. He looked furious.

"I didn't buy this fucking town. I wanted out of this God forsaken place," he said. His hands balled into fists and Paisley tensed, waiting for him to strike. "I hate it here. I have always hated it here. That asshole, Craven, hung this town around my neck like an albatross. He gave that slut all the money, and gave me the deeds to my own personal hell!" Hollis leaned down and grabbed Paisley's foot, spinning her around and then back toward the fire. Paisley grabbed at the ground to try and find something to hold onto.

"Stop!" she yelled, but he didn't listen.

"You are just one more thing that I have to get rid of. I would have liked to use your stupid vlog to get the word out, but Hyacinth's death will be covered enough that people will hear about it. So now you're just another problem to deal with." Hollis pulled up on her leg, ready to toss her into the fire, when a sound broke through the wind. It was a siren. It was *multiple* sirens. Hollis stopped. He looked down the mountain. The trees were too thick, and they were too far away for him to see them coming. He looked down at Paisley.

"Did you call the cops?" he asked. He seemed slightly insulted. Paisley tried to pull her leg free, and groped at the ground behind her. Her hand hit something thin and cool under the leaves. She wrapped her fingers around it.

"I didn't have to," she said, and flicked her head upward, suggesting that there was something above him. He looked up and there, in the night sky, were four tiny blinking lights. Two green and two red.

"What the fuck is that?" he said.

"That's an auto-adjusting hectocopter, with an 8K camera on a five-axis gimbal, and the ability to track a cell phone--Hyacinth's cell phone, to be exact. And all while live streaming to whatever social media site I want."

Hollis looked down at her. The fire reflected in his eyes and made it look like his soul was ablaze. He clenched his teeth and tightened his grip on her ankle. It hurt, but she wouldn't show it.

"That's right, it followed Grover up here, and that's how I found you. But don't worry, the world definitely saw you kill him." Paisley kept her left hand wrapped around the thing beneath the leaves and shoved her right hand into her pocket and pulled out her phone. She turned it to face Hollis. He grabbed it with his free hand and looked at the screen. It showed an overhead view of him, standing there, holding Paisley's leg, perfectly lit by the roaring fire. A comment came across the screen.

WhyItHurts: *Smile, motherfucker. You're on Candid Camera.*

"Bitch!" Hollis yelled, and threw the phone into the pit.

"Now, *I'm* not your fucking problem, the hundred cops who've been watching on the live stream, and are now flying up that hill, to come here and kick your ass, are your problem," she said.

Hollis glared at her.

"I didn't enjoy killing those women, but I have a feeling I will enjoy killing you," he said. He pulled her ankle so hard that she felt something in her leg snap. She wasn't sure it if was ligament, tendon, or bone, but it hurt. He spun her toward the fire again. He dipped low to get the leverage to flip her into the pit, and that's when she struck. She swung her left hand forward, the prong of the long campfire fork glinting in the fire light before stabbing into Hollis's thigh. He screamed and let go of Paisley's leg. Her foot dropped to the ground in an explosion of pain. She had lost the fork as it was now sticking out between Hollis's blood-covered hands as he tried to pull it free. Paisley tried to stand, but her leg was worthless and she fell back down.

Hollis ripped the fork from his leg and threw it into the trees. He walked to Paisley and stood over her. His face was an expressionless void. He reached down, grabbing her by the neck and lifting her effortlessly off the ground. He held her so that her face was even with his. She couldn't breathe. The light started to fade at the edges of her vision. She clawed at his face, but his grip didn't loosen. The sirens were still too far away to save her. This was it. Her death was going to be live streamed on the internet. She had accepted the fact that she was going to die, knowing that Hollis wouldn't get away with it.

Something moved. Something big. A shadow behind Hollis. Paisley tried to hold on, but her eyes rolled back into her head.

55

Sounds danced around, but Paisley couldn't make them out. People's voices. Someone calling for a medic. Fire crackling. She couldn't see, but she could feel the pain in her leg as someone held it carefully. She felt pressure around it as someone was splinting it.

"Get the stretcher up here," someone in the distance called. There was a response too far off for her to hear, but whoever had called for it yelled back toward where she lay, "They say they can't get it up the hill."

"It's okay." A soft, deep voice came from just inches away from Paisley's face. It sounded similar to Hollis's. She tried to pull away at the thought.

Paisley tried to scream, but only a rough croak came out, accompanied by what felt like glass shards in her throat.

"Miss Mott, please, calm down. Everything is going to be okay," the voice said. "You've suffered a broken leg and some damage to your neck. It's probably best if you don't talk. They can't get the stretcher up here, so I'm going to carry you down the hill. It'll be okay, I promise."

That voice. It was so much like Hollis's that she had to see who it belonged to to make sure it wasn't him. She forced her eyes open. It burned to do so, but she managed.

The man above her was handsome, like Hollis, but more rugged. Had he had black hair she would have assumed that it was Hollis, somehow playing a trick on her. Instead he had dark red hair. His face was covered in thick, dark stubble. He smiled and she knew who it was. She reached up and touched his face. She wanted to touch that smile. She had seen that smile before. It was Hyacinth's smile.

"Rowan," she said through the pain.

His smile widened and he took her hand.

"Yes, Miss Mott, I am Rowan Bloom. It is a pleasure to meet you," he said.

Paisley sat up quickly, nearly head-butting Rowan in the process.

"Hyacinth?" she croaked.

"She's going to be okay, thanks to you," Rowan said. "Now, if you don't mind I'll carry you down to see her?" He tried to slide his hand beneath her legs and under her arms. She pulled back. She looked up. The drone was still there.

"Help me up," she said.

"You've got a broken leg," Rowan said.

"Yeah, so I may need to lean on you going down the hill, then. Help me up," she said. She wasn't about to come this far and let the world see some man carrying her out like he saved her.

"Are you sure?" he asked. She didn't need to respond-- the look on her face said it all. "As you wish."

Rowan stood and reached out his hand. Paisley froze for a moment before looking at that hand. She was afraid she was going to look and it would be Hollis's hand at the end of Rowan's arm. That these brothers would share more than just similar faces. She looked at his hand. It was strong, work-worn, not soft, like Hollis's. She reached up and grabbed it. It was rough. The hand of a carpenter. He pulled her up and held her hand while she steadied herself on her good leg.

"I'm going to need to lean on you," she said.

"That's perfectly fine," Rowan said, taking his place next to her. She looked around and noticed that Hollis was gone. They began the very long walk down the hill. She could see flashing lights in front of the cabin. There were police cars everywhere, and a few ambulances sat idling. When they got to the clearing she allowed herself to be put on a stretcher and wheeled the rest of the way down the hill. She was grateful to be off her hurt leg. As they rounded the house she could see two ambulances. There was someone in each one. In the back of the closest she could see Hyacinth, sitting up on a stretcher. There were IV tubes in her and an oxygen mask on her face. When she saw Paisley she smiled. She tried to wave but looked too weak.

"You saved her life," Rowan said. He had not let the stretcher get more than a foot from him since she got on it. "Thank you."

The doors of the second ambulance slammed closed and a paramedic slapped the door.

"Move!" the paramedic yelled. He turned to one of the medics pushing Paisley toward the ambulance Hyacinth was in. "If they can get him to an operating room quick enough, he's got a chance."

"Hollis?" Paisley squeaked. She hadn't seen him by the fire, but she had hoped he was dead.

"Grover," Rowan said. Paisley turned to look at him.

"The axe struck the crash plate in his bulletproof vest," he said. "Hit hard enough for it to pierce the metal and bury itself into his sternum. Crushed his ribs, one of which

310

punctured a lung. He lost a lot of blood, but he has a chance." Rowan and the paramedics loaded the stretcher into the ambulance and locked it in place next to Hyacinth. Paisley reached out and took her hand.

56

Paisley was in the hospital for two days. Her leg wasn't fully broken, but she did have a pretty bad spiral fracture. They put it in a cast, but let her walk around on crutches since she refused the wheelchair. Though Paisley was released from the hospital she chose to stay with Hyacinth in her room.

Hyacinth had suffered a lot of cuts and bruises, but when they brought her in she was dehydrated and starving. Her body had begun to shut down. A nurse said that if Paisley hadn't found her she would have died of dehydration within fourteen hours or so. What everyone knew, however, was that had Paisley not found her she would have been butchered and left in the woods a lot sooner than that.

Paisley told the authorities about Nathan Steiner, and when they went to recover the body they found another body under the floor. It was the corpse of the male companion of the victim Hollis had left in the woods the day after Paisley arrived. She remembered seeing the plastic bag when she'd been down there, and now was very glad she had been too scared by the skeleton to look.

Paisley had been told all about the shooting, and when

she heard Boyd had been killed she cried. She asked about Pilot and found out that Rowan had taken her to live with him and Hyacinth. They were close siblings, and before Hollis had framed Rowan and he had gone into hiding, he had lived at Raven Bloom with her. Their father gave Hyacinth controlling stock in Harris Mining and Oil, which made her a very wealthy person. He gave nothing to Rowan, who had despised the way his father had done business and instead of going into the coal business he went to school for history, archeology, and criminal justice, against his father's will. Cecil was given nothing since he ran away after his mother had been considered the first death that was attributed to the sasquatch. But Hollis-- Hollis couldn't run away. He was there running his father's church after he died. He wanted nothing more than to leave the town. The congregation was shrinking, and once it was gone, so was he.

And then Craven gave him the very thing he hated most in the world. The town he wanted to get away from. Hollis had made it his mission to bring people back to the town. Once it was a thriving tourist trap, of his own making, he would sell to any developer willing to take advantage of the townsfolk, and leave. He had planned to have Paisley come out and vlog about the sasquatch. Then, while she was there, she would end up covering the death of her host, a very popular internet personality, at the hands of the very sasquatch that she was there to cover. What he hadn't planned on was the resilience of Paisley Mott.

Rowan had grown worried when he hadn't seen Hyacinth, who was scheduled to bring him food and battery chargers for his phone and the battery-powered satellite internet setup. When he hadn't heard from her he'd ventured down toward town, hoping not to be

313

spotted. He had no luck, but when he returned to the cabin and found that it had been rifled through he called Grover. Which, Paisley assumed, was the call that Grover got when she was trying to tell him about finding the body. Grover had known Rowan was up there, and he was turning a blind eye to it, as he knew his deputy was innocent.

WhyItHurts had been the one who saw the live stream first and called in the cavalry. Hundreds of thousands of people had watched the video live after Hyacinth had been tagged in it. Rowan saw the tweet alert, and when he clicked it he saw what was happening. He saw Hollis throw the axe at Grover. He also saw Paisley Mott, the woman staying with his sister, save her life.

There were conflicting reports from Rowan and a deputy about who arrived on scene first. Rowan claimed that there was a deputy already on site when he got there. The deputy claimed that when he got there Rowan was already in the woods behind the cabin.

The live stream went on for a minute after Hollis dropped Paisley. It was unclear what grabbed him on the footage. But whatever it was picked Hollis up and carried him away, quickly. The drone skimmed the tops of the trees but couldn't see into the darkness. It lost connection when the phone went into the lake. The phone was recovered, but no one knows if Hollis was with it when it was thrown in. The body was never found. When Paisley was asked about what she saw, she would just say she didn't remember. Though she would never forget the dark gold eyes that looked back at her in the firelight that night.

315

ABOUT THE AUTHOR

Kalvin Ellis spent a generous portion of his childhood in his parents video store. When not watching movies in the back room he would be next door at the used bookstore hidden under a shelf and reading a mix of Calvin and Hobbes, Stephen King, and MAD Magazine. It was in these two places that he developed his love for storytelling. Kalvin has lived a tragic life and now lives by the mantra from one of his favorite films, The Iron Giant.

"You are who you choose to be." ~ Hogarth

Kalvin lives in Denver, Colorado with his family and is currently working on a number fiction and nonfiction books. You can check in with him at KalvinEllis.com

Paisley Mott will return!

Made in the USA
Coppell, TX
13 April 2021

53678228R00187